ALSO BY KATT ROSE

THE LOSS
BUILDING IT UP
A FATHER'S DAUGHTER

Forget
Me
Not

KATT ROSE

Country Roads Publishing
Vancouver Island

ISBN-13: 978-1-9993994-3-6
FORGET ME NOT
Copyright © 2019 by Katt Rose

Country Roads Publishing are trademarks used under license and registered in Nanaimo, Vancouver Island, Canada.
www.countryroadspublishing.net

Cover design by BespokeBookCovers.com
Formatting by Polgarus Studio
Author Photo taken by Kyle Trienke

CHAPTER ONE

I've always hated these walls. They have no color. I crave color; I like the warmth but he has no patience for it. Everything in this house is arguably flawless, but it's cold and it bears no character. The walls shine with white. Is white even a color? I don't think it should have that right. White walls, white furniture, even the paintings that hang have no meaning, no life. They simply represent a number. And what is that number? Simple….expensive.

I shifted my heavy eyes to the clock. The loud, ticking clock. Its incessant noise rang loud in my ears. It was just after three p.m. and here I was, alone at the kitchen table. I let out a heavy sigh; this was not how the day was supposed to play out. I was not supposed to sit here in our house so completely broken, knowing my world had shifted. For you see, today my mother did not recognize me. I knew this day would come, but I didn't expect it to come so soon. Seven months ago my mother was diagnosed with Alzheimer's and though she had begun to fade in and out, she always knew who I was. Always.

But today, I fell from her thoughts. I was nothing. I simply disappeared. I squeezed my eyes shut and thought back to earlier in the afternoon. My mother's kind brown eyes were heavy in confusion as I let out a sob at her simple question. "I'm sorry, do I know you?"

"I'm your daughter, Emmy."

My mother fluttered her thick lashes once , clearly perplexed. "No, no you can't be. I'm sorry but I don't have any children."

And in true motherly fashion, she leaned forward and placed my hand within hers. She stroked it comfortingly. "I hope you find your mother."

I snapped my eyes open and shoved back the kitchen chair. The legs scraped against the tiled floor and protested with a high-pitched squeal.

"Emmy! Be careful. That floor isn't cheap." Sean, my boyfriend strode in and gawked at me like I was a disobedient child.

I stared up at his immaculate features, he too, like this house was flawless. Sean's skin tone was forever kissed by the sun. His dark brown hair fell perfectly and matched his eyes. His physique was hard earned but he wore it effortlessly. Despite his physical perfections, he lacked genuine emotion, mostly sympathy. Work and finances were his true love. They gathered all of his attention; I merely was the cute trophy attached to his arm. Sean would not notice that I was emotionally devastated, not unless it affected him personally. And my mother held no connection to him whatsoever.

"Sorry," I muttered. "It was a rough day." I took a shattered breath and my mother's vacant look flashed through my mind once more.

Sean raised an eyebrow and took a step closer. "Your mother?"

"Yes. She...she forgot who I was today."

"Well, that's common for her condition, right?"

I bristled at his matter of fact tone. "Yes, but that doesn't make it any easier."

"Look on the bright side of things. You don't have to visit her as often, she won't know the difference."

My jaw gaped open and I stared up at the man I shared a roof with. His eyes fell to me and he shrugged his shoulders carelessly. "It's true Em. And you know it."

"How can you even say that to me? She's my mother! She will have some good days; I want to be there for *all* of them. I don't know how many she will have left…"

"Suit yourself. "Sean checked his watch. "Oh great. I'm behind schedule. I'll be home late, I have a meeting at the office today."

"Of course you do," I whispered.

"What was that?"

"Nothing. I hope it goes well."

But he was already gone. And once again, I was alone with the ticking of the clock.

⌘

"Emmy, honey. How are you?"

My heart skipped a beat at my mother's words. She knew who I was today. "Hi mom, how are you?"

My mother raised a brow. "You're avoiding the question. I asked you first. How are *you?*"

"I'm good."

"No you're not. Don't you lie to me young lady. Sit down and spill it."

I couldn't help but smile and did as I was told. I flopped into the plush seat across from my mother. I took my time staring at the vacant white walls and furniture. Everything in this room was clinical and sterile. I began to tap my fingers nervously on the couch and avoided my mother's eyes. "I've been better. You…you didn't recognize me yesterday."

The color drained instantly from my mother's features and her knuckles turned white as she gripped onto the sides of the chair. Her face twisted with agony and sheer terror. "No." She gasped. "No!"

Guilt tore through me and I rushed to her side. My mother stood up abruptly. "How could I forget my own daughter? No! This can't be possible. How could this happen to me?"

As my mother's voice continued to rise a nurse came rushing in. "What's happening? Audrey, are you okay?"

My mother turned half wild towards the nurse. "I forgot my daughter yesterday? How could I do that? The doctor said I would have more time!"

The nurse spoke in a soothing manner. "Audrey, there is no textbook time line on a thing like Alzheimer's. We try our best to understand it, but each case is unique."

My mother took the words in and her brown eyes fell to me. "I'd like to be alone with my daughter please."

The nurse studied the situation and nodded. "Okay." She left the room and shut the door quietly behind her.

"Sit down Emmy. Please."

The sombre tone in which she took left no room for argument. I sat back into my seat and watched as my mother composed her features. When she looked up at me, all the fear she possessed earlier was gone. Her delicate angles looked soft and calm.

My mother cleared her throat. "I don't know how much time I have left. Well, moments that I'll remember anyways."

"Mom, ple—"

My mother cut me off sharply. "Emmy, please just listen to me. First and foremost, you are my heart. I am so proud of who you are as a person and I love you to the moon and back. When my mind disappears, I don't know where I go. I simply don't remember it. It's like I'm asleep and everything goes quiet. It doesn't entirely feel real to me."

I swallowed back the tears that had begun to form. My hand clutched my heart and I had to bite my lip to stop it from trembling. My mother met my gaze and she smiled, ever so softly.

She cleared her throat once more and continued. "Please don't ever think that I could forget you; that is simply not possible. You are with me wherever I go. When I do not remember the world around me, or the words I speak, and the mother you know is no longer here, remember one thing. She is not I. She may take my form, but her memories are not my own. Her feelings are not my feelings. You, Emmy, are my world. This disease does not change that. Ever."

Through my blurry-eyed vision, my mother held herself with the grace of a swan. She reached across the end table and grasped my hand. "I'm not done yet. There is so much to say in such little time."

"What else could there be?" I choked.

"Leave him."

My back stiffened and confusion took over my features.

My mother went on quickly. "I am stuck with a disease that I did not choose. My mind is going to be muddled, and my life will be compromised. That is against my will. But you Emmy, you're world has been compromised for a long time by *him* and that is your choice. You can fix it. It is time for

4

you to walk away. He is your disease, and you hold the power to change it."

The reality of her words struck me cold. I knew Sean wasn't her favourite person but she had never shared her true thoughts with me. When most people first met Sean, they were taken in and charmed by his good looks and seductive smile. But that had never swayed my mother, for she saw him for what he truly was. An anchor.

"You haven't been happy for a very long time, Emmy. You surround yourself by miserable people in his world. Shallow and petty; they are not your friends. Your hobbies have long since been erased. I have watched over the years silently, but I can't do it anymore. Time is running out." She took a deep breath.

"I have watched him take little pieces of you over time and bury them away. He was smart about it, I'll give him that. The pieces he chipped away at first were so small, you didn't notice. But over time, those tiny fragments add up to who you once were, *are*, as a person."

My mother took a heavy breath and suddenly looked old. "I fear that you are lost. You need to get out, get out now. Being alone isn't a bad thing. Give yourself time to find yourself. A true partner in life will not stifle who you are, they will nourish it. You need to find your spark again. I did not raise you to settle, I raised you to be a force that dared not be reckoned with." Audrey took a shaky breath and raised her eyes to mine. "I need to know that you will be happy. Please, Em, try to understand it from my point of view."

The words carried with them a heavy blow. My heart ached in a way that I had never felt before. In the depths of my stomach something twisted into a sharp, painful knot. Her words were true, this I knew, and I had known it for quite some time. But it was hard to walk away. I had dreamt of doing so many times, but he always drew me back in. And it was warm, loving, cozy, and safe. But it never lasted long. Once he felt I was compliant once again, things would go back to being the same. Cold, distant, and I became nothing more than his puppet and trophy.

It wasn't always this way. In the beginning, I was excited to be seen on his arm, to next to him. No one had ever noticed me before, and all of a sudden, everyone wanted to be me. For once in my life, money was never an issue. He gave me all the clothes and shoes I could only dream about. With him by my side, no place was to far; no dream was out of reach. People envied us. They wanted to be us. Women's eyes would drink him in, and I could feel men's stares brush against my skin. But we weren't the pretty picture we appeared to be. They didn't see what happened when the dancing stopped and the music came to a halt.

My mother's words rang with the harsh truth. Over time, he had taken little pieces of me and put them on the shelf. My new wardrobe quickly replaced my old one. My worn jeans with holes were tossed away, forever erasing my roots and where I came from. A personal trainer was then assigned to me. He moulded me into all the women that frequented the galas and benefits we attended. The next thing to change was my hair. I had thick, espresso hair that brushed against my collarbone. It was the ideal length for a lifetime spent in the barn and on the circuit. But no, it wasn't good enough. Extensions were put in, and the color was lightened to an unnatural blonde. My blue eyes were heightened by the color, but when I looked into the mirror; I no longer saw myself staring back.

"Do you like to dance?"

My mother's voice tore me from my thoughts. My brows pulled in confusion at her question. "Since when do you dance, Mom?"

As I studied my mother, my smile fell. Her bright eyes looked faraway and distant. She hummed along to a song only she could hear. My mother suddenly stood up as if she weighed nothing at all. She moved to the song inside her head. Despite knowing that her mind had drifted into a time before me, I was mesmerized by her movement. Her body moved with the strength and grace of a ballerina. She floated over the floor in such a skilled way, I realized at some point in her life she had formal training as a dancer. As I watched her, I wondered why someone so talented would have ever stopped, nonetheless tell me about it. Despite the beauty in the show, sadness overtook me. I wrapped my arms around myself and knew that my mother was temporarily gone. Her mind had taken her away from me, but I took a small comfort in the fact that she looked happy. If she were to slip away forever, I hoped her mind would always take her here, to this place in her memories.

The nurse entered the room and stopped in her tracks. She, like I, was taken by the talent sweeping across the floor. I gave the nurse a small headshake and she nodded in understanding. I watched in silence as the nurse approached my mother and took her by the hand.

Hesitation filled my mother and she planted her feet firmly in one spot. "Wait," she cried out and looked toward me. "Am I in?"

Confusion once again overtook me. "Are you in where?"

"The dance academy! Did I make it?"

I stared at my mother. Her petite body quivered in anticipation, and she wore her heart on her sleeve. I offered her a sad smile. "Congratulations Audrey. You are in. The dance was beautiful."

My mother went weak in relief. Her eyes filled with wondrous tears and her hands covered her heart. "Thank you. I promise, I won't let you down."

The nurse smiled at me and gently took my mother by the hand. She allowed herself to be dragged away. All the while, she wore a beaming smile as her mind drifted into the dark.

CHAPTER TWO

I drove home in a daze. How could my mother not share this part of her life? Why would she lock up such a talent? So many questions rattled through my head, but loudest of all were my mother's harsh yet honest words. They dug under my skin and latched on tight. The pain they created made me wince. I applied my blinker and turned onto the familiar street. The large, nearly identical houses loomed over me in the setting sun. Shadows bounced off the immaculate structures and carried with it a darkness that clouded over my spirits.

I stopped in front of the iron gate and punched in the code. As I pulled up the long paved drive I noticed a familiar black sports car parked next to Sean's. I let out a sigh and checked my reflection quickly in the car mirror. My features looked tired and worn. I reached into my purse and applied a fresh coat of mascara, as well as some lip-gloss. I clicked open the glove box and pulled out a hairbrush, and quickly ran it through my over processed hair. One of Sean's coworkers was here, which of course meant I had to be presentable.

As I stepped out of my car and headed toward the house, I wanted nothing more than to crawl into a hot bubble bath and soak with a glass of wine. But that would not be happening anytime soon. Even though I didn't understand the business talk, I would be expected to sit next to Sean and put on a happy face. As I stepped through the front door, I pressed it closed as quietly as I could. My heels clacked against the tiled floor and as I approached the closet, I kicked them off happily.

I pressed my bare feet into the cold floor and enjoyed the feeling of my arch resting flat. I wriggled my toes and smiled. It was a simple act, but it brought a rush of contentment. Loud voices tore my attention away from the other room and I did my best to position a smile on my lips. I followed the noise and stepped into the room. Sean, and his co-worker Will, both dressed in suits turned at my presence. Will smiled but Sean studied my tired appearance and frowned, just for a split second.

Sean stood up from his chair and wrapped his arm around my waist. "There she is." Sean pressed his lips against mine. "Come, take a seat. We're discussing some new companies we've invested in."

"Sounds exciting." I sat next to him quietly and gave Will a warm smile.

As their voices carried on, my eyes fell to my manicured nails. I almost scoffed at how ridiculous they looked on my hands. They would be useless in the barn, dirt would get under them constantly, and the polish would be scuffed. My eyes continued to study my hands, my smooth, flawless hands. I ran my finger over the palm of one and felt empty. I no longer had calluses from the many hours of hauling a wheelbarrow or from tossing bales of hay. Those days had long since been erased now. The familiar clacking of heels stole my attention upwards. I looked up to see Nikki, Will's secretary stride in with two mugs of coffee. She placed the black liquid in front of the men and smiled sweetly.

A tight feeling overtook the pit of my stomach. I hated her. I could feel my features pull in disgust at the mere sight of her. She, like I, had fake long, over bleached hair. Her makeup was heavy and flawless, her clothes designer. I studied her thick lash extensions and realized with a sick jolt that we looked strikingly similar. My eyes continued to sweep her features, all the while comparing my own. Nikki was the one to push the idea into Sean's head that I needed a trainer. And so, he got me to work with hers. Nikki was tall and graceful, her frame fit, and her chest gathered attention. I looked down at my own chest quickly, and knew I didn't have much in that department. She had recommended her surgeon to me, in apparent small talk, but I refused volatilely. Though my frame was fit, it would never be model lithe, like her own.

Nikki quickly gave me the once over and raised the pitch in her voice. "Emmy, it's so nice to see you. I feel like I haven't seen you in ages."

I hesitated before answering. "Hi Nikki. It's nice to see you too."

Nikki raised a manicured brow and studied me. "Huh." She reached into her purse and pulled out a small bottle. She leaned over the table and rolled it toward me. I glanced at the tube that lay in front of me.

"It's concealer. It does wonders to hide the dark circles. You can have that one if you'd like."

My blue eyes burned into her and she smiled her flawless smile. But I saw the two-faced gleam hiding beneath the makeup. Sean cleared his throat and I hesitantly looked his way. His lips were pressed together tightly as well as his hands. This seemingly simple act of Nikki was a personal hit to Sean. His trophy wasn't gleaming like he came to expect.

I picked up the tube and placed a smile on my face. "Thanks. I'll have to try it sometime."

Nikki smiled coyly. "It's like sleep in a bottle."

"Fantastic."

Sean's eyes bore into me for a moment. I looked away and focused my gaze to the table. He seemed somewhat satisfied with my response and continued on with where the men had left off earlier.

⌘

"Do I not give you enough?"

I groaned at the sharp tone of Sean's voice. "You give me more than I want, Sean."

"Well then I'm confused. All you have to do is look put together. You're appearance reflects directly upon me."

"If you would take a step back from your work, for once in your life, maybe you'd realize that I'm dealing with a lot right now. And it's been extremely hard on me."

"Is this about your mother again?"

"Of course it is!"

"Em, there's nothing you can do about it and I'm paying for the care.

What exactly do you have to worry about?"

I sucked in a sharp breath. And there it was. It always came down to the money for Sean. "I never asked you to pay for it. I could go back to work again. Don't you forget that you're the one who asked me to stop."

"Of course I asked you to stop. You taught people how to bend at unnatural angles. Yoga isn't a career. Money's not an issue, don't worry about it."

I backed away and sat down on the edge of the bed. Sean stopped pacing and looked my way. "I need you with me, Em. You're my other half. You know that, right?"

He took another step closer and placed his hand against my cheek. "I can book you a day at the spa, would you like that?"

"Not everything can be fixed with money, Sean."

He pulled his hand away. "Well then what? What do you want?"

"I need a distraction. I need to do something."

Sean darkened. "Do something? You have a lot on your plate already."

I barked out a laugh. "Like what? Shop? Workout? That's not a life. I need more than that."

"Since when?"

I ran my hands through my hair in frustration. "Since always! You took everything away from me that I love. I need more than this!"

"We have a fundraiser to go to this weekend. That should give you something to look forward to. Everyone will be there, it will be huge."

Disappointment knocked at my heart. "That's not what I mean. I need more."

Sean took three large strides toward me. He slipped his hands over mine and stood me up. "I'm sorry I've been so busy working lately." He pressed his lips to mine, and his hands began working against my side.

"I'm not in the mood, Sean."

"You will be."

I wriggled out of his grasp. "Not tonight."

Sean blew out a frustrated breath. "You're impossible. I'm going to bed, I have an early morning."

He stormed past me and slammed the bathroom door. Frustration coursed through my blood. I grabbed my laptop and placed it under my arm and marched downstairs. I stretched out on the couch and flicked open the screen. The bright blue light from the screen stung my eyes against the blackness of the night. I fumbled my fingertips against the keys and began to search my mother's disease. None of what I read was comforting to me. I slammed the laptop shut and stretched out on the couch. I closed my eyes and let sleep and the heaviness of the day take over.

⌘

"Do you think you'll ever stop dancing?"

"Not as long as I'm breathing."

"You really love it, don't you?"

My mother's features took on a dreamy look. "It's apart of who I am. The passion I have for dance seeps into my very core. Why do you ask?"

"I'm just wondering what it's like to love something so much."

My mother raised a brow and studied me. "You look sad. Don't you have anything, anything at all that you love to do? You strike me as someone who would have a passion."

"I used too." I whispered.

"Tell me, what is it?"

"I used to ride horses and compete. I got pretty good at it actually. I had a bad fall six years ago and had to take quite a bit of time off from riding. My doctor recommended yoga to help aid with my recovery, and I fell in love with that as well. I actually became an instructor for awhile."

"Yoga is kind of like dancing. "My mother tilted her head to one side. "You don't do either anymore?"

Emptiness gnawed at my flesh. "Not so much anymore."

"Why not?"

"Life took over I guess."

"Nonsense. If you love something that much, you never let it simply stop."

I couldn't help but smile, just a little. "I suppose."

My mother looked deep in thought and frustration overtook her. "I don't remember your name but you seem familiar to me, somehow.."

"My name is Emmy. You and I visit frequently."

"Emmy? That's a pretty name."

"Thank you."

"Emmy? I'm feeling tired. I think I may have a nap. Will you come visit again soon?"

"Of course I will."

"Okay, good. Oh, and Emmy?"

"Yes?"

"Go find the things you love. You're too young to look so lost."

I forced a smile. "I'll try my best."

More often than not, my mother no longer recognized who I was. Though she couldn't recall my name, she always took comfort in my presence. We enjoyed long talks and laughter and she still gave me words of wisdom. Despite knowing that my mother was fading away, I still sought out the comfort in her presence and relied on her to help guide me through the dark. Deep down, my mother still lingered in the fog…she was just living in a different time, but the core of who she was still remained and I hung on to that like a lifeline.

As I sat into the driver seat of my car, my phone rang. "Hello?"

"Hi Emmy, it's Nikki."

My lip curled in disgust. "Ah. How are you?"

"Oh, I'm fine. I'm calling on behalf of Sean. He's asked that I accompany you shopping for this weekend's event."

"Oh?"

"He knows I have impeccable taste. So, are you free right now?"

And what, my fashion is chopped liver? I clenched my fist together and gritted my teeth. "Sure." I spat out.

"Fantastic. I've also booked you a hair appointment. Meet me at the salon in half an hour. Bye darling."

The phone clicked and Nikki's overly sweet tone faded away. "Who does she think she is?" I muttered.

I raised my eyes to the mirror in the visor and opened it up. I studied my reflection and gently ran a hand through my hair. I tilted my head from one side to the other and smiled softly. My mother's voice ran through my head and I nodded to myself. It was time to start finding myself again.

CHAPTER THREE

I arrived at the salon to find Nikki pacing in her high heels and skin tight dress. I turned off the car and took a deep breath of patience. "Here we go," I whispered.

I pressed myself out of the car and met up with the impatient blonde. Nikki's eyes widened and she grabbed me by the arm. "It's about time you showed up. Hurry up!"

I allowed her to drag me inside the salon. The familiar scent of hair products and shampoo filtered my lungs. Nikki placed a dazzling smile on her face and let go of me immediately. She began chatting with the hairdressers and tossed her platinum hair over her shoulder.

"Emmy? Are you ready?"

I turned to my hairdresser Lonna. "Yes."

Lonna struck up a conversation as I settled into the chair. I listened quietly and gave her my two cents when needed. She draped the black gown over me and began to comb out my long, fake hair.

"The usual?"

"Actually, no."

Lonna looked taken aback as the comb paused mid air. "Oh? What were you thinking?"

"I want the extensions gone and my original hair color back."

Lonna shifted her weight and her eyes flew to Nikki. "Are you sure?"

"Yes. It's my hair after all. C'mon Lonna, work your magic."

"I wasn't expecting this is all. Don't you have a fundraiser this weekend?

It can be risky to make such a drastic change before a big event."

Impatience reared its head. "Look Lonna, if you won't do it I'll go somewhere that will. It's my hair, I can do whatever I want with it." I cringed as the words escaped my lips, knowing I sounded like a spoiled child. But for too long decisions had been made for me. For too long, I went ahead with everyone else's vision. It was time for me to start making my own.

"Oh, of course you can. No, no. I'll do it."

"Thank you."

As Lonna began to take out my extensions, I glanced over at Nikki. She was so deep into her conversation she wasn't even aware of what transpired around her. As long as she was the center of attention, all was right in her world.

"Okay, they're out."

I stared into the reflection and smiled. My natural hair fell just below my collarbone. I raised my fingertips to the ends and touched it ever so gently. I tossed my head from side to side and smiled. "It feels so light. I love it!"

Lonna smiled, just a little. "Are you sure you want to change the color as well? Too much change in one day might be a little overwhelming."

"Nope. Bring me back to my natural color. I've always hated the bleach look."

Lonna bit her lip, and then reluctantly nodded. "I'll go and grab the color samples. I'll be right back."

"Thank you."

Lonna appeared a moment later and handed me the book of colors. I studied them and my eyes fell to one particular color. The color was a rich brunette, the color of espresso. I smiled broadly and tapped a polished nail. "This is the one."

"Are you sure?"

"Lonna!" My tone was sharp.

"Okay, I'll mix it up."

I nodded briskly. "Thank you."

At that moment, Nikki's eyes had strayed ever so slightly from her conversation and they fell on me. Her mouth formed into a perfect "O" as she stomped over.

"What happened?"

"What do you mean?"

"To your hair!" she snapped.

I shrugged my shoulders and smiled. "Nothing. I wanted the extensions out. I miss my real hair."

At that moment, Lonna entered the room mixing the color. Her steps faltered as she took in the scene. Her body went tense and I could tell she wanted to flee. "Lonna!" I snapped. "Don't even think about it."

Nikki's eyes landed upon her and she took in the bowl of color. "What is this?" she growled.

"I wanted a change." I replied immediately. "Back off Nikki and let her do her job."

Nikki's sharp gaze challenged me but I held on strong. A moment of uncertainty crossed her features before she stormed away. Lonna took her place beside me and began painting on the color. There were no more attempts at conversation to be tried. I waited until the color was applied and Lonna wrapped my hair into a tight bun.

"I'll be back in twenty minutes."

"Sounds good." I settled back against the chair and waited for the minutes to tick by. From behind, Nikki sat in the waiting area, cutting her fuming gaze into me the entire time. The timer eventually went off and Lonna came over. She nodded to the sink and I followed. Once my hair was washed I took my place in the seat once more. I kept my eyes to the floor the entire time. I didn't want to see the color until my hair was completely dry. My heart began to beat rapidly in my chest, enough so that I heard it loudly within my ears.

"It's done."

"Oh my god, what have you done? Sean is going to kill me!" Nikki screeched from the background.

The stress in her voice brought me great joy as I raised my eyes to the mirror. My reflection caught me off guard and I let out a surprised gasp.

"Oh, I knew it! The change is too much, isn't it?" Lonna wailed.

I leaned closer toward the mirror and studied myself. The Espresso color was a rich shade. Depending on how the light hit it, there was the faintest shimmer of red. The blue in my eyes shone royally and the color complemented my skin tone. It brought out the slightest of freckles across the bridge of my nose. I let out a light laugh and stood up. I turned to Lonna and wrapped her in a bear hug.

"Thank you so much! I feel like myself again."

Lonna let out a sigh heavy in relief. "You're welcome."

I tore the cape off and grabbed my purse. I walked up to Nikki who continued to glower at me and I gave her a hearty slap on the back. "Bill it to Sean."

"Where do you think you're going?" she whined.

"Shopping apparently."

"We were supposed to go shopping together."

"I think I'll choose my own dress." With that, I let the salon door slam behind me.

⌘

Once I left the salon, I had every intention of going dress shopping. It wasn't until I caught my reflection in the side mirror that a wave of emotion sucker punched me and I had to pull over. I didn't need another dress, I had a closet full of them, and if I I'm being truly honest, I could care less to have one more. I slid my gaze to the small rear view mirror and studied my reflection. It was only a change of hair color, but to me it was so much more than that. It was a small step toward the girl I used to be, the girl I used to be proud of. The girl who knew where she was going in life, who had a voice of her own and would never slip into closets and cry alone in the shadows.

The tears began to slip away as I let the past three years hit my heart. My stomach turned as the knot deep inside twisted tighter. My limbs began to tremble and my heart raced. The loud thumping in my ears beat like a drum as I struggled to take a steady breath. This was a feeling I had begun to know all too well. It happened when I took a long and hard look at my life. Sean's presence somehow erased my own and I became nothing more than a shiny item he could call his. How on earth did I let that happen? My voice became nothing more than a whisper, my ideas were unrealistic and shot down, even my own personal appearance got altered. It was alarming knowing that not only did I let this happen, but at the time he made me think it was what I wanted. And I somehow believed him.

Sure, financially I never had to worry anymore. But it came with such a strong price. *My happiness. My freedom. Me.* My choices were no longer my own, my day was structured minute by the minute with meaningless tasks that were designed to make me feel useful. Panic attacks would often find me and I would slip away, unnoticed by the one I shared a life with. When they finally passed, I would cry for hours. And then my mother got sick. It was another thing being lost, only this was one I could never replace.

My life before Sean wasn't without its struggles. I competed on my horse and when we did well at shows, the money was half decent and it got us by for quite sometime. In the meantime to make ends meet, I took on a part time gig as a yoga instructor and took photos for local events. I loved my life, I was happy then. The choices were my own, and I was doing what I loved to do, complete with a solid support group of friends. Of course, they didn't fit into Sean's "crowd" and I let him erase them over time as I allowed him to pull me away from everything I had loved.

Thinking back to it all, the day I sold my horse was the day a large part of my identity died. I remember feeling a physical ache the morning I loaded my boy into the trailer. When the rumble of the engine started and those truck tires pulled away carrying away my precious cargo, I broke. My knees faltered and I fell to the ground as I watched my hopes and dreams get lost amongst the gravel dust.

I shook my head fiercely as the memories came out to haunt me. I wiped the tears away briskly from my swollen eyes and started the car. I stepped on the gas hard and began heading to the care home where my mother stayed. As I drove to the familiar building, I hoped and prayed with all my might that her mind would be here with me today. I needed to talk to someone who was in my corner more than ever. As I entered the parking lot I raised my foot off the gas and coasted into a vacant spot. Once my feet hit the pavement I took off running and arrived breathlessly into my mother's room. The noise startled her and she jumped.

"I'm sorry, I didn't mean to scare you."

My mother turned and her eyebrows rose. She stood up from her chair and walked over to me with the smallest of smiles. She raised her hand against my hair and smiled. "There she is. It's been awhile."

I was unsure of how to answer. Did she even know who I was? She must have sensed my hesitation for she let out a chuckle. "That blonde washed you out something terrible. And the length was too much; it looked like you were hiding beneath a curtain. "

It was then I realized my mother was lucid, and once again, my tears fell freely. Only I couldn't feel an end to them. Sobs escaped my lips and my body racked from the effort.

"Emmy, honey. What's wrong?"

"I-I-I..."

"Come here. Shh, it's okay. I've got you. It's all going to be okay."

Though my mother was small, she wrapped me in a hug that rivalled any bear. She led me to the couch and I stayed in her embrace until the tears stopped and my breathing quieted.

"Are you worried what he'll think?"

"A little. It seemed like a good idea at the time, but now..."

My mother scoffed. "Emmy, I think you need to ask yourself if you're in a good relationship. All you did was change your hair color and now look at you. Honey, it's only hair. What made you do it?"

"I missed feeling like myself."

"I missed seeing you like this. You shouldn't be worried to do things for yourself. It's your life, you don't need to walk on eggshells it's not healthy. It's only hair for heavens sake."

I let out a deep sigh and sat upright. "I know."

"To be honest I'm surprised you've made it this long. You were never one to play within the rules for very long."

A smirk crept up. "I remember."

"Emmy?"

"Yes, Mom."

"I need you to really listen to what I'm about to say."

"Of course."

"Please don't stay here just for me. I've been watching you for quite some time and there is nothing more heartbreaking than watching your own child drown in front of you. I need you to break free of whatever it is that is boxing you in, and for the love of God, please live your life. Find what makes you happy and do it."

"Mom, I am happy."

"That's an outright lie. Do I look like an idiot to you?"

I hung my head and lowered my voice. "No, you are anything but."

"Emmy, look at me please."

I raised my eyes to her and she nodded. "Good. My darling daughter, look around you. Look where I am. Life is too short and precious to spend it being so miserable. It's a waste. You are not a weak, frail girl. You are smart, driven and determined. You wanted your life to be an adventure, and so my girl, go find it. Leave the nest, spread those wings and fly already! "

Before I could respond my mother stood up and grabbed my hands. "Stand up."

I did as told and watched her in shock. "Mom, I-"

"Shush. Don't say a word. Just give me a big hug."

I didn't have an option in the matter as she drew me close and tight. I threw my arms around her and gave her a tight embrace. My heart faltered slightly and tears began to form. "Mom, what's happening?"

She broke the grasp and stood back. "Come back and see me when you've found the joy within yourself. I'm not going anywhere. I do not want to see you until those eyes of yours have some light again. Do you understand?"

I knew better than to argue with her when she took on that tone. No matter how old I was, I was still her daughter, and she would always be my mom. I nodded feverently. "I promise."

"Good. Now give me one more hug."

I did as asked. As I turned to walk away I stopped at the door. "Mom? Is it okay to be scared?"

"If you aren't scared than you're not doing it right."

I blew out a breath. "Okay." I managed a small laugh. With one last smile, I turned away and left my mother standing alone in her room.

⌘

The house was near empty when I stepped into the foyer. The housekeeper bustled in the next room and I gave her a gentle wave. Sean was still at work no doubt. Out of habit, I entered the walk in closet and pulled out a royal blue dress. I slipped out of my day clothes and stepped into the elegant garment with the low cut back. Once I zipped the dress on snug, I sat down on a soft seat to apply my makeup for the evening. I gazed at my reflection and ran my fingertips through my new hair. How was Sean going to react to this? Would he like it? Would he hate it? The small flutter of butterflies began to stir and I tried my best to shake them away. *No! No! No!* It was *my* hair, on *my* body. It didn't matter what anyone else thought. This was all me.

For years I had kept my hair pin straight. It was how he liked it. But tonight was a night of embracing the old becoming the new. I rushed from my seat and ran back to the closet. I stood up on my tippy toes and pulled out an old shoebox. I rummaged through my old memorabilia and found a bottle of sea salt spray. The sight of the familiar bottle brought a flood of memories back to when my life had no restrictions. I spritzed the spray into my hair and crunched the hair within my palms. The sea salt brought out my playful waves. I continued to scrunch my hair until I reached my desired look.

"Emmy?"

The shock in his voice sent me whirling in his direction. "Sean! You nearly gave me a heart attack! I didn't hear you."

Sean's eyes stayed wide as he continued to study me. I grew uncomfortable with the silence and began shifting from foot to foot. "Well," I began cautiously. "What do you think?"

Sean closed his mouth and shook his head. "I-you look so different." Sean ran his hands through his hair in frustration. "Maybe we can still fix it in time."

"Fix what? My hair?"

"Don't be smart with me. Of course I mean your hair. People won't recognize you!"

"But I like this look."

Sean blew out a frustrated breath. "Fine, get your shoes, we have to go."

The drive over was uncomfortable, not a word was spoken. The noise of the tires on pavement filled the small cab. I did my best to ignore Sean's disapproving gaze and set jaw by keeping my eyes glued to the world outside as it blurred by.

The party was the same old thing. The same faces, same smiles, same boring chatter that I wasn't truly apart of. I ignored the silent stares and whispers from the bystanders. *She's rebelling. Who does she think she is? What is she trying to prove?* For christ sake, it was only hair. But you see, in a world where everyone is so desperate to be the same, change can be a scary thing, no matter how small. Throughout the night Sean grew tense. His smile was strained as he glanced my way. He gripped my hand a little tighter than necessary as he dragged me from conversation to conversation. I looked around at the dining hall. It was packed to the brim, noise from laughter and alcohol induced chatter began to echo off the walls, and I had never felt more alone. Finally the night came to an end. I followed Sean to the car and slid into the passenger seat, kicking off my heels.

"That was a rough night, Em."

"I thought it was the same old thing to be honest."

Sean gripped onto the wheel tightly; his eyes were laser focused on the road. "If you planned to intentionally embarrass me job well done."

My hands flew to my hair by instinct. "If this is about my hair, I think we need to let that go. It's not that big of a deal."

"It is to me Em. We are a couple. You stand beside me, you represent me."

His words squeezed my heart. It was just hair...my hair. How could something so meaningless have such a big impact? How could his voice, his tone actually make me feel guilty?

Sean cleared his throat. "Can you change it back?"

I could, but I won't. Not for you. Not anymore. Tears welled in my eyes. "No."

Sean stole a nano second of a glance my way. "I see. I'll try to get used to it then."

I nodded curtly. "I looked like this when I met you. Why are you so bothered by it now?"

Sean didn't take his eyes off the road. "I've always had big plans for you. Don't stray from them now."

"Whatever happened to asking me what I want?" I whispered. But my voice was lost amongst the revving engine and disappointment.

CHAPTER FOUR

I didn't know him anymore, more importantly, I didn't know who I was anymore. I had gotten lost over the years and it was getting harder and harder to find the exit. I pondered on the thought and wondered if there was anything more heartbreaking than feeling completely alone while sharing a life with someone. *No, there isn't.*

Sean was out like a light next to me, sleeping blissfully. I envied how easy sleep came for him. When darkness fell, my mind unleashed the beast. Thoughts of my mother and everything I was loosing ran rampant; all of my fears and worries took over. The tears, as usual, began to fall and I was too tired to hold them back, but this was nothing new these days. Countless nights I cried myself to sleep with Sean at my side, only he never noticed, or didn't care. I could never tell. I let out a shuddery breath and let the heaviness close my lids. The darkness crept in until I finally dozed off.

I dreamt of him. I hadn't dreamt of him in over a year. I tried not to think about him, for selling him had stolen a piece of me. It was the scene I wanted to forget, the day his new owners arrived. He was tied in the alleyway of the barn, groomed to perfection. His copper body gleamed like a new penny, his black mane and tail as smooth as any vain women's hair. My hands trembled as I placed his stable quilt over his well-muscled frame. I remember I couldn't breath as the sobs had stolen my very breath. Ace knew something was up. He danced in agitation and his warm brown eyes filled in concern. "Be a good boy. I'm so sorry. I love you. Never forget that."

I gave his neck a hearty pat and planted a kiss on his nose. His expressive eyes followed my every move. *What's wrong?* They seemed to say.

"Emmy?"

I flinched at the sound of her voice, his new home. His new person. "I can't do it." I fumbled.

"I know. It's okay. I can load him."

I stole one last look at my pride and joy. "Please take care of him. Be kind to him."

"I will. I promise."

My eyes drank him in for the last time. I had to force my dead limbs to walk away. I grabbed my purse half hazardly and swung it over my shoulder. My muddy boots marched unsteadily beneath my feet and the smell of leather and hay rushed past me. I stepped out of the barn and turned the corner. I couldn't make it to my truck. Instead I pressed my back against the barn and heard Ace calling for me. The sound tore a hole in my gut. I knew his sounds; this one was full of concern. He wasn't going to make this easy on his new person. I could tell from the high pitch he had used. Another neigh tore through the barnyard. I heard his hooves clack as he tried to bolt. I peeked around the corner and saw his new girl keeping a firm hand on the lead rope as Ace danced in nerves. He held his head high, his neck tense. A man walked up to Ace's new person, I'd guess it was her boyfriend. I never asked nor did I care. I watched as they tried to reassure my horse. Ace relaxed his neck ever so slightly, but even from a distance I could see how wild his eyes were. The two of them walked Ace up to the empty trailer that awaited his arrival. Ace balked and put the brakes on. Again he called. *Please load. Be a good boy and step into the trailer. Please.*

I watched for fifteen minutes as my horse worked up a sweat and his voice grew hoarse from calling. I buried my head in my hands and let out a curse. I did not want things to end this way. I did not want to be the one who had to load him into the trailer; I did not want to be the one to close the door and block out his sunshine. *Fuck Ace.* I forced my heavy body away from the barn and I took off running, towards him.

"Ace!" His body came to a halt and he let out a loud neigh. "Easy boy, it's okay. I've got you." I tore the lead rope out of his new owner's hand and pressed myself against him. "We're okay. You got this buddy." I gave a gentle tug and walked towards the ramp. Ace followed but he was hesitant. I stared into the dark trailer and felt Ace let out a heavy sigh. He could feel the change. He could sense the end.

His hooves gingerly stepped up the ramp and into the trailer. I secured him inside and took his head into my hands. "Be a good boy. Promise me." I silently counted to three and backed out of the trailer. As soon as Ace realized I had left, the trailer began to clang and rattle. He pawed at the ground and desperately tried to turn around, toward the exit, towards the light.

"Shut the door, Brian!" Ace's new people slammed the door and locked it in unison. She shot me a stressed smile. "Thanks for the help. We've got to get a move on."

I watched in horror as the trailer swayed side to side. I watched until the black truck disappeared down the drive, carrying my precious cargo. As the truck rumbled out of sight, Ace's attempts in trying to fight the metal box that carried him away echoed in the empty day. My body could take no more. My legs gave out and I met the cold ground heavily. I tucked myself into a ball and squeezed my eyes shut, desperately wishing I could forget what I had just witnessed. A strong, warm grip grabbed my elbow and pulled me up. "Emmy. It's going to be okay. It's going to be okay."

"You didn't see him, Chase. You didn't see him. What have I done?"

Chase wrapped me in a tight embrace. "We'll get through this." And I believed him. With everything I had, I believed him.

⌘

The sound of the incessant alarm drew me from my restless slumber. I sat up groggily and blew the hair out of my eyes. I slipped my cold feet into my morning slippers and trudged to the kitchen. My lifeline, coffee, was calling my name. As I waited for my brew to finish the front door slammed shut. Sean strolled into the kitchen wearing a pair of athletic shorts and a t-shirt. His skin was flushed and his hair damp. The veins on his muscled limbs were prominent, a tell tale sign that he had completed a recent workout. Sean gave me a quick nod. "You look tired."

"Jee, thanks. Morning to you too."

Sean slipped past me and got to the coffee before I could. I watched as he poured the steaming liquid into his mug. Sean felt me watching him. He set down the coffee pot and studied me. "What's wrong?"

"Nothing. I just had a bad dream."

"Oh, that's it?"

I stepped past him and reached for my favourite mug. "That's it."

"When's the last time you got in a workout?"

I bristled at his scolding tone. "I dunno. Four days ago, maybe."

"Well, I know what you're doing today."

"I'm sure you do." I mumbled. *Jump when I say jump. Smile when I tell you too. You're mine; I own you.*

"You've got a closet full of gym clothes. Besides, a workout might be just what you need. You've been kind of uptight lately."

I slammed my mug on the counter. "Excuse me? I've been *uptight*? Are you not aware of what I'm going through?"

Sean let out a heavy sigh. "See this is what I'm talking about."

"Screw you."

Sean's face darkened. "Be careful how you speak to me, Em. You're walking a fine line. Just do what I say. I know what's best for you."

I threw my hands up in the air. "How could you possibly know? You're never here!! I have to go through everything on my own."

Sean stepped toward me in a swift movement, knocking my mug in the process. I watched in slow motion as the mug teetered the edge. Gravity won and the mug shattered into tiny pieces across the kitchen floor. Sean blew out a frustrated grunt."Great. That's just great."

"That was my favourite mug," I whispered.

"It was old and a piece of junk. It didn't match anything in the rest of the kitchen." Sean glanced at the time. "Can you clean it up? I have to shower and run to work. We've got a big meeting today."

I stared at the tiny sharp fragments. "Sure."

"Oh, Em? Don't forget; make sure you get in a workout today. Make it your priority."

I didn't bother with a response. I reached for the broom and began sweeping up the mess into the dustpan. I stopped at a larger chunk of glass where the faded painting of a horseshoe was still nearly visible. My heart tugged and a knot formed in the pit of my stomach. I picked up the paint shard and turned it over carefully. I could still hear Chase's voice and see his smile as he gave the mug to me, wrapped in a gift box. I closed my eyes and briefly saw the carnival lights flash. *Better days. They are no more.* I dropped the piece into the garbage can and tossed the broom into the closet.

I found myself in my gym clothes. Sean's words were beat into my brain along with his disappointed tone. I slid into my vehicle and started the engine. My dream from the previous night was still with me. *Ace.* As the years passed I had lost touch with his new owners. Whether they moved and changed their number, or they blocked me I wasn't sure. I had kept my presence to a minimum, but I liked to ask for an update every once in awhile via text or photo. The disappearance of his new owners had always bothered me, but I knew I had no more rights to him. I gave them up the day they handed me the cheque.

I drove in a daze. I pulled into the packed parking lot of the gym and saw the dedicated people through the large glass windows on the exercise equipment. Skin flushed, breathing hard getting the job done. My hand paused on the door handle and I sighed. My heart wasn't in it. I stuck the key back in the ignition and backed out of my parking stall. I knew where I would end up. My skin itched at the thought; my heart sped up and twisted with excitement and guilt. The only barn in town was an upscale riding academy, the complete opposite of where I used to frequent. I pulled into an empty spot and stepped out into the brisk air. I shuddered quickly and zipped my jacket up as far as it would go. The thin athletic layers were not built for the current temperature. As I stepped into the flawless barn, goose bumps nipped at my skin. The sweet scent of hay teased my nose and curious horses peeked their heads over the stalls. My eyes took in the barn and I whistled in admiration. Nothing was out of place, not a speck of dirt was to be seen.

"You sure are a lucky horse, you know." A curious bystander poked its nose at my shoulder. I smiled at the familiar scent of equine. I pressed my hand against its forehead. My fingers automatically began playing with the horse's forelock. Warm brown eyes watched my every move but there was no sign of distrust. My heart flopped and I stepped back as if I had been stung.

"I can't do this. I can't be here." I turned on my heel and ran back to my car. I slid inside quickly and slammed the door with more force than necessary. I stared at the gray sky, I had nowhere that I wanted to be; no one that I could run too. I was stuck in an endless circle. The walls were closing in, and I couldn't escape it. I rested my forehead against the leather steering wheel and stayed there for quite some time. *This can't be my life. This can't be my forever. I want to go home.*

Home. It's a funny thing isn't it? The place that I considered home, the place I missed most was no longer mine. I had to leave it all behind, and right now; I would give everything I possessed to have it back. I sat upright and hit my hand against the dashboard in frustration. The blow felt good, and I hit it again and again. "Damnit!" I cried. "God damnit how did I get here?"

My phone jingled. The sound pulled my attention from my self-pity. I glanced at the message and my throat suddenly felt tight. The message was from Elayna, my best friend from back home, or at least she used to be before I cut myself off from the world. *"It's almost Aarons day. My thoughts are with you and your mom. We hope you two are ok. Please don't be a stranger. We're all going to visit him at the usual place. I hope you can make it this year. Please, Em. I miss you. We all do."*

I read her message three times through before I gently put the phone down. I stared at it like it was a wild predator. *Aaron. You bastard, how could you?* Rage and devastation hit me like a ton of bricks. It had been five years since Aaron left his mark. He had been a part of the reason I had to sell Ace, we were in a tight spot and I needed the financial help. Anything and everything counted at the time. My mom had begun to show signs of Alzheimer's and she had to leave her job much earlier than anticipated. Her medical costs were piling up and after what Aaron had done; it put a real strain on the family unit. A part of me blamed Aaron for my mom's rapid decline, the emotional strain he caused elevated all the negatives. But on the other hand, at least she was able to disappear into a time before all of this was a reality.

I decided not to respond to Elayna's text. I brought the car to life and drove to my mom's care home. *Screw the promise of finding my happy.* Sometimes, you just needed to see your mom, no matter how old you were. I walked down the familiar halls to her room. She was perched on her favourite chair; her legs were curled under her as she stared out the window. Though I could only see the back of her head, I sensed the sadness in the room.

"Mom? Are you okay?"

"I didn't see it coming Emmy. I did not see it coming."

"None of us did, Mom."

"I should have, I am his mother. It's my job to protect my children and I let him down. And now look? Where is he, Em? Do you know where he is? He will never smile again, he will never laugh. He is left forever in the dark. In the cold."

I watched as my mother rose from her chair and began pacing frantically, she was slowly coming un-glued. Her voice began to rise higher and higher into a manic state. I had seen this before and I knew what would come next, the total breakdown. For once in my life, I wished for my mother's disease to take over and blacken her mind. I didn't want her to relive this, I didn't want to go through this again, I couldn't take it. I wasn't strong like I once was.

"Mom, look at me, please."

She carried on as though I weren't even here. Her voice continued to rise and to my horror she picked up a glass vase and hurled it at the wall. The explosion of glass filled my ears and I watched as the fragments of sharp shards fell to the floor. My mother let out a scream of agony and the tears began to fall violently. Her small frame began to tremble uncontrollably as her sobs took over.

I ran to her and wrapped her in a tight embrace. "Breathe, Mom. It's okay, everything is going to be okay. You are not alone, I'm here."

Her sobs grew wild and she let out another unearthly wail. I tried to keep her calm, keep her quiet but I could no longer control the sorrow that had taken over. The nurses ran in and their trained eyes took in the situation with worry. They pushed me back and without a second thought, they administered a needle with clear fluid into her skin. It didn't take long for her to quiet. She focused her eyes on me and bore her stare into mine. "I need to see him, Em. Take me to him! I need to see him! Please!" she sobbed.

One of the nurses stepped over to me quickly. "What happened?"

I shook my head and stepped back, watching as the other nurse took my sedated mother to her bed. "She remembers."

"Remembers what?"

"Betrayal. Tragedy. Why do you need to know?" I snapped.

The nurse seemed to be taken aback. "We're just trying to help. I've never seen her like this."

"I have." I whispered.

My mother turned to her side on the bed. Once again she locked her gaze on me. "Take me to him, Emmy. Let me see him."

I said nothing. My tongue felt leaden and heavy. Instead I watched her as the drugs took over and her eyes fell closed. I took a shuddery breath and the horror set in. I realized I would be going home after all.

CHAPTER FIVE

My hands shook uncontrollably as I sat at the kitchen table. I was on my fourth glass of wine by the time Sean got home from work. My phone lay by the near empty bottle of wine and I stared at it like it would be coming to life at any given moment to bite me. I reached for my glass and took a long swig, allowing the buzz from the alcohol to take over. I welcomed it.

"Em?"

I nearly jumped out of my seat at the sound of his voice. My body twitched and the glass of wine tipped over. The red liquid oozed across the table. "Oh shit." I cried.

I lunged for the paper towels and in my haste my knee slammed against the table leg and it was enough to send the glass falling for the floor. For the second time that day glass spewed across the kitchen floor. "Oh god." I gasped. It was too much, everything I had tried to escape was rising to the surface and I couldn't stop it.

Sean for once sensed something was wrong. His arm held me back and he reached for the broom. "Stay back I've got this."

I felt my breaths coming in quick and haggard. I was on the verge of hyperventilating. I pressed my back against the wall and slid onto the kitchen floor. I pressed my knees against my chest and buried my hands in my hair. I watched Sean as he worked quickly and efficiently, cleaning up my mess. His eyes flicked between me and each time our eyes met, I caught the look of worry. Sean dumped the glass into the garbage and he slid beside me.

"What the hell happened today, Em."

I shook my head and bit my lip. I saw it all over again, playing like a movie. "Aaron. She remembers. It was terrible. They had to sedate her."

Sean tensed beside me. He knew about Aaron. "Oh shit. That's coming up isn't it." He squeezed my knee. "I'm sorry, Em, I really am. But...." Sean took a careful breath. "You normally don't let it get to you. You sweep it under the rug and act as if it's just another day."

"I know. It's different this time. She wants me to take her to him."

Sean shook his head. "I don't think that's a good idea. What are you going to do?"

"I'm going to do as she asks. I suppose it's time for me to go back. I always knew I would have to at some point. We still have the house. Maybe I will finally be able to sell it once and for all."

"Are you ready for it?"

"No."

Sean looked at me with something close to tenderness. I hadn't seen him look at me that way in a very long time. He reached out and tucked a strand of hair behind my ear. "I'm going to lose you, aren't I?"

His words surprised me. "Why would you say that?"

"I know what waits for you back there."

"Nothing."

"No, it's not nothing. I've seen the faraway look in your eyes. I know you go back there in your mind. I know where that mug came from."

I forced my eyes to meet his. "Sean..."

"I see a lot more than you think. I just think you're better than all of that. I want you to *be* better. I want you to be mine. But you've been fighting me every step of the way. I'm not sure you will come back and all of my hard work will have been for nothing."

And there it was. The bottom line, what it all boiled down to: himself. It always came back to how it affected him. He was not used to losing. His image was everything and winning was the ultimate goal.

"Do you even love me, Sean?"

"What kind of question is that?"

"An important one. Do you love me? Or am I merely a challenge, a trophy you want next to you?"

Sean stood up. "That's a stupid question."

"No it's not. Can you say the words? Look at me, Sean."

He did, but not a single word escaped his lips. I kept my eyes locked on his. "Because I don't. I don't love you. You have left me to drown time and time again. Not once have you stepped in to save me. Not once have you been there, and I mean really been there for me. I am alone, even when you are physically beside me, I am alone."

Sean's mouth opened slightly. I could see him desperately looking for the words that failed to come to him. I stepped forward and raised my hands to his face. "I can't do this. I am so tired, Sean. Exhausted is an under statement. I don't know how I'm going to get through this but right now I just need to breathe. And I can't breathe with you. I just can't. I need all the strength I can get right now. And I am stronger alone."

I watched my words sink in. His face furrowed in confusion until the anger took over. He slapped my hands away. "Are you ending this?"

"It's been over for a long time."

Sean shook his head rapidly. "You're not thinking straight."

I folded my arms in a protective stance. "I'm sorry but I am. I shouldn't have let it get this far."

The rejection set in. I saw him recoil. "You're making a mistake. But let me make one thing clear; if you go back there, you will fall and you will fall hard. "He ran his hand through his hair. "You could never make it in my world. You'd get eaten alive. I should have known better. I wasted a lot of time and money trying to blend you in. It was doomed from the start." His eyes grew hard as he looked me over.

In that very moment I knew I was doing the right thing. His words left me at peace. I had to leave this behind, no matter what happened this would never be worth coming back too. Sean had proved that time and time again.

"You're right, Sean. I should have aimed higher than you. You were never strong enough for me."

He let out a snort. "I hope you enjoy your fall, Em." He grabbed his keys and left the room. The slam of the front door echoed throughout the home.

I looked around the house one last time and shuddered. It felt colder than usual, I felt strongly out of place. *Leave. Get out and run. Now.* My feet took action and I ran for the bedroom. I grabbed what little items that I owned; the things that were originally mine before Sean. All of the fancy clothes and shoes would stay. They would act as a reminder to him that he could never change me. I won. I gathered my things and headed for the front door. I took my spare house key off the chain and left it on the end table. With one last glance behind me, I said a silent goodbye. I swung the front door open and shut it quietly behind me. I stepped into the chilled air that threatened snow. And for the first time in a long time, I felt like I could finally breath.

⌘

My breath swirled like white smoke in the brisk night. I bounced from foot to foot as I waited for my gas tank to fill. I stomped my foot impatiently until the pump clicked alerting me it was full. "Oh thank god." I placed the pump back into its cradle and quickly launched myself into my warm car.

Now what? Step one was complete, cut the ties that burdened me. Step two…well, that would be the hard part. Going backwards, from everything that I ran away from. *Who in the hell goes backwards? What happened to moving forward? Place one foot in front of the other, just keep moving, don't go back. Never go back. Leave it all buried in the ground.* But I no longer could. The past can never stay buried. It will always rise to the surface and demand to be seen. It needed a proper farewell and I couldn't say no to my mom. I simply couldn't. She too, like me, had tried to keep the past locked away. But something had shifted. Her mind needed to see it; she needed to face what she could no longer keep in the dark. And I would go back for her. I had no other choice.

I reached for my phone. I brought up Elayna's text once more and looked it over again. I glanced at the time, it was late. Without a second thought I dialled her number. *Please be sleeping. Please let me get an answering machine.*

"Emmy? Is it really you?"

I hadn't heard Elayna's voice in so long. The familiarity of it fell over me like a warm blanket. I had missed her so much."It's me. I'm so sorry." My voice broke in an instant.

"What's wrong? Where are you?'

"I'll be coming home soon."

"What's wrong, Em? I can hear it in your voice."

Her gentle tone unleashed everything in a single instant. "Everything. My mom, for a start. She's sick. Alzheimer's; it came on quick but tonight she remembered Aaron. They had to sedate her. God, Elayna, you should have seen her. She completely fell apart. And I left Sean tonight. I have nowhere to go. I just got caught up in the moment, you know? It felt so good to say good-bye, but my god, I actually have nowhere to go. There's no one here in this city that I trust. Oh, Elayna, what have I done?"

"Take a deep breath, Em. I'm so, so sorry. Why didn't you tell me about your Mom? You always have a place here with us. Come over. We have room. Bring your Mom too. Please, come back. You don't have to be alone. Please come home."

I silenced my tears. Why had I cut myself off from her? She had always been like a sister to me, and I could only imagine the hurt I had caused her when I left without so much as a word. Over the years she had tried to make contact, and I was always the one pulling away and yet here she was, giving me a safe place without a second thought. It was so Elayna. And running was so…so me.

"Em, are you still there?"

"Yes. I…I just need to pick up my mom from the care home."

"Let me know when you're on the way."

"I will. Thank you."

I hung up the phone feeling somewhat hopeful. The next big task: taking my mom away from the place that held her safe. *What the hell am I doing?* I took a determined breath and started the engine. It was now or never. This was the point of no return.

CHAPTER SIX

The Nurse thought I was crazy. I got into a heated argument with her and was referred to the manager of the care home. I explained in great detail of the situation; more so than she deserved to hear. Her stone face barely shifted, barely made a motion. I stared at her dumbfounded wondering if she had a soul. By the end of the conversation she merely gave a small nod and a wave of her hand in dismissal. As I rose from my chair her hard tone stopped me.

"Emmy?"

"Yes?"

"If anything happens to your mother this is on you. We are not liable for the events that take place outside this facility."

My jaw dropped and I stared at her in slight disgust. How times had changed. Here I was, now getting a lecture from a stranger on what I could and couldn't do with my mother. I shook my head at the silliness of the thought, I had to ask, no beg for approval for time alone with her. "Do you want me to sign something that washes your hands clean of any mishaps?" I snapped.

She slightly twitched, as though the words hit a nerve. She briskly slid a piece of paper toward me. "I wouldn't quite use those words, but yes, I would appreciate if you would sign this before you take her."

I picked up a pen and glanced over the paperwork, it was full of legalities to cover their ass. I signed the dotted line and left the room without looking back.

⌘

Loading up my mother was easy. Her every muscle was tense in anticipation as we left the care home. We both walked with urgency in our steps. I tried to keep my eyes locked only on the exit but my eyes couldn't help but wander to the patient rooms as we left. Confused, lost faces stared back at me. The sounds of raised voices echoed down the lonely halls. I stole a glance at my mother and she set her jaw in a determined motion and kept her eyes locked to the door that held her freedom. Though she held her posture in a confident manner, she had a slight tremble in her hands. When we stepped into the winter air, she stopped abruptly and clasped onto my forearm. She looked at me in slight wonder and took a deep breath as though she hadn't been able to breathe in a very long time.

"Mom, are you ok?"

She nodded. "Yes, Emmy. I am." She turned her body toward me. "We're going to see Aaron right?"

I flinched at the sound of his name. "Yes, I promised you we would."

Her body relaxed. "Good." Her eyes scanned the parking lot. "I-I don't know what you drive anymore."

"Follow me, Mom."

She did. I took the bags from her hands and placed them in the trunk. My mother hesitated slightly before getting in the shiny car. She wrinkled her nose and let out a giggle. "Oh, Em. This is so not you."

I placed my hands on my hips. "What is that supposed to mean?"

"You've always been drawn to the older, er, more "vintage" vehicles if you will. This is the polar opposite. It's so…so…shiny and new."

I rolled my eyes. "Sean talked me into it." I let out a shrug. "Get in the car, it's good on fuel and the heater works and trust me where we're going, we're gonna need it."

My mother slid inside and clasped her hands together neatly. I started the engine and backed out of the parking stall. As I made my way to the freeway the butterflies began to flutter. *What are you doing? You're in so far over your head you have no idea. What happens when your mother's mind goes into the dark? Can you watch over her? Are you ready to face Aaron? Get ready for it, Em. You're about to drown.* I gave my head a rough shake and clasped my hands tighter against the steering wheel. We drove in near silence, with nothing on but the radio. A part of me was scared to attempt a conversation with my mom, I didn't want to hear the exact moment that her mind left. Truth be told, I had no idea what to expect, no idea how everything worked.

"Thanks for getting me out of there, Em."

"You're welcome, Mom."

"It was an awful place, you know? I feel like I got lost amongst those walls. The choices were not my own. Everything was forced upon me."

I winced slightly. I had been the one to put her in the home. Her mind had gotten fuzzy rather quickly and I began to fear for her safety. When I got the phone call from the police that she had driven her car into a pole; it was the final straw. I remember that day so well. I arrived on scene and my heart flopped into the pit of my stomach. Her car was crunched into a light pole and glass was everywhere. My mother was disorientated as the crimson blood ran down her face. She had been crying and fear was etched across her skin. She didn't remember how she got there, or where she had been trying to go. When she saw me arrive she bolted from the paramedics and fell into my arms.

"Take the keys away from me, Emmy. I need help, look at this mess! It's happening faster than we thought. I can feel it taking over. It's a monster. I could have killed someone! Keep me safe, Em. Keep the world safe from me."

Those words still cut me like a knife. I glanced over at my mother who dozed quietly. Her chest rose and fell in a steady rhythm. I kept the music to a low volume and focused my eyes back on the road. I stole a glance at the luminous grey sky that threatened snow. "Three more hours to go," I mumbled to myself. "Three more hours."

The drive was breathtakingly beautiful. I watched as the grey swallowed the clear blue sky; the promise of snow hovered from above. The snow covered mountains loomed in the distance, and the never-ending trees stole as far as the eye could see. Even though the heater kept the cab of the vehicle toasty, the road glittered from the ice that lead us into the mountain town that I left so long ago. My mother still slept soundly, and for that I was grateful. My heart beat uneasily at the thought of her waking up; I wasn't entirely sure who she would be. As the familiar landmarks began to come in view, an overwhelming sadness took hold. Memories and flashbacks of those I walked away from began to take hold.

"We need more lights on the roof line!"

I grumbled as I attempted to untangle the knot of Christmas lights. "I'm not going up there, I don't do heights."

Aaron jumped into action and shoved me. As I stumbled he wriggled his eyebrows playfully. "You're such a girl. Leave it to me."

I shook the memory out of my head and took the exit that held our destination. Though it had been years, I was fairly confident I knew where to find Elayna. Nothing changed much in this ski town with its chateaus, resorts and walkable tourist friendly villages. I drove through the snow-dusted roads looking for a gas station. I pulled next to the pump and braced for the cold. The sharp wind nipped at my skin and sent the flakes falling from the sky, dancing every which way. I took a deep breath in, and it burned my lungs. As I filled my tank my eyes landed on the snowboard shop across the street. I watched as happy people fuelled by excitement entered the store. The sting of hot tears filled my eyes as Aaron entered my mind once more. That shop was his second home. *Jesus, why the hell did I ever come back here?* I swear I could still see him with his tousled hair, tall frame and forever smile.

"Where are we? I'm cold."

My vision broke and I turned to see my mother hopping from foot to foot with her arms crossed tightly against her torso. "We're home, Mom, well sort of."

Audrey's face furrowed. "It's colder than I remember."

My body relaxed and I let out a light laugh. "You and me both."

Audrey stood next to me and studied her surroundings. "Can we grab a snack and a warm drink? I'm famished."

"Sure thing. There's a really good café around the corner, well at least there used to be."

Audrey nodded to the fuel pump. "Hurry up and fill this thing and we can find out. I'll be waiting in the car."

Once the tank was full, I slid into the drivers seat and rubbed my hands frantically together. "Holy crap! The temperature is not forgiving here."

Audrey smiled slyly. "Look at us, we've been gone too long. We're a couple of light weights now."

I laughed freely. "It appears that way." I started the car and sighed happily as the heat spilled out of the vents. "Oh man does that ever feel good."

"It does. Now let's go! I'm starved."

"Me too." I pulled the car out and circled the block until I found the café. We pulled into a parking stall and ran into the warmth of the shop. We placed our orders and found a seat by the fireplace. My mother took a long lingering look around her, and the familiar shadow flashed across her eyes. I knew she was thinking of him.

"Mom? Are you ok?"

She closed her eyes tightly and her chest rose up and down in a laboured manner. When she opened her eyes my heart caught in my throat. She was the definition of torment. "Mom?"

Audrey rose quickly and a hand flew to her mouth. "Why? Why did this happen to me, to us? How could this happen?"

Curious bystanders gazed at us with interest. I sent them a dark glare and stood in front of my mother. "Mom, I think we should go and get some fresh air. What do you say?"

"Fresh air? The cold is bloody unwelcoming out there. Emmy, why? Tell me why? Please, I need to know." Her voice broke and the tears began to fall.

Shit. I knew this was a bad idea. As much as I mourned the loss of my mother's mind, in that moment, I wished with everything I had that her mind would fade. I didn't want her to remember *that* day. But she wasn't that lucky. In the distance the bell above the door jingled indicating another customer walked in.

My mother's sobs rose above the soft music that played quietly in the background. "How does this happen? How can the world keep moving while ours has stopped completely? How am I supposed to get out of bed and keep breathing when I want to die? Emmy, my heart, it hurts so much. How could this happen?"

Dread took over once I realized what was happening. Her mind had faded from the present; however it was stuck in a time loop at the worst possible moment of our lives. Anger quickly took hold of me. As if we weren't going through enough. As if this stupid disease wasn't robbing me of my only family member it had to leave her with this memory, one I wished her muddy mind would have the decency to erase forever.

A male voice spoke behind me. The warmth of the tone pierced my skin. "Emmy? Is that you?"

Chase. I turned in disbelief as I stared up at the familiar face I hadn't seen in so long. His grey blue eyes were marred in concern as he looked from myself to my mother. His dark hair escaped his toque and his face was full with a beard. *Damn you, you can still make my heart skip a beat.*

My mother's cries tore my attention back to her. "Mom, we need to go outside."

"Aaron. Take me to him, I need to see him now!"

Chase looked at me in question but he broke the stare abruptly. With a single stride he took hold of my mother's arm and led her out the door. He spoke into her ear with words only made for her to hear.

I followed slowly and stepped into the falling snow. Chase attempted to quiet my mother. I watched the scene unfold before me and I had to look away. I've seen her like this more times than was humanly kind. Exhaustion hit me like a ton of bricks and it became hard to breathe. I looked away and focused on the large flakes that floated to the ground. I took comfort in the power something so small could have as they buried the world flake by flake. *Screw you Aaron, you did this to her. You broke her. Are you happy now? This is all on you.*

I took another step back and buried my hands in my hair. I didn't want to be here, I knew we should have never come back. It was too familiar; the hurt was still too fresh. If I had things my way, I would never have come back to this godforsaken place. I was so caught up in my thoughts that I didn't even notice Chase as he stood beside me.

"It's been a long time, Em. I never thought I'd see you back here."

I kept my eyes focused on the shops in front of me. "I never planned on coming back."

Chase tensed next to me. Another wave of guilt hit me as I realized my words had bite. He was quiet for a moment before he spoke. "I got your Mom to sit in my truck. She's pretty worked up."

I bit my lip to keep from crying. "Thank you."

"Your hands are trembling. Em? Can you look at me please?"

I didn't answer nor move for a moment. I slowly complied and raised my eyes to meet his.

"What's wrong with her? It's like it just happened."

I couldn't ignore the steel gaze. "She wanted to come back to see him."

"That's not the whole story. You're missing the part why you look like you haven't slept in months."

"So you're telling me my anti aging beauty creams aren't working, huh?"

"Em, please. I haven't heard a word from you in years. You owe me this."

I broke the gaze. "Alzheimers, okay? She has Alzheimers. Her mind is a bloody mess and more often than not, she doesn't know who I am. I have been watching her fade away in front of me and there's nothing that I or anyone else can do."

I threw my hands up in the air in frustration. "And for some damn reason her mind is stuck on Aaron. She is reliving it over and over and she was hell bent on coming to see him. So, here we are. Is there anything else you would like to know?"

"Is there anyone helping you?"

"It's just me."

"Em, you can't do this alone. Why didn't you call me?"

"I have to go. Elayna is expecting us."

Chase studied me for a moment longer and let out a perplexed sigh. "Can you at least let me drive your mom to Elayna's? She's calm now. You can follow me."

I didn't have the energy to argue. "Okay. Thank you."

Chase gave me one last look that was filled with pity and a hint of anger before he turned for his truck. I collapsed into the drivers seat and watched as his truck rumbled to life. I placed the car in drive and followed from a safe distance. *Here we go.*

CHAPTER SEVEN

Elayna and her husband Jay, child hood lovers stood on their front porch in anticipation, Chase must have called to alert them that we were on our way. I killed the engine and stepped outside. As soon as Elayna's eyes locked on me she ran with a child like giddiness. Her arms enclosed my shoulders and she squeezed the breath out of me.

"It's so good to see you. We've missed you so much."

I pulled back and managed a smile. "I've missed you too. Thank you for letting us stay over tonight, I'm sorry it was such short notice..."

Elayna waved her hand in the air. "Don't be silly, you are always welcome. She took me by the hand and dragged me to the house. "C'mon, its warm inside. We've had the fire going all day."

I allowed Elayna to drag me where she wished. I passed Jay and gave him a small smile. He nodded in acknowledgment. Chase helped my mom get out of the truck and he took her hand firmly. I gave him a look of gratitude. He nodded briefly and looked away. Chase was always the one to remain calm; he was the man with the plan no matter the situation.

The warmth from Elayna and Jay's small home made my skin tingle. Elayna began talking a million miles a minute and pranced into the living room gesturing me to follow. I found myself giggling and my sprits lifting; thankful that time hadn't changed Elayna. She was always the free spirit of the group. As soon as Chase entered the room Elayna swirled around and walked over to my mom and wrapped her in a warm hug.

"It's been a long time, Audrey."

My mom studied Elayna for a split second. Her face broke into a warm smile. "It's nice to see you too, honey." Her eyes fell to Jay. "I see that you were able to convince her, eh?"

Jay let out a laugh. "I always knew she would say yes to me sooner or later."

Elayna winked in his direction. "He has always been overconfident."

Chase cleared his throat and shifted uncomfortably. "Uh, Em, can I talk with you for a sec?"

"Sure."

I followed Chase into the kitchen and kept a safe distance. He turned to me and respected the barrier I created. "I know this is none of my business but what are you doing back here exactly?"

"I don't know to be honest. Mom was doing fairly well at the home and then....I dunno. She broke down."

"I see. And you figured the best remedy for that was to remove her from her care?"

Anger swelled inside me. "Please don't judge me, okay? I'm doing the best I can here. I—she kept going on and on about Aaron. For some reason she has become fixated on him after all this time. She wouldn't quiet down until I agreed to bring her here."

Chase nodded slowly. "I really wish you would have reached out earlier. I'm sorry that you've had to go through this all alone, I really am. For what it's worth, you will have help here. My concern though is that you may not be able to handle this on your own...your mom may need 24/7 care, y'know?"

I pinched the bridge of my nose and closed my eyes. "I haven't figured out everything yet. She was miserable in the home, in that place. I don't know what my next move will be just yet, but I'll figure something out. We have to take this day by day, step by step." I broke off my words and let out a huge sigh. I forced myself to look at him. "I'm so tired of being scared all the time. I'm so close to coming un-glued, I don't know how to be brave anymore." My shoulders slumped and I felt the weariness take over. That was the difference between Chase and Sean; I never had to put on a front with Chase. I could always tell him everything, but then again, we grew up together. We've been through it all.

Chase broke the barrier and took me in his arms. I breathed in his familiar scent and let the warmth of his body take over. He kept the embrace short and sweet before releasing me. "You're not alone in this. You have us. We'll figure something out, I promise."

"He's right. You have us, we just wish you came back sooner." I jumped at the sound of Elayna's voice.

I turned toward her kind eyes and let out a sad smile. "I don't know what I did to deserve you guys in my life, but I'm so grateful."

My mom cut the moment short. Audrey stood in the doorway looking slightly uncomfortable. "I'm sorry to interrupt, but I'm feeling rather tired. I haven't had a day this exciting in well, since I can't even remember. Is there somewhere I can turn in for the night?"

Once again Elayna took over. She bounced over to Audrey and took her by the hand. "Follow me."

I watched them disappear around the corner. Chase cleared his throat and nodded to me. "Walk me out at least for old times sake?"

A chuckle arose from somewhere within. "Why not."

The brisk cold assaulted my delicate skin. I shuddered deeply and followed Chase to his truck. He paused by the door and stared at the graying sky. "Snow's coming."

"Feels that way. I don't remember it being this cold."

Chase snorted. "You're a light weight now. You better remember your roots, Em or you won't make it."

I tossed his shoulder lightly. "Hush. I'll be fine."

He rolled his eyes. "Yeah, I know." The truck door opened in protest as he slid in the front seat. "Get some sleep. We'll figure this out."

A warm sensation replaced the cold momentarily. For once, I didn't feel alone. "Chase?"

"Yeah?"

"Thank you for today. "

"Anytime, Em. It's good to see you back here."

I went to respond but the loud rumbling engine over shadowed my voice. With a quick wave Chase drove away.

⌘

It was the smell of this place; home. I loved it yet I also hated it. I felt like I was stuck between worlds; happiness and fear. My last memory of being home was anger, shock and a pain that was worse than any heartache. But here I was. I had no idea what was going to happen, what my mother hoped to accomplish, hell what I was going to do. It was so unlike me. But my life, our life was now full of unknowns. We were now living moment to moment, not knowing what lurked around the corner.

My mother slept soundly upstairs in the warm house. Elayna and Jay had turned in for the night; I was the only one awake. I paced the house aimlessly, unable to welcome sleep. I curled up on the couch and tossed a blanket around my shoulders. The fire crackled, decorating the room in a faint orange glow. I watched through the window as the darkness outside lightened from the falling snow. The moon bounced off the white hills and the world looked magical. A creak from the floorboards above sent me upright. I took the stairs two at a time and peeked into the guest bedroom.

"Mom?"

Audrey stepped away from the window and twirled around facing me. "It's beautiful isn't it?"

I nodded. "Yes."

"I remember when you and Aaron were little. I had such a hard time keeping you guys inside when it snowed. You two could have played out there for hours on end."

"I remember."

For a moment, Audrey's soft features looked fierce. "So do I." She shook her head and closed her eyes. "I remember, I always want to remember," she whispered to herself.

My throat caught and the tears welled in my eyes. Life was a cruel thing. Being a good person did not guarantee you kindness in return, it did not promise happiness. It promised you nothing but surprise. It was a crapshoot at best.

"I feel it, you know."

My thoughts focused back to my mother. "Feel what?"

"It. Deep inside. I can feel it fighting to take over. It's like a hungry monster that dwells in the shadows. I'm trying my best to keep it locked away but it's strong. It wants to break free; it wants to live. It's a sneaky bastard."

"Mom, I-"

"Emmy, I want you to live. I want to see you happy, I want to hear you laugh before it takes over, and I mean really laugh. Screw the rules and bloody live. Trust me, take it from a woman who is battling time."

My mother stepped beside me and took me in her arms. "I need to know that you're going to be okay. I am so damn proud of you and the woman you have become."

I broke. As my mother's petite frame held me, I cried as if I were a child. She stroked my hair and shushed me. Gently rocking me back and forth like when I was a little girl. The tears eventually stopped and I pulled back, wiping my eyes. My mother gave a sleepy smile. "There's my girl."

A laugh of disbelief forced its way out. "You must be exhausted. Let's get some sleep."

"Sounds good to me. Sweet dreams, Emmy."

"Night, Mom."

I crawled into the second bed and nestled under the thick blankets. My eyes blinked heavily and I was gone.

CHAPTER EIGHT

I awoke to the smell of bacon. My eyes fluttered open and I shifted to my side. My eyes flew to my mother's bed and I jumped up when I saw that it was empty.

"Shit!" I scrambled to the door and managed to stub my toe on the door jam. "Dammit!" I hopped from foot to foot as I tore the door open and ran into the hall. I took the stairs as quickly as I could. My steps slowed from the sound of happy voices.

I rounded the corner and relief swelled over me. My mother was sipping on coffee with Jay and Chase. Elayna danced in the kitchen as she fussed over the open stove. The conversation fell silent as all eyes were on me. I straightened my posture and began running my hands through my hair in a half attempt to tame the bed head.

"Good morning, sunshine." Chase drawled.

Heat flushed my cheeks and I pulled at the edge of my nightshirt. "Er, good morning everyone."

Elayna came toward me with a crooked smirk. She passed me a cup of coffee. "He's completely checking you out," she whispered.

The redness crept to my nose. "Oh, god."

Elayna laughed and grabbed my arm. "Come, come. I need some help in the kitchen." She gave Chase a quick wink and he looked shocked that he was caught.

"Oh how I missed you kids." Audrey's pearly laugh filled the room. The sound gave me great joy, followed by a tug of emptiness. How long would it last? Would she ever make that sound again?

Elayna noticed the change in my mood. "Hey," she nudged me. "We got this, k?"

I half-heartedly smiled. "Okay." I looked around the chaos that was the kitchen counter. "What can I help with?"

"You're on pancake duty. Apple cinnamon."

"That I can do."

The room was infectious with happy energy. Laughter and upbeat music seeped through the walls. I got lost in it and found myself swaying to the rhythm as I mixed up the thick batter. It had been years since a house felt like a home. Sean rarely let loose to laugh, he was all about work and maintaining control. *Love.* That's what had been missing. But right now, this quaint cabin was filled with it and I drank it in like an alcoholic on a binge.

"Foods ready!"

It didn't take long for the food to be gone. The clean up began and the men stepped up. Jay noticed my incredulous look and shrugged. "I'm well trained, what can I say?"

"I am impressed."

Elayna smiled like a proud peacock. "What can I say? I'm good."

Chase cleared his throat and stepped between us. "Can I steal her for a moment?"

Elayna waved her hand in the air. "Sure, sure take her away."

I followed Chase into the hall. "What's up?"

He fished something out of his back pocket. "Hold out your hand."

I did as asked and smiled coyly. The sharp, cool metal erased the smile immediately. I stared down at the keys that lay lifelessly in the palm of my hand. "Are these....?" My voice drifted off.

"Yeah. I've been doing my best to keep the place somewhat in order. I haven't had much time but it's all secure."

My breath caught and I looked up at him. "Thank you, I really mean that." I stared at my feet. "I-I don't know that I can go back there."

"Audrey will want to go."

"I know." I bit my lip and peered around the corner at my mother, who was the picture of content. I knew how it would change in an instant.

"I'm not ready, Chase. Here, take them back."

He shook his head. "I have a copy. You keep these."

My voice hardened. "I don't want them."

"Don't want what?"

I flinched at the sound of my mother's voice. "Umm…"

Her quick eyes took it all in. "Oh. I see." Audrey smoothed her shirt down. "Emmy, I would like to see it. If you're not ready I completely understand. But I *need* to see it."

My patience and strength wavered. All I wanted to do was throw the damn things into the depth of the ocean. I wanted the water to swallow them whole and bury it from the world.

"I'll take you."

I gave Chase a sharp look. He ignored it. "You might want to bundle up, the cold will take your nose right off."

Audrey gave him a thoughtful look. "Give me a few minutes." She disappeared up the stairs.

"What do you think you're doing?" I hissed.

"I'm giving you a break."

"Do you know what it's going to do to her when she's there? You don't know how to handle her!"

"Actually I do." He lowered his voice. "I was there too, Em. I remember the both of you that night."

I snapped my mouth shut and stepped back. "Right."

Audrey stepped down the stairs and her happiness was replaced with solemn determination. "We'll be back honey."

"Okay. Mom? Be careful."

"Always."

Chase gestured her out the door. "I'll see you later."

"Call me if you need me." I whispered.

He shut the door quietly behind him. I ran to the window and watched as he helped my mom hoist herself into the truck. It shuddered to life and crawled down the drive. *Crap.* She was going home.

⌘

Two hours passed. Two. I heard nothing from them. Chase ignored my phone calls. Anxiety fuelled me as I paced a path in the deep snow. Did my mother have a break down? Did she bolt? Was she crumpled on the ground devastated all over again? It was the not knowing that drove my wild march; back and forth, back and forth. My boots crunched loudly under the frozen snow but I paid no attention. My breathing began to labour and escaped in a white puff like dragon smoke. I squinted against the glittering snow and peered down the drive, waiting. Forever waiting. I glanced at my watch once more. Two hours and ten minutes. The sound of tires caused my heart to stutter. I froze mid step and watched the old truck come toward me. I made no move as the truck halted to a stop. The engine went silent. For a moment, no one moved. Chase watched me from the truck but I could read no emotion from him. I glanced to the passenger seat and saw it was empty. *Oh god. She's gone.* My knees wavered but I somehow willed my body to co-operate. My faltering walk quickly became an awkward run. I slammed my body against the driver side door and pulled it open with everything I had. Chase slid out.

"Where is she?"

"Calm down Em, she's-"

"Chase, where the hell is she? I knew this was a bad idea." I covered my face in my hands. ""Oh god, if she hurts herse-"

"Hey, that's enough. Stop. Look at me."

I let my hands fall from my face and pulled my sight to him. Chase loomed over me and his grey eyes grew serious. *I know that look.* I released a trembling breath and nodded. "Okay. I'm listening."

"Get in the truck."

"Excuse me?"

"Get in the truck. Now."

I did as told. I slid into the passenger seat and slammed the door with more force than necessary. Chase got in and started the engine. He reversed and pulled a tidy turn as we headed down the drive. He didn't speak. I narrowed my eyes at him and watched his body language trying to decipher his hidden words.

"Chase, what gives? Where are we going? Where is my mom?"

"Stop giving me the death glare. Audrey is fine." He quickly glanced my way. "Put on your damn seatbelt."

I clicked the seat belt angrily into place and crossed my arms like a bratty child. I listened to the hum of the vents as the heater worked tiredly blowing warm air into the cramped cab. "Someone was there."

Chase's voice sent prickles down my arms. "What do you mean? Like a squatter?"

"After I took Audrey to the house we went to see Aaron. Someone else was there."

"Who?" I whispered.

"Your aunt, Samantha."

"Aunt Sam? What's she doing here?"

"Your mom called her last night. She asked her to be here in case things get bad. Em, she doesn't want all this on you."

Oh mom. Aunt Sam was the complete opposite of my mother. She was a strict Christian, who lived her life by the Bible. My mom was a free spirit who believed in the healing power of oils and karma. She went where the wind blew her. Still, I knew why aunt Sam was here. She was a nurse. She had the knowledge, the connections. She would know what to do when things went south.

"You okay?"

"I'm fine."

"Okay."

And that was another reason why Chase held a piece of my heart. He knew when to push and when not too. This was one of those instances. He could read me like a book. He knew when I said no and meant yes. When I wanted help and when I didn't. He knew how far he could string me along and when too simply stop. I arched an eyebrow. "Chase?"

"Yeah?"

"How was she at the house?"

Pain crossed his features ever so briefly. "At first it broke my heart. She sobbed as soon as we pulled into the driveway. I didn't push her; if she wanted to turn around I would have taken her out of there. I gave her some time and she pulled herself together. She went into the house and took in everything silently. I kept my distance, it....it felt almost intimate, y'know?"

He shook his head. "She went into his room and shut the door. She was in there for awhile. I didn't hear her cry. To tell you the truth, I had to go outside to catch my breath and clear my head. I wanted her to be able to say or do whatever she needed without me hovering." He stopped and his gray eyes looked at me in disbelief. "I don't know how the hell you've been doing this on your own for so long. That prick of a boyfriend was useless. How are you still standing?"

His words hit me. It was a compliment but it also was a side jab. "I don't know. It's the hand we were dealt and I've been trying to live as best as I—we can."

The truck suddenly came to a halt. My body lurched forward and the seatbelt locked, stealing the breath from my lungs. The tires locked and we skidded forward five feet on the slick road before coming to a standstill. Chase threw the truck in park, stormed outside and slammed the door so hard the vehicle quivered. My eyes grew wide as he cursed in the silent day. He marched to the box of the truck and laid his arms wearily over the edge. He slammed his palm against it once before hanging his head. I instinctively went to his side.

"Chase? Are you okay?"

"No, Em I am not okay." He forced his gaze to me, and my heart cracked. "You left. You left everything. Aaron was a part of my life too. It didn't just happen to you. I was there, I was right there but you didn't see me. You didn't see anyone. And all this,"he gestured to the openness of nothing. "Is bullshit. Your mom's a good woman and this shouldn't be happening to her, not after everything else. And you, you wasted years of your life being miserable with an asshole who left you to pick up the slack looking after your mom. Why the hell didn't you reach out? Fuck!" He slammed the side of his truck again and I jumped. He tore off his tuque and ran his hands through his hair. It was almost comical how it stuck out every which way, but nothing was funny about this moment.

His voice lowered. "I should have checked in on you. I should have known how damn stubborn you are."

Everything about Chase in this moment would be forever burned into my memory. How he was visibly wounded like an animal left for dead. I stood next to him and laced my fingers with his. "I am so, so sorry. I admit, I didn't think of anyone else during....well, you know. I just needed to get away from everything and everyone that reminded me of how life used to be. Sean was a stupid mistake, one in which I paid for greatly. He was my karma in a sense." I let out a heavy breath and leaned against the truck. "And in regards to my mom, you're right it isn't fair. Nothing about it is fair. But we have no choice. None. We have to cope and move forward as best as we can. My selfish hope is that if her mind goes, she disappears to a happy time in her memories, one where she doesn't hurt or is vividly aware that her body has betrayed her."

Chase draped his arm over me and squeezed me close. "You've done good, Em. I'm proud of you."

"Thank you. I'm glad life hasn't changed you. You're one of the good ones."

He let his arm fall away. "Let's get back in the truck, I want to take you somewhere."

"What about my mom?"

"Your aunt and her need to catch up, they had a lot to go over."

"Okay, at least she's in good hands."

The truck chirped to life and off we went. I leaned forward to turn up the radio. I let the music float around me and let my mind get lost. I watched the icy roads pass by, admiring the homes as smoke drifted from the chimneys. I noted the white fields and watched in wonder as the light caused the snow to glint like diamonds. The road continued to wind taking us further into the countryside. My interest was slightly peaked as barns appeared up ahead. Chase entered the long drive and killed the engine. A large walnut colored barn stood before us.

"Where are we?"

"A barn. What does it look like to you? C'mon, let's go."

Chase sensed my hesitation. He sighed and grabbed me by the hand. "You deserve to do something you love. Let this be an escape for you. I don't want you to end up on the bottle; I'm amazed it hasn't happened yet to be honest."

I shook his hand off and gave him a shove. "Hey!"

He chuckled and regained his grip, towing me along with him. "Follow me."

I allowed myself to be led away, my eyes taking it all in. As soon as the barn door opened my body nearly went limp from the familiar smells of barn life. Horses stood in the stalls with their thick winter blankets. They pulled lazily at hay from the nets. The familiar snorts of content trickled into my veins.

"Oh wow." I whispered in wonder.

"Missed it?"

"Yes."

"I know the owner of the barn, she's a good lady. C'mon there's one guy here who could use some exercise."

"I'm allowed to ride?"

Chase sighed. "When I surprise you with something, I go all out. You should know this by now." Chase stopped and pointed to the stall on the end. "Call his name."

"Excuse me?"

"Watch the stall on the end and say 'Ace.'"

My heart flip-flopped. "Chase Havens, if you are toying with me right now, I will kill you right here, right now."

He laughed. "Go on, what are you waiting for?"

I clasped my hands together and gave a small hop. I turned my attention to the stall on the end and gathered my courage. My heart was pounding so loudly it was deafening. "Ace! Where's my handsome boy?"

A shrill neigh cut through the alley. A loud thump followed as a copper horse slammed his chest against the stall door. His perked ears were tipped as far forward as they could go, listening. He was on full alert as he craned his neck and head toward my call.

"Oh my god it's him. It's really him!!" I smacked Chase and took off toward my old best friend. "Ace! I'm here buddy, it's me."

I slowed my steps as I approached him. He let out another neigh and his eyes widened in excitement. I held out my hand and ran it down his neck. He lowered his head and I wrapped him in a hug. "It's so good to see you, bud."

I tore my gaze away and found Chase. He stood behind us smiling from ear to ear. "Did I do good?"

"You hit it out of the park. How did you find him?"

"It's a small town. I saw his ad and recognized him immediately."

"He was for sale?"

"Yeah, the lady who bought him from you kept him all these years. She recently had a kid and no longer had time for him. What can I say? I got a good deal."

"*You* own him?"

Chase shrugged. "You could say that. Like I said, I got a good deal."

"I don't know whether I hate or love you right now."

"I'll take the latter. What are you waiting for? Take him for a spin."

My eyes settled to Ace. "What do you say buddy? Wanna go for a ride?"

Ace tore a mouthful of hay from the net and chewed methodically. "Sorry bud, but you've got no choice in the matter." I reached for his halter and stepped inside the stall. After years of being away, I was somehow given back my happy place.

CHAPTER NINE

"You guys are looking good. How does it feel?"

"Amazing." My smile grew so wide my cheeks hurt. Ace loped easily around the arena; his thick black mane blew back in an easy rhythm. His black tipped ears were kept forward, enjoying every moment. I leaned forward and gave his sweaty neck a heavy pat. "Good boy, bud."

I slowed him to a walk and pointed him toward Chase. "How much do you want for him?"

Chase shook his head. "Oh no. He's not for sale."

"Excuse me?"

"I can't have you running away on us again."

"So you're going to essentially hold me hostage here?"

"Not at all. I just know you won't willingly run away on us now."

"I hate you, Chase Havens. You know that right?" I swung my leg over the saddle and dismounted neatly. Ace rubbed his sweaty head against my side and I let him.

"You love me and you know it."

I shook my head and clucked for Ace to follow. "I've got to brush him down and tuck him in."

"I'll help."

We worked together methodically knowing what to do, like old times. Ace twitched his ears back and forth listening to us. He let out a hearty sigh and fully enjoyed the pampering he received. I tossed on his winter blanket and secured the clips. Ace followed eagerly to his stall, which held fresh shavings, clean water, and hay. I gave his neck an affectionate pat. "There you go boy. I'll see you tomorrow."

I locked the stall door behind me but my feet couldn't find it in them to move. Not yet. I folded my arms over the stall door and watched him eat. Chase followed suit.

"How long have you owned him?"

"Five months."

I raised an eyebrow. "Were you ever planning on contacting me?"

"Every day but I could never make the call. I dialled your number but I couldn't find it in me to push the last digit."

"Why not? We've known each other forever. It's not like I'm a random stranger."

"Things didn't exactly end on a good note, Em. The last image I had of you stuck in my head nearly killed me, and it was stuck playing on repeat. You were completely broken; you were just done. With me, with everything. I didn't know what to expect if you heard me on the other end of the line. I chickened out, plain and simple."

I looked away and nodded. "I'm so sorry, Chase. I never meant to hurt you."

"I know that now." He forced a smile that wasn't real. "Time has passed."

"A lot of time."

"I heard rumours things weren't going so good for you. Once I saw that Ace was for sale it seemed like the perfect gift. I remember the day you sold him. I know how hard that was for you. I wanted to give you something that could take you away from all the crap, so you could feel like yourself again. I know how you get, so stuck in your mind. You needed an escape and he was it."

My eyes began to feel the sting of tears. "You know me to well. I can never thank you enough for this, you're aware of that right?"

"You don't have too. I hope it helps you fix the broken parts, slowly make that smile you had on earlier a regular fixture."

"I hate how well you know me."

"No, you don't. You love it."

"Stop saying that."

"I can't help but speak the truth."

I sighed and watched him from the corner of my eye. His smile turned smug. "What?"

"Are you seeing anyone?"

Chase's face dropped in surprise. He snorted and pushed up the sleeves of his jacket, revealing a tattoo sleeve on a firm forearm. "It's been a long time since I've been on a date." He furrowed his eyebrows in thought. "Huh, yeah it's been awhile. After you left I licked my wounds for about a year."

I flinched. "I-"

He held up a hand to stop me. "The last relationship I had lasted four months. It didn't end well."

"Really? Who was it with?"

"Miranda Brooks."

My face fell in disgust. "Miranda Brooks? Oh, Chase. You can do so much better than her." My face rumpled in disappointment. Miranda and I hated each other. There was no significant event that led to the mutual feeling; we simply had never gotten along. Miranda was smug with her good looks with her forever-tanned skin, flawless makeup, fake mink lashes, and shiny brown locks. That woman was always done up to the nines and she wore it well. Men drooled over her wherever she went.

"Why the long face?"

"I can't believe you dated her. Who ended it?"

"Me. She was not easy company."

I laughed a high, giddy laugh. "Excellent. Ah man she must have been so angry with you, no one dumps her."

"Yeah I got that from her reaction. She tossed my favourite mug against the wall."

I giggled. "I'm so sorry."

Chase wiggled his eyebrows. "She was aiming for my head. She's going to love that you're back."

"Mm, no I'd like to avoid her if I can."

"Unless you hide at Elayna's the entire time here that's not going to happen."

"Lovely."

"Come on, we should get out of here. Are you hungry?"

"I can't remember the last time I ate. I think it was breakfast?"

"Tsk tsk. It's dinnertime. C'mon, let me buy you dinner."

"In town?"

"I was thinking the pub."

My jaw dropped. "Saddlers Pub?"

"Only the best for you."

It was the most popular pub in town; a hit with tourists and locals alike with its cheap but delicious food, and welcoming interior. It was also a frequent stop for local artists to perform.

"Everyone will be there." I let out a sigh and Chase tilted his head. "Are you embarrassed to be seen with me?"

"No, not at all."

"Just checking. So, are you in or out?"

I held a hand on my empty stomach. "In."

"Excellent. I'm starved."

Chase took me by the hand and began to jog. His long legs moved easily in a relaxed pace whereas mine had to work twice as hard to merely keep up. We both slid into his truck in sync and he backed out of the drive. A familiar song came on the radio and he began to sing along. His voice sent a shudder across my skin. Memories of the past began to flood back and my cheeks flushed. I looked away quickly, hoping he wouldn't see. Some of my fondest memories of Chase were reserved to him and his guitar. The first night he performed in front of an audience was the night I knew I loved him. Despite all the people in the room, I was the only one he saw.

"Do you still perform?" I asked almost shyly.

"Almost every Thursday night."

My mouth gaped. "Really?"

He laughed. "Jee, don't look so shocked. Am I that bad?"

"No, just the opposite. I must say, I'm shocked your single; a guy with your looks who not only plays guitar but sings as well. The ladies must be clawing to get you."

Chase smirked and I could tell he ate up the compliment. He shrugged half heartily. "It worked for you."

The blush came back. "Hey, we have known each other since we were what, five?"

"Yeah. We both saw each other go through the awkward stages in life. Did I surprise you with how well I turned out?"

I rolled my eyes. "Get over yourself."

He checked me with his shoulder."You turned out pretty good. I questioned it when you were, oh, about twelve. "

My eyes widened. "Hey now. Be careful with what you say. I'm a fragile woman."

"You are anything but fragile. We're here. Let's eat."

I sat in the truck and stared at the rustic chalet style pub. The lively music from inside seeped into the parking lot. Chase stood outside, rubbed his hands together and waited for me to follow. My appetite disappeared in an instant. I knew without a doubt that I would run into the people I grew up with. Most had stayed in town and worked in tourism. I didn't know if I was ready to deal with all the questions I knew would surely follow.

"Hey are you going to come in or what?"

I took a breath and gave myself a mini pep talk. "Yeah, I'm coming." I shoved the door open and stepped into the frigid temperature. "After you." I gestured.

He winked and took my hand. "Let's go."

Chase's hand enclosed around mine tightly and he gave me a reassuring squeeze. The warmth of his body transferred to mine quickly. Even though we had been apart for years, we were falling into an old familiar rhythm without a second thought. I don't know if I found comfort in it or fear. The lines were becoming blurred the more time we spent together. I watched him as he led me confidently into the warmth of the pub and wondered if it was natural for him to reach out for me, or if he was testing the boundaries. My thoughts became broken as the crowds of people yelling to each other over the music took over. I did a quick inventory of the crowd and couldn't make out any recognizable faces. It was well into the snow sport season; most of the faces that filled the building were tourists.

Chase bent down to my level and placed his lips against my ear. "Wanna sit in the back?"

I nodded and allowed myself to be dragged away. As he navigated us through the crowd my eyes locked with a familiar set of brown eyes that were filled with disbelief. Her perfectly glossed lips formed a perfect "O." *Shit. Miranda.* Chase found us a table near the window and he placed his hand against my lower back, scooting me to my chair. I turned and grabbed his jacket.

"How long have you and Miranda been apart for?"

Chase tilted his head. "Why does that matter?"

I looked behind him urgently. "Because she's marching our way now."

His head snapped back. "What?"

"Quick," I hissed. "How long?"

"Three months."

"Three months! That's it? Jesus, Chase she's out for the kill."

Before he could respond a smooth, silky voice wafted over. "Emmy? Have my eyes failed me or is it really you?"

I forced a smile. "Nope, it's me." My eyes quickly assessed her. She was still as put together and gorgeous as ever. She no longer wore her dark hair long; it was cut into a long lob. Time, it would appear had been rather kind to her. Damn. Why couldn't she have gotten fat? The image of her flawlessness standing next to Chase in his rugged good looks made my stomach queasy. They looked like something straight from Hollywood.

"I never thought I'd see the likes of you back here." She placed a hand on her hip and stared at me from head to toe, long and slow.

I shifted uncomfortably from her laser gaze. "Oh, you know just looking for a change."

"I heard you were living it up in the city with some rich guy," She stopped and gave me another steel look. "I guess it's not for everyone."

My back stiffened. "No, I didn't like the fakeness that soiled that world. You would've gotten a kick out of it."

Her eyes narrowed and Chase stepped in. "We're just grabbing a bite to eat."

At the sound of his voice, Miranda uncoiled. She put on her best smile and her gaze filled with mild longing."Old habits die hard I see. I'll see you around, Emmy."

I didn't bother responding. I watched her saunter away and hoped she would fall flat on her face. "She's still hung up on you, you know."

"Yeah right. She hates me."

"Just the opposite," I mumbled.

"Hey," he nudged the menu my way. "Choose something."

I read the menu unenthusiastically and settled on a chicken wrap with an in house brewed raspberry beer. I sipped on the cool, fizzy liquid and watched the crowd for entertainment. Everyone was in good spirits; most sported wind burns from the goggles worn while skiing or snowboarding.

"Do you miss it?"

"Miss what?"

"This place? This used to be us," Chase gestured to the crowd. "We would spend all day on the mountain and come back here to wind down."

"I remember." I scanned the room one more time. "Yeah, I miss it."

"Do you want to go?"

"Snowboarding?"

"Yeah. Would you like to go with me?"

My nerves kicked in as I realized Chase's tone had changed. It was softer, hopeful, vulnerable. "Oh, I don't know. It's been years since I've been on a board."

"It's like riding a bike. What do you say, would you like to go with me?"

"Um.....sure. Okay, yes, I'll go. I don't have my gear anymore I'll have to rent."

"That's alright. How about tomorrow? I can pick you up at 5:30?"

"AM?"

"Yep."

"Gross."

Chase smirked. "I'll see you tomorrow before the sun rises."

⌘

"I think I just said yes to a date with Chase."

Elayna's eyes widened and then she burst into a musical laugh. "I like where this is going. It's like no time has passed at all."

"It feels that way sometimes, although…"

"I know." Elayna reached out and squeezed my arm. "Your mom and aunt came by today."

"I figured as much."

"She thanked us for the hospitality but she went back home."

I let out a heavy sigh. "I don't know how she can stay there."

Elayna softened her voice. "The memories weren't all bad there, there's a lifetime of good, happy times all around her in that house." Elayna paused."You can stay with us as long as you like."

"Thank you. I'll get everything sorted out, I promise. I don't want to burden you with my mess."

Elayna snorted. "Don't be ridiculous."

"I should probably pop in and say hi to aunt Sam and check in on my mom."

"Do you want company?"

"No, this is something I should do on my own."

Elayna squeezed my arm in reassurance. "Good luck."

I stood abruptly and tried to stretch the kink out of my back. "Thanks, I'll see you later."

Elayna gave a sympathetic smile and waved. I reached for the car keys and quickly snuggled into my winter jacket. I swung open the front door and winced as the cold scratched my exposed skin. "I hate winter," I muttered angrily as I high tailed it for the car. I slipped into the driver seat and started the engine, praying for the heat to kick in soon. I drove with caution, holding my breath every time the car became one with the ice. By the time I reached home, my hands hurt from the death grip on the steering wheel. I cut the engine and pried my hands off the wheel. "You used to drive in this all the time, Em. You're okay," I whispered to myself.

My eyes studied the all to familiar house before me. My stomach took a nose dive. The aged farmhouse's white paint had begun to peel and the faded blue trim looked tired amongst the winter scene before it. Smoke billowed from the chimney, and the faint glow from the lights inside illuminated softly against the early darkness of winter. Silhouettes moved hastily behind the curtains and though I wanted to go inside and feel the heat of the blazing fire, I could not move. My eyes moved from one end of the property to the other and a cold shudder shook my bones. Aaron was everywhere. Memories were everywhere. I felt unwelcome.

"You can do this. One foot in front of the other. You can do this." I repeated the chant until I stood on the covered porch. I raised my hands to knock on the door but could not make contact with the weathered metal. I let my hand fall to my side uselessly and took a step back. I stared at the dull door before me and did nothing. Absolutely nothing.

After some time the creak of the door echoed amongst the silence. I raised my eyes and found myself staring into aunt Sam's sympathetic eyes. I had not seen aunt Sam in a very long time, and the strikingness she bore to my mother caught me off guard.

Aunt Sam studied me and gave a sad smile. "Emmy, it's so nice to see you again. You have grown into a beautiful young woman."

Her soft voice erased some of the chill that gnawed its claws into me. "Hi aunt Sam. It's nice to see you, too." I bit my lip unsurely and lowered my voice. "Thank you for being here."

Aunt Sam opened the door wider. "Would you like to come in? It's freezing out here."

I hesitated for a moment. Aunt Sam did not push me; she simply waited with a patience that I did not possess. I shuddered and nodded. My heart began to beat wildly as I crossed the threshold and stepped into the warmth. Aunt Sam closed the door quickly behind me and suddenly my breath felt restricted. I unzipped my jacket hastily as if it were the one choking me. My breath became staggered as my eyes scanned the room wildly. Aunt Sam's face filled with concern and she grabbed onto my forearm tightly.

"Emmy, you're okay. Take deep, slow breaths. Can you hear me?"

I did not look at her, could not. I saw him everywhere. I closed my eyes tightly and felt my chest tightening. "Emmy!" the voice was louder now.

"Open your eyes and look at me! Emmy, open your eyes girl!"

Aunt Sam's voice hammered in my ears and my eyes flew open. "How can she stand it?" I croaked.

Aunt Sam's brows furrowed. "I don't follow you."

"Mom. How can she *want* to be here?"

She lowered her voice. "She finds comfort here. Not everyone has the same coping mechanisms. God creates us all differently."

I felt myself tense at the mention of God. I had nothing against religion, people were free to believe what they wanted, and if they found comfort by the thought, good for them. My issue was with people who pushed it upon others and accepted all the shit life throws your way to be a part of some "plan." Over the years aunt Sam and my mom had butted heads for that very reason.

I was not in the mood to get into an argument, so I let the comment slide. "She and I clearly aren't wired the same." I sighed. "Where's Mom?"

"Talking to Aaron."

"Excuse me?" I snapped.

"Like I said, everyone seeks comfort in different ways. She's in his room."

"God dammit."

"Emmy! Watch your tongue."

I held my hands up wearily. "Sorry, I didn't mean to offend you." I sank tiredly on the couch and it creaked in protest. I sank my face into my hands. "I feel like everything is spinning out of control and I can't stop it. I don't know where I would even begin."

"Emmy, you are only one person. The world doesn't expect you to have all the answers, neither does your mother."

I sat up rod straight and the heavy sadness took over. I studied the pictures on the wall and shook my head. "We left in such a hurry, everything here remains as it was, from the photos on the wall to the furniture in this house. Everything looks the same, but nothing is the same. Absolutely fucking nothing."

Aunt Sam tensed beside me at the language but did not protest. My eyes landed on a particular picture and I stood, making my way toward it. The magnetic pull was strong. I studied the photo of Aaron and I. Our heads were pressed together, and we were laughing. Snow covered our tuques, and Aaron's blue eyes were electric. I remembered that day well. It was the first time I had been able to keep up with Aaron down a black diamond hill. My fingertips traced the frame carefully, softly. His laughter echoed in my memory and a sudden bitterness replaced the fragile memory. In a matter of seconds, I lost control of my actions. The careful tenderness I had earlier for the photo dissipated and I tore the picture off the wall and threw it across the room. An angry yell came somewhere from the depths of my soul as the glass shattered against the wall.

"Samantha what was that, I-"my mother stopped in her tracks and stared at me with a look torn between disbelief and sudden grief. "Oh, honey…"

My hands began to shake uncontrollably. My eyes widened in slight fear as I stared at the broken glass across the floor. "I-I'm sorry. I don't know what came over me."

Aunt Sam bustled to work without a word. My mouth fell open as I met my mother's face. "Mom, I'm so sorry."

She embraced me with a hug and stroked my hair. "I think that's the first time I've seen you release the anger you've been nurturing. Oh, honey. Don't keep it bottled up anymore, let it out. You can never move forward if you don't forgive."

My body shook as the tears fell. I suddenly felt so small and insignificant in this world. What was happening? Why was our family dealt another shitty hand? We had been through so much already. So much. Too much.

I wriggled out of the hug and felt a sudden urgency to feel the fresh icy air in my lungs. "I'm sorry, Mom, I need to go. I can't stay here."

My mother's angelic face fell. Weariness filled her features and she nodded heavily. "I understand. You're not ready for this yet but I'm going to stay. I need to stay; this is my home. Our home. I know you can't understand this yet but this is my safe place, Em. There is so much joy here, my heart feels content."

"I know. But I can't stay, you're right; I'm not ready to be here. I just needed to see that you were okay."

"I appreciate that. You go, I'll see you later?"

I nodded and put on my jacket with a quickened haste. The walls felt like they were beginning to close in, I needed to get out. "I'll talk to both of you later." I gave them a quick wave and slipped out the door.

The cold had never felt so good. I let my lungs take in a deep breath, thoroughly enjoying the way they burned in protest from the frigid air. I jogged to my car and slammed my key into the ignition. There was no more hint of caution as my foot pressed heavy on the gas pedal. The car skidded sideways but I regained control. I tore out of the driveway and before I knew it, I found myself alone in the parking lot of Saddlers pub. "Fuck it, I need a drink."

The warmth of the pub stung my thawing skin as I forced my way through the crowd to a quiet table near the fireplace.

"What can I get you?"

"Whisky on the rocks."

"Anything else?"

"No."

"Coming right up."

A moment later the waitress placed a glass in front of me. My lips sipped at the strong amber liquid before me. I swallowed greedily as the drink burned its way to the depth of my stomach. By the time my third beverage came round, my head began to buzz from the effects. It had been a lifetime ago that I let myself loose control. I let the feeling take over.

"Holy shit, Emmy is that you?"

I turned to the familiar voice. "Cole?"

"It is you! Wow! Stand up and give me a hug."

My limbs responded to his request before my brain had time to process. Cole wrapped his familiar arms around me and gave me a tight squeeze. He pulled back and smiled his playful grin. "It's been a long time. Too long."

I stared at him and for a split second, I saw Aaron's cheeky grin next to his. The two of them had been best friends since childhood. They were the mischievous duo in town, always getting into trouble but managing to skirt the consequences due to the innocence they managed to hold on too. I studied

Cole and felt a slight pain. The memory of his devastated face flashed behind my eyes. It was one of the first times I had seen a grown man break down.

But here he was. He had grown up, matured. He wore a slightly crooked smile and gave me a playful nudge. "You're still as hot as I remember."

"Cole!"

He laughed loudly. "Aw c'mon, take the compliment." He scanned my table and the way I wobbled unsteadily. "Are you here alone?"

"Yep."

He eyed my near empty drink. "How many of those have you had?"

"About three, I think."

"I see. How much food have you eaten today?"

"Not that much."

"Gotcha. C'mon, the gangs all here."

He grabbed my arm and began to tow me away. I skidded my feet in protest. "Wait, please! I don't think-"

Cole stopped and concern flitted his face. I sighed heavily and rubbed a hand over my face. "My mom's sick, it's Alzheimer's. She's back at home, our home. I went to go see her and I couldn't....I just couldn't stand to be there. It felt wrong."

Cole's face fell. "Em, I'm so sorry. I wish you had called. You guys were like family to me, I hope you know that." He pulled me in for another hug, and I breathed in his scent. "Does this mean you're back?"

I let the warmth of his embrace spread. "I'm sorry. You've always been family to me too. And yes, I-we are back."

Cole released me and lifted my chin with his finger. "It's about time. C'mon, say hi to everyone. They'll be glad to see you."

"Well....sure, why not."

"Excellent." He gripped my hand and led me through the chaos to a large table. Heads turned toward us and surprise filled the faces. I suddenly felt like the new kid at school, that terrible moment when the teacher asked you to stand up and introduce yourself. Somehow this was worse, as the faces staring back at me were all familiar; they represented a different life. One that was long dead and buried.

I put on my best smile and waved. "Hey strangers."

Squeals and laughs of disbelief broke out before me. I got swept away in hearty pats on the back followed by quick hugs. The faces blurred together and the voices blended into one. Once I was released, I took an unsteady seat. The whisky and empty stomach began to make itself known.

"What are you drinking there, Em?"

"Whisky on the rocks, please."

"Got it!"

Soon enough another full drink slid my way and I began to sip the burning liquid. The voices began to fade as I scanned the room, trying to tune out the noise that was everywhere. My eyes evaluated the table I sat at. I jumped in surprise when a scowling Miranda Brooks stared back at me. I straightened my posture and looked away. How had I not noticed her sitting there? She rose gracefully and slid beside me.

"So, you've found your way back for good, huh?" She pursed her lips. "Welcomed back with open arms, I see."

"Nice to see you to, Miranda."

"I mean, really. You wasted no time at all. You have Chase wrapped around your little fingers already. I don't know how he could even consider taking you back after what you did to him."

I prickled at her comment. "Be careful, Miranda. I'd tread lightly if I were you." I turned my eyes to her and threatened her with my gaze. God, how I hated her. Time had not changed her entitled beauty. At all.

Miranda loved a challenge. She tossed her luscious hair over her shoulder and sneered. "You ran because you were a coward. You left him, and after what happened with Aaron, well it doesn't speak very highly of your character, does it?" Miranda stopped to let out a dramatic breath. "You deserve everything that's coming to you."

I stood. "Who do you think you are? How dare you mention Aaron!"

As our voices rose the groups happy chatter ceased to a silence. "Em, is everything okay?" Cole prodded.

Miranda stood to her feet to mimic my stance. "Everything's fine," she drawled. "I'm just reminding our dear friend Emmy of the responsibilities she left behind." She looked at her nails in thought before continuing. "I don't know how you can sleep at night honestly. Rumour has it Aaron had been reaching out to you, but you didn't get the message in time. You didn't even have the decency to be present for his day. The whole bloody town was there, all but you."She pressed her finger into my chest.

A tremor tore through me and anger swelled like it never had before. A beast inside was suddenly released. I lunged toward Miranda in one swift move and knocked her to the ground. She cried out in surprise and our bodies hit the floor in a jumbled heap.

"Get her off of me!" Miranda cried. She wriggled desperately. I sat atop her and pinned her arms above her head. "Get this bitch off of me!" She kicked her feet uselessly like a flopping fish.

Strong arms wound tight against my waist and began to lift me. "Let her go," the voice was soothing in my firing ears. "Em, let her go."

Any anger I had possessed began to drain away. I knew that voice. It had the power to diffuse me, make me laugh, make me feel safe. *Chase.* He released his hold and his lips were set in a hard line. "What are you doing?"

Miranda scrambled to her feet and clawed me from behind. I tried to dodge out of her way but her hands locked on my hair. She yanked me toward her in one powerful motion. I squawked in surprise.

"That's enough of this bullshit." Chase grabbed her forearm. "Let go."

Miranda pouted. "Did you see what she did to me?"

"I did. I also heard what you said. Let her go."

"No."

Chase took an unsteady deep breath. His body tensed as he bent toward her. "Let her go or I won't step in to help you when Em gets her hands on you."

Miranda hesitated as her eyes looked my way. My body went rigid, ready to fight. She looked back at Chase uncertainly. "No."

"Fucking let her go. Now."

Miranda stomped her foot and I felt the sweet release of her loosened grip. She glared at me. "You should have never come back." She grabbed her purse and pulled herself together."Well boys, looks like my nights over."

We watched her strut away and the realization of the scene I caused came crashing down on me. I gingerly met the gazes around me. "I-"

Cole cut me off. "You still know how to make one hell of an entrance."

My jaw dropped and I began to laugh nervously. "I don't know what came over me."

"It's not the first time you two have duked it out. Remember in Grade 12?"

Heat flushed to my face. "Does this town forget nothing?"

"No."

"Clearly," I mumbled.

Chase cleared his throat and placed a hand on my lower back. "I think I should take you home."

Home. The word sent my stomach into a downfall. I couldn't go home, it no longer housed any comfort. "I can't go back," I whispered. I turned to face Chase hurriedly. "Please don't bring me back there, I can't. I'm not ready."

Chase placed his hands on my shoulders. "I meant Elayna's."

"Oh." Relief rushed through me. "Okay."

"I'll drive you there, you shouldn't be behind the wheel."

"What about my car?"

"It'll be fine. We'll get it tomorrow after snowboarding."

My face wrinkled. "That's going to be a rough wake up for me."

"The fresh air will do you good, c'mon."

Chase found my hand and clasped on firmly. I followed him out into the darkness of the frozen night and climbed into the safety of his truck. We drove in silence before he broke the spell. "Rough day?"

"I went home to see Mom."

Those words told the entire story. He nodded and lowered his voice sympathetically. "I'm sorry. For everything."

I sighed and leaned against the seat. "Me too. Mom seemed happy enough."

"That's a good thing, Em."

"I know, it just seems so wrong to me."

Chase nodded. I stole a glance at him, and his gray eyes remained focused on the road before him. Whether it was the whisky coursing in my veins or long buried feelings, I suddenly craved for the warmth of his body next to mine, and his deep breaths of slumber lulling me to sleep. How I missed those strong arms wrapped around me, holding me safe.

The truck halted to a stop. I stared at the dark house before me, not wanting to move. "I'll walk you to the door."

Before I could protest Chase was out of the truck and opening up my door. He held out his hand and I clasped on to it, gingerly finding my footing on the frozen snow. He led me to the front door with steady steps as I fumbled for my keys.

"Have a good night, Em. I'll pick you up in a few hours."

I deflated. "Yeah, sure. See you in a bit." I leaned against the doorframe and watched him walk away. His tall, strong frame moved lithely and his truck roared to life assaulting the stillness of the night.

"And I walked away from *that?*" I cursed myself as I shoved the front door open. I kicked my boots off and stumbled to my temporary room. At the sight of my bed, my body went weak. I collapsed like a falling tree and was out before my head hit the pillow. My last thought was of Miranda Brooks' horrified look and I smiled.

CHAPTER TEN

"Wakey, wakey.."

"Go away," I mumbled.

"Wake up, there's this hot bearded guy downstairs waiting for you."

My eyes flew open and Elayna sat next to me, her hair tousled with an amused grin on her face. "I knew that would wake you," she sang.

I glanced for the time. "Oh no, what time is it?"

"5:25 am."

"Crap, I was supposed to be ready to go." I scrambled out of bed and finger combed my hair. "What am I supposed to wear? My wardrobe isn't what it used to be."

Elayna laughed. "Go wash your face, I'll dig out something of mine you can wear. We're the same size."

"You're a life saver. Oh, Elayna?"

"Yeah?"

"Do you have any Advil?"

"Rough night on the town?"

"You could say that."

Elayna smirked. "Uh-huh."

My face fell. "What have you heard?"

Elayna shrugged. "Oh, you know. Something about the return of a certain resident tackling another."

My jaw dropped. "My god, does nothing stay quiet in this town? It happened mere hours ago."

"I'll be back with some clothes and Advil. Sit tight."

I groaned and quickly set to the task of brushing my teeth and washing my face. Elayna came back and dropped an outfit before me. I dressed quickly and tossed down the pain reliever. I glanced in front of the mirror quickly and gave a nod of approval. "As good as it's gonna get."

I rounded the corner and hopped down the stairs. Chase was bundled up in a thick jacket, his hair tousled under his toque. His gray eyes fell to me and he smiled. "Well, well look who made it up. I bring coffee." He held up two travel mugs in a peace offering.

I reached for a mug in approval. "Thank you."

He smiled his playful smile. "Ready to go?"

"Ready as I'll ever be."

"Excellent, let's get a move on."

⌘

"Move! Get of the way! Oh, crap!" The tip of my board caught in a snowdrift and I went tumbling into the snow for the umpteenth time that morning. I sighed in frustration and let my head fall into the cold white powder. My body ached and the pounding in my head returned with a vengeance.

"C'mon, get up. That was the longest run of the day so far."

I grumbled as Chase smiled brightly. I pushed my way to an upright position and groaned. "I forgot how hard this was."

"Nah, you're doing fine. It'll come back to you."

"Doubtful."

Chase shrugged off my protest. "I think we should take a break and get some food, what do you say?'

"I think that's the best idea you've had all morning."

He rolled his eyes and took off down the hill. I managed to keep up without eating snow. Once we were at the end of the run, I kicked off my board and eagerly made my way to the cafeteria. We found an empty table near the window and placed our order. I stared out the window and I had to admit, the view was breathtaking.

"Beautiful, isn't it?"

"It sure is."

"How are you feeling?"

"Sore. Everywhere."

Chase chuckled. "It'll be even worse tomorrow unfortunately."

"I don't see how that's possible."

Chase grinned wider. "My advice, take a long, hot bath tonight with epsom salt. It should help."

"Noted." My phone beeped and a feeling of forewarning fell over me. I fished the phone out of my pocket and saw a missed call from aunt Sam. My face fell.

"What's wrong?"

"I have a voicemail from Sam." I dialled the code and listened to the far away voice in my ear. *Hi Emmy, it's aunt Sam. I know you don't feel comfortable here but I think it's best to keep you in the loop. Your mom had an episode this morning, she, well her mind isn't in the present right now. Call me when you can.*

"Em?"

I stared at the phone in silence. My shoulders slumped in defeat. My childish hope of bringing my mother back to where it all started had failed. I had this unspoken wish if I could bring her back to the beginning, it could wash away the battle for her.

"Emmy?"

I forced my gaze to meet the man before me. "Can you take a picture of me?"

Chase furrowed his brows. "Excuse me?"

"Can you take a picture of me? Not here, outside in the snow."

"Uh-sure."

"Let's go."

He followed me into the winter wonderland and I grabbed my board. I gave him my phone. "I'm ready."

He held up the phone and I heard the click of the shutter. I watched as a woman began to walk our way. "Excuse me, would you mind taking a picture of us?"

"Not at all."

"Thank you." I stood next to Chase and gave him a small grin. "Smile."

He looked at the phone held in our direction and gave an awkward grin. The woman returned the phone. "I took a few for you."

"Thank you."

I studied the photos and smiled. Those would do. Chase's voice brought me back. "Do you care to tell me what's going on?"

"My mom's mind left this morning."

"Oh, shit. Em-"

"Nothing can stop it, Chase. It's not going to stop, its only going to get worse. There will be a day when it leaves for good. One day, she won't remember who I am. I can't let that happen."

Recognition filled his features. "That's what the pictures are for."

"Yes. I'm going to make her a photo album. This way she'll have something with her at all times. Hopefully she can find comfort in it, even when her mind let's me go."

Chase placed his hand on the small of my back. "I don't think she'll ever let you go. Even on those days when she can't remember your name, I think you will always be familiar to her; the bond is deeply rooted."

"I hope so. Do you mind if we go?"

"No, I'll take you back."

"Thank you. We need to pick up my car anyways."

⌘

"Looks like your cars still here safe and sound."

"Yeah." I unclipped my seat belt and forced a small smile. "Thanks for today, it was fun."

"No problem. Are you going to be okay?"

"Yeah, I'll be fine." I opened the door and left the warmth of the truck.

"I'll call you later then?"

"Sounds good." I slammed the door shut and watched Chase drive away. The snow swirled slowly around me and I ambled toward my car. I scowered my trunk for the ice scraper and began to uncover my windshield. I dusted the snow off my hands in satisfaction and slid inside the cold car. The engine faltered in protest but finally caught. I let my head fall heavily against the headrest and waited for the heat to fill the cab. *Why. Why is this happening to us? Aaron….why aren't you here? I don't want to do this on my own.* Sadness filled my veins like ice water. *Shit. Shit. Shit.* I slammed my palm against the steering wheel and let out a curse to the sky. I stuck the car in drive and headed to my place of solace. I walked down the aisle way of the barn and kept my eyes to the ground; I was in no mood to make small talk with anyone.

Ace stuck his head over the stall door. His black tipped ears perked forward and his eyes were bright with curiosity. "Hey, handsome boy."

Ace craned his head to the side and let out a neigh. I stepped into his view and his nostrils quivered with low excitement. "Hey bud. Want to go for a ride?"

I entered the stall and tossed his halter over his delicate head. He stood quietly as I gave him a quick brush down and saddled him up. Once I swung into the saddle he began to prance restlessly. He seemed to sense the unease that boiled within me; the need to run, to escape. To simply disappear. I kept Ace at a slow walk as we left the barn; the clip clop of his hooves on the concrete echoed around us. Once we were outside the snow silenced everything. It muffled the sounds from the outside world from us. I let Ace transition into a smooth trot as we headed for the open field. I fell into an easy rhythm with Ace's bouncy movements as though no time had passed at all between us. He responded to the slightest movement from my body, our minds melded into one.

Emmy. Where are you? Emmy, please don't leave me here. Come back, please, come back. I shook my head as the memories began to unfold. My mind was beginning to waver being back here. Everything I had worked so hard to forget was now an open wound. A wave of panic tore through me. I felt like a caged animal, restlessly pacing, wanting, no needing to escape. No matter how I played it in my head, there was nothing left I could do. I simply could not take my mother's mind, place it in a box and keep it safe. It was a living thing with a mind of its own. It was a ghost, it had no shape, no physical form for me to chain to her. It could slip away through the cracks anytime it wanted. It was not fair. It should be attached to her soul, her body. It should keep her safe. It was her home. But it failed her-her own body had failed her; it was the ultimate betrayal.

My thoughts transitioned to my body and Ace felt it. Ace's pace grew choppy and my muscles tensed and tightened in response. I leaned forward over his neck and wrapped my hands in his course mane. "Let 'er fly."

That was all he needed. He remembered our years together, the cues I had given him so long ago. In one quick burst he plunged forward into a dead run. The bitter wind nipped at my skin and stole my breath. The tips of my fingers began to numb but I did not care. My mind stilled as Ace outran my broken memories. The tears I had suppressed for so long began to fall and I worried they would freeze. I let Ace run until he slowed to a walk. He let out a loud snort and tossed his head.

I leaned forward and gave him a hearty pat. "Good boy, bud. Ready to go home?"

Once we were back at the barn I took time giving Ace a good brush down and tossed on his winter blanket. I placed a few extra treats into his dinner and tucked him in for the night. "See you tomorrow, Ace. Thanks for taking me away."

I walked slowly to my car and had every intention of heading back to Elayna's for the night. However, an internal battle waivered inside of me. Guilt for leaving my mother alone when she needed me the most weighed heavy on my heart. Selfishness whispered loudly in my ear. Would she even notice if I didn't come around? A part of me, a rather large part did not want to be around her when she disappeared. I did not want that burned into my brain. I did not want to see my strong shell of a mother wither away in front of my eyes. I did not want to care. I did not want to deal with it anymore.

With one voice ringing louder than the other I drove straight to the pub.

CHAPTER ELEVEN

The alcohol warmed me from deep within. The rosy flush danced across my skin, making me feel temporarily alive again. With each sip I took, the guilt got quieter and quieter. A drunken smile appeared on my lips. "I win." I whispered to myself.

But the memories became louder in my head. They banged loudly against the cage I had locked them behind. The familiar surroundings I had walked back into were making them harder and harder to silence. My eyes felt heavy from emotion and lack of sleep. I let them drift close and he appeared. *Aaron.* I saw his confident grin and heard his sparkling laughter. "Lighten up, sis. It's only life. Don't let it get you down." My eyes fluttered open and a familiar face stared back at me. I jumped in surprise.

"Sorry, gave you a fright huh?"

My mind groggily began to filter names through my head. "Craig?"

"The one and only." Craig narrowed his eyes as he stared down at me. "You a little drunk are ya?"

"Maybe," I muttered.

"Becoming a habit I see."

"Excuse me?"

"I heard you jumped my sister a few nights ago."

"I wouldn't say I jumped her. I warned her to stop talking about Aaron but she wouldn't keep her mouth shut. Surprise, surprise. She always did like to hear herself talk."

Craig's jaw tightened. "She was talking about Aaron?"

I stood up to my full height and sighed. "If you're going to go around and accuse people of unwarranted actions, get the whole story first."

"What did she say about Aaron?"

It was my turn to narrow my eyes. "What does it matter?"

"It doesn't."

I glared at him. "Then don't fucking ask." Anger coursed through me. "What is it with you Brooks'? Stop mentioning him to me. Just. Stop."

The noise in the pub had come to a near silence. I looked around the room and flashes of curious bystanders gazed upon us. Craig looked uncomfortable and shook his head. "I think I should take you home."

"Don't touch me." I shook off his hand.

"Emmy, can we please not make anymore of a scene than we already have?"

I glowered at him and dug through my purse for my phone. "Give me a minute," I muttered. I dialled Elayna's number and got her voicemail. "Dammit."

Craig cleared his throat. "I can drive you."

"I think not." I held up my finger to silence him and dialled Chase. *Don't pick up. Please don't pick up.*

"Miss me already, huh?"

He picked up. Crap. "Funny story...do you think you can give me a ride home?"

"Where are you?"

"The pub." Silence filled the other end. I waited for what felt like an eternity and Chase had yet to respond. "Chase, are you still there?"

"I'm on my way." The line went dead but his tone was not pleased.

Craig cleared his throat. "I'll wait with you outside."

I didn't argue. I let him weave me through the crowd until the night air slapped me. Craig leaned against the pillar and crossed his arms. "So," he began. "Picked up where you two left off, huh."

"Shut up."

"Touchy subject."

"No, it's none of your business."

"Not normally. But you know my sister was seeing him for a bit."

"So I heard."

"Broke her heart when he ended things. I don't understand myself what the big deal is with Chase Havens. Poor taste in my opinion."

I forced myself to look at him, smug smile and all. "I forgot how much of an asshole you are."

Craig took a bow. "Emmy?"

"What?"

"Why are you back?"

His question jolted me. "I'm sure you've heard about my mom."

"Yeah, I did. I am sorry."

"She wanted to come back, she wanted to go home. She wanted to see Aaron."

Craig stiffened. "Why?"

"Why does it bloody well matter to you?"

"It doesn't. I just think some things are better left alone."

"That's one thing we can agree on."

"Em?" Chase rounded the corner and he did not look happy. His eyes drifted between Craig and I. "You okay?"

Craig smirked. "Don't worry bud, she's all yours."

I glared at him. "Go away."

Craig held up his hands. "My pleasure." His smirk deepened. "Its nice to see you back round here." Craig turned on his heel and shoulder checked Chase as he left.

Chase's eyes evaluated me in a calculated manner. "What happened?"

I shrugged my shoulders. "Dunno. I went to the barn and took Ace out; I needed to clear my head. I had every intention of going to see my mom but that clearly didn't happened. Drinking sounded better apparently."

Chase shook his head slowly. "C'mon, lets get you out of here."

I didn't argue. "Okay."

Chase helped me inside his truck. My head fell heavy against the headrest and the world began to spin. I closed my eyes and I hoped for nothingness; but my mind betrayed me. I wanted to see nothing but darkness, anything but what my mind conjured up. Instead, I saw Aaron and my mother with their bright eyes and carefree smiles.

"Sooo, what do you think?" Aaron drawled.

Audrey put her hand on a hip and smirked. "The Jeep suits you. Are you going to take me for a spin, or what?"

Aaron brightened. "Hop on in and hold on tight."

I squeezed my hands into fists and shook the memory away. Those days were dead and gone. No more, never again. My eyes flew open and I was surprised as the salty warm water dripped down my face.

"Em? Are you okay?"

"No, I'm not. I don't know what okay feels like anymore."

Chase squeezed my knee and started the truck. I watched the frozen world speed by and pleaded my brain to quiet. I wished desperately that I could run away from it all: the worry, the fear, the anger, the guilt. Everything. I wanted a break from my life, from me. I had hoped the alcohol would help me reach my destination of numbness but my attempt had been cut short.

"We're here."

Chase snapped me away from my thoughts. I stared up at the quaint A frame log house before me. I squinted against the night looking from left to right. "Oh." My heart stilled. "You finished it."

"I did."

"Oh." I shoved the truck door open and stood in the frozen snow. I took careful steps toward the house as my boots *crunched crunched* in the white powder. My eyes began adjusting to the hazy darkness slightly lit by the winter white backdrop. I noted the detached shop in the distance. Chase fell into step with me as we stepped onto the covered wrap around porch. He unlocked the door and gestured me inside.

The warmth from the house tickled my skin as I began to thaw instantly. A roaring fire crackled in the living room, which was the heart of the home. I let out a low whistle. "It's beautiful."

"Thanks."

I took my coat off and hung it on the rack. I took a quick walk around and noted the country style kitchen, washrooms, large picturesque windows and the loft upstairs, which held the bedroom. The house felt warm, personally touched by Chase. "I mean it, Chase. This place really suits you."

He shrugged."I should hope so, since I built the damn place."

I stifled a gasp and ignored the feeling as though I was socked in the stomach. I began to take a closer look at the finer details. Nothing was spared. "Wow. You did it; you really did it, didn't you? This house is built by joinery isn't it?"

No nails, or screws were used. Every joint was hand crafted by his hands to fit and lock together like a large puzzle. I stared at the beams above in wonder. *He did it without me.* While we were together, we had bought a piece of land. This had been Chase's dream, *our* dream. And while I left and my world fell apart, he had picked himself up and marched on while I was left gasping to keep my head above water.

Chase noticed my face change. He took a step closer and wrapped me in his arms. "Em, it's okay. Shh, it's okay."

I didn't know I was sobbing. As his arms held me, I fell apart. No matter how hard he squeezed, he wouldn't be able to hold me together, not tonight. "I'm scared Chase. I'm terrified to see my mom disappear; I'm scared of how easy it is to leave her alone. I don't know what I'm doing anymore. I'm scared all the damn time."

"I know you are. There are no rulebook here. Let yourself feel whatever it is that you need to feel. Give it time."

I wriggled out of his embrace and met his eyes. "Time isn't the friend here. *We* don't have time."

Chase flinched. "I'm sorry. Poor choice of words."

I fell onto the couch behind me. Chase sat across from me in the single recliner. My eyes fell onto him and I let them take their time taking him in. His hair and beard were slightly dishevelled. His blue gray eyes met mine and didn't look away. "I don't know how I ever left you."

Chase's body tensed slightly. "Em-"

"Look at what you did, Chase. This is incredible. I'm so proud of you. You pulled it together and made the dream a reality. I don't think I could have done that."

"You were what fuelled me to do this, Em. You are as much apart of this home as I am."

"What do you mean?"

"I was there. Your family is like my own. I loved you with everything I had in me. When your family fell to pieces, I felt everything you felt. It hit me too." Chase stood up and ran his fingers through his hair. "I think you forgot that. I needed you just as much as you needed me, but you left. You left like a damn thief in the night. No goodbye, no note, no god damn nothing! How do you think that made me feel?"

His gaze settled on me and hurt filled his eyes. "Apart of me understood, but I thought you would come back within a few days. I always thought you'd come back to me. But you never did."

The deep ache within my stomach began to twist and turn. My heart fluttered uneasily in my chest and it suddenly got hard to breathe. Truth be told, when I left I didn't think how it would affect him at all. Our dreams, our future, it didn't cross my mind once. Not once. I had blinders on; all I could feel was the shock and anger of a moment that changed everything. Being here, seeking comfort in those who knew everything felt suffocating. I had to leave it all in hopes to move on. But instead of moving on, I lost it all. It wasn't until the anger wore off that the reality of what happened stood before me. My mind had begun to clear and that's when my heart began to ache for my best friend, Chase. I missed his voice, his touch, his soul. But I didn't know how to go back, I didn't know that I ever could. And then my mom got sick. Once again, everything changed.

"Sorry doesn't even begin to make up for what I have done to you, Chase. I am truly sorry from the depths of my soul. I didn't know how to face the betrayal of what I had done to you. And then my mom got sick and I lost it. A small part of me wonders if its karma. Life is levelling the playing field; taking those I love away for hurting someone who means everything to me."

Chase let out a deep breath and fell beside me in the couch. He was silent for a moment, his eyes taking in his home. "The anger and hurt you caused me kept me going with this place. I thought if maybe I built this, you would come back."

I sat silent and forced myself to look at him. "I did come back."

His face fell. "When?"

"Three months after I left. It took that damn long for the doctors to figure out what was happening to my mom. They hustled their investigations after my mother drove into a pole and couldn't remember what happened. Then I was forced to arrange care for her..."

"I came back for you. I needed you beside me. I missed my best friend. I never meant to stay away for so long, but like I said shit happened. I was in so over my head and I needed to apologize to you for what I had done. A phone call wasn't going to cut it. But when I came back..." I let my voice trail off.

Chase rubbed the back of his neck; a nervous habit he formed. "Keep going."

"I saw you. With *her*."

Chase blew out a breath. "I wish you had come to me. Em. I wasn't with a soul for about a year after you left. What you saw, it was just typical Miranda trying to cozy up to me. I was hurt, so I didn't push her away."

I let out a forced laugh. "All I saw was you, with my mortal enemy Miranda Brooks. I knew then how much I had hurt you. I assumed you hated me and I fucked off. And it was that very day I met Sean." A wry smile formed my lips. "Funny how life works, hey? It has a sense of humour, a cruel one but at least its something."

Chase tucked a loose strand of hair behind my ear. "Are you going to look at me?"

I raised my eyes to his. "I saw you kiss her."

"I wish you had kept watching. You would have seen me push her off. When we did eventually get together, things between us didn't last long. I was trying to fill a void. It didn't work."

"I am truly sorry, Chase. For everything."

"I know you are. I am too." He gave me a small grin. "I was downright pissed off at you. I had never been so angry with anyone. And now here you are, on my couch."

"And?"

"And what?"

"Do you still hate me?"

Chase studied me. His finger trailed my jawline. "Hardly."

I smiled. "So, it worked then."

"What did?"

"You built the house and poof, I appeared."

I scooted closer to him until our faces were mere inches from each other. *I missed you so much.* "I forgive you, Em. I always have."

I closed my eyes and pulled back. "Can we do this?"

Chase sighed. "Do what?"

"Go back to where we left off?"

"I'd like to try. You don't have to be alone in this anymore. Let me take some of the load off. You're drowning."

I let out a heavy sigh and rested my head in his lap. "I don't deserve you."

"You did back then and you do now. Stop being so hard on yourself. You can't dwell on the past, it will only weigh you down." He gave me a tight squeeze.

"When did you get to be so philosophical?"

"I was forced to have a lot of time to think."

I stretched out and let the heaviness take over my body. "So you should be thanking me then?"

"Ha, for what?"

"For forcing you to grow up and become who you are now. I did good."

"Only you would find a way to pat yourself on the back. Em?"

Chase's voice became muffled in my ear. For once I was drifting away into a sea of blackness, my mind stilled. I welcomed the quiet; the pure nothingness and I let it take me under.

CHAPTER TWELVE

"What's it like where you go?" I sat next to Aaron, allowing my feet to hang over the edge of the fence. The tall grass swayed gently in the spring breeze, the smell of life reawakening.

"I don't know. I don't feel any pain. My body and mind are kinda numb. It feels good, safe and comforting, y'know?"

"No," I whispered.

Aaron softened. "How's mom?"

"I don't know."

"Have you been to see her?"

"I'm scared to be around her."

"You have to stay close, Em. Don't leave her. She needs you and you need her."

The old familiar tug in my heart appeared. "I know. Aaron?"

"What's up, sis?"

I stared at my left forearm and traced my finger over the raised scar. "I'm so sorry."

Aaron's carefree expression fell. "Don't be sorry, you did everything you could." He stood and pulled me off the fence. "Come here, kiddo."

I fell into his arms and hugged him tightly. Aaron stepped back after a moment and stared into the distance. "Watch over mom, k?"

A wave of loneliness cracked my heart. He was going to leave me again. "Is it that time already?"

"Yeah. I can't stay, you know that."

"Aaron?"

"Mm?"

"I love you."

Aaron broke into his childish, carefree smile. "Who wouldn't love me?"

I laughed. "Don't be a jerk."

He winked at me. "Love you too."

"Don't forget us," I whispered, as my words were lost in the breeze.

⌘

Heat radiated against my skin from the warm body next to me. I stretched out happily and squinted my eyes open. Chase was on his side, his head propped up by his hand. "Morning sleepy."

I smiled widely as I took in his tousled hair, and still half asleep gaze. A lifetime of memories flooded back to me in a split second. "Morning, stranger."

"How did you sleep?"

I sat up gingerly, working the kinks out of my neck. "It's been a long time since I passed out on a couch. I can't believe we both fit on this thing."

"You're tiny. It was a good excuse to have you close."

I grinned, and then grimaced. "My head is throbbing."

"Ha, can't handle the alcohol like you used too. Aging is a bitch." Chase hopped over me and stood, stretching. "I feel like my body belongs to a 50 year old some days."

"Time takes away so much," I said to myself.

"Coffee?"

"Yes please." I flopped back down and shifted onto my stomach. I watched Chase, still in the clothes from the night before bustle in the kitchen. The aroma of freshly brewed coffee began to fill the house. I took in a deep, appreciative breath and met him in the kitchen.

Chase handed me a steaming mug. "Here you go. Drink your way to alertness."

"I will, thank you." I took a careful sip of the heated dark liquid. The familiar taste filled my senses and promised to kick my brain into gear. My eyes drifted out the large kitchen windows and grew wide at the beauty before me. Mountain views stood in the distance, offering a panoramic view. The fields glistened in the snow-draped rug, and areas of the property were clustered with tall evergreens and bare twisted maples.

Chase stood behind me. "Beautiful, isn't it?"

I craned my neck around the corner and made out a small barn and wood shed. "How many acres is this again?"

"Twelve."

I turned to face him. "Twelve. Twelve acres."

"Yep, and a small creek borders the neighbouring property."

"I forgot how beautiful this place was."

He gazed at me softly. "Yeah, you have." He took a step forward and my heart began to hammer like a jack. A loud knock at the door broke the trance and caused us both to jump.

"Dammit," Chase muttered under his breath and left to answer the door. Elayna burst into the room. Her worried features fell and she grinned as wide as a cheshire cat. "There you are, I've been calling you like mad. I had a hunch you'd be here."

My cheeks flushed instantly. "Sorry I didn't call, I was, uh, well..." I gestured helplessly.

Elayna smiled widely once more before her features fell. "Your aunt came by this morning."

My stomach dropped. "Is everything okay?"

"I don't know, she wasn't willing to talk with me very much. She left pretty quickly."

"Crap, thanks for letting me know."

Elayna's eyes danced from myself to Chase. "Anywho, I guess I should be going." She took a step forward and wrapped me in a bear hug. "I'm so glad you're back. I guess I'll see you later?" She smirked at Chase, "or maybe not."

I rolled my eyes. "I'll talk to you later."

"Uh-huh."

Chase shot me a look and walked Elayna to the door. "Thanks for popping in."

When Chase rounded the corner, escorting Elayna outside I grabbed my cell phone. *10 missed calls. Shit.* I dialled my aunt Sam and paced restlessly.

"Emmy is that you?"

"Yes. I'm sorry I missed your calls. How's mom?"

Aunt Sam let out an exasperated sigh. "She's asleep now. It was a rough night, Emmy. She went completely blank, and she was quite upset. She had no idea where she was, who I was. I was hoping you could come by and try and talk to her. I wonder if she just needs someone familiar near her, you know?"

"You're her sister. Aren't you familiar enough?" As soon as the words were out guilt slapped me across the face,

Chase rounded the corner and caught the tail end. His expression looked pain. I shook my head and mouthed *I'm sorry.* I pressed the palm of my hand into my forehead. The line remained quiet. "Aunt Sam?"

Sam cleared her throat. "While I am her sister, we have spent years apart. The bond we have is nothing like yours. I have chosen to be with my sister during one of the hardest battles of her life."

Her words were steeled and they were meant to hurt. They did. They sliced my insides like a paper shredder. *Fuck.* I spoke quickly. "Can we all meet for lunch, or a mid afternoon coffee?"

"I was hoping you could come by the house, actually. I thought it would be nice to get things out of storage and set up the home a little more. I think it could help your mom on a sub conscious level to have the house feel lived in like it used to be."

I slumped onto the granite counter top in defeat. Her words made perfect sense. "Sure," I sighed. "I can be there in a few hours."

"Good. See you then."

The line went dead and my body grew cold. I felt Chase's presence behind me, battling whether it was safe to come closer or not. "Em? You alright?"

"I have no idea." I turned to face him. "Can you come with me?"

"Of course I will."

Relief flooded my veins. "Thank you, thank you so much." I let out a small laugh. "I mean this is ridiculous isn't it? I'm scared to go home, to see her…"

Chase took a large step forward and wrapped me close. "We'll get through it. Step by step, k?"

I leaned aginst his arms and craned my neck upwards to meet his eyes. "Thanks for being here. I don't know how I could do this on my own."

Chase ran his fingers in my hair. "We should pick up your car then and take you back to Elayna's for a change of clothes."

I smirked. "I look that bad huh?"

"Naw, y'look good. But you might want to get your grubbies on. I think I overheard heard we're setting up the house?"

I wrinkled my nose. "Yup. Time for the items to see the light of day." I crossed my arms and leaned back against the counter top. "I think apart of her always knew she'd come back. She refused to let me sell the house and our belongings. I fought with her bringing most of it into storage, I just couldn't understand why she would want to hold on to everything. There was no need."

"Do you regret it?"

I shook my head. "No. I just wish we were here for a different reason."

"I know. I'm going to change clothes and have a quick shower, do you mind? We can head out in 15 minutes."

"Sounds good. I'll wait here."

Chase nodded and took the stairs two at a time. From above, I heard the shower start. I lingered at the bottom of the steps and glanced upward. Chase left the bedroom door opened and was unaware I was watching. He tore off his shirt and grabbed a towel from the hall pantry. I admired his taut back muscles as he disappeared behind the corner.

"Still looks good," I muttered to myself. I tore myself away from the stairway and made my way to the fireplace. I grabbed the fire poker and shuffled the ashes, revealing embers. I strode into the kitchen and quickly slipped on Chase's clunky slippers. I unlocked the glass sliding door and grabbed a handful of wood from his neat stack. Once inside, I placed the wood strategically in the fireplace and helped bring the fire to life by blowing on the embers like a birthday candle. The embers began to smoke, until at last, a small rush of flames bursted to life. The wood began to snap and crackle as the fire roared to action. I sat on the cool tiled floor and hugged my knees to my chest. Intense warmth followed by butterflies began to beat in my stomach. This felt all too familiar; being with Chase no matter where we were, felt like home. I wrapped my arms around my torso and hugged tightly. It was too soon. I could not expect to pick things up where we left off. I was not ready for that. Time had changed a lot of things and my world was so unsettled. I needed him that I could not deny. I spent nearly every waking moment regretting what I had done to Chase, but at the time I'd believed it was necessary. Life had pushed us away but now here we all were, we had come full circle.

"Hey, look at you. You're still the fire queen I remember."

I stood up stiffly and forced a smile. "Yeah."

"What's wrong?"

"I'm just feeling a little uneasy about today. It's nothing. Come on, we should get my car. I should get changed into something warmer."

Chase raised an eyebrow but didn't push me. "Okay." He grabbed a toque and motioned me out the door. I hopped in the truck and tried to ignore the uneasy flopping of my stomach. I stared out the window in silence as we headed into town, trying to focus on deep breathing. A firm squeeze on my knee caused me to jump.

"Em, it's going to be alright. I'm with you. Loosen up; you're knuckles are turning white you're clenching your fists so hard."

"What?" I looked at my white knuckled grasp. "Oh. Oops." I unclenched my hands and rotated my wrists in an effort to loosen up. The nerves began to bunch and build and before I knew it, my knee was bouncing in a rapid pace. "Jesus!" I cried in frustration. "I can't keep still."

Chase nearly whispered. "Just breathe, it will be okay."

His words lacked the conviction I yearned to hear and I couldn't help but notice his own grip had tightened on the steering wheel. My nerves were like an infectious disease; spreading and taking hold of those who were near.

Soon enough he pulled next to my frozen car. "Are you going to be okay to drive?"

I nodded. "Yes, follow me to Elayna's?"

"K."

After a few attempts my car awakened. I stuck it in gear and began the drive to my temporary home. *Where do I belong? I feel like I'm stuck in limbo. I have nowhere to call my own.* It was a short drive from town to Elayna's. I parked quickly and Chase pulled in behind. We entered the vacant house together.

I looked around and called out a greeting. There were no signs of life. "They're probably at work."

"Most likely. I'll wait here for you."

"Okay, make yourself comfortable. I'm going to have a quick shower."

"Okay."

I took the stairs two at a time and grabbed a pair of leggings and warm sweater. I escaped in the washroom and turned the shower on full blast. The house was aged and the pipes often took awhile to warm up. Once the water held a trace of heat, I scooped my hair and fastened it into a loose topknot. I stepped under the mild water and hoped the warmth would quiet my trembling hands. A feeling of forewarning had taken over. I had a sickening foreboding that I would soon be left to face everything I had long since fled. And I wasn't ready. I would never be ready.

CHAPTER THIRTEEN

We arrived at the storage facility. We worked in rhythmic silence loading up the truck. Chase threw glances of concern my way but said nothing. He knew how hard this was for me. He also knew me well enough that I didn't want to talk about it; there was no way to predict how this would go. It all would depend on my mom's current state. Would she be present in the moment? Or would her mind have been robbed of her essence?

"Truck's full," Chase said quietly.

"Let's go."

We hopped inside the cab and Chase hesitated starting the ignition. "Are you sure you're ready for this? I can deliver all of this myself if you want."

"As tempting as that is, and believe me it's *so* tempting, I should see her."

"Here we go then." The truck tires crunched the ice below and away we went.

⌘

"So do not fear, for I am with you; do not be dismayed, for I am your God. I will strengthen you and help you; I will uphold you with my righteous right hand. Isaiah 41:10"

"What the hell is this?" I exclaimed.

Sam looked at me in outrage. She put the Bible down gently and marched toward me, grabbing my elbow. She dragged me into the kitchen. "Do not speak to me that way, Emmy. I am trying to offer your mother some comfort."

"Aunt Sam," I said in exasperation."I'm beyond thankful that you're here,

I truly am but you know as well as I do that Mom isn't the religious type. She's always been more of a free spirit. Religion is your comfort, not hers."

Sam took a forced breath. "Emmy, there is no better time than right now for your mother to form a relationship with God."

Before I could say another word, my mother's tinkling laughter filled the house. Sam and I looked at each other in question before we went to investigate. Chase stood next to my mother; his body language was clearly uncomfortable. His cheeks were filled by a deep hue of red.

Sam and I watched as Audrey took another step closer to him and twirled the end of her hair. Her voice softened into a purr as she reached out for his forearm; I gasped in horror as I realized she was flirting.

Chase sent me a look of help. "Oh god!" I moaned. *Gross, gross, gross.* I scurried between them and gave Chase a gentle push backward. I sent him an apologetic look and faced my mom. "Mom? Chase is my, uh, friend."

He rolled his eyes and stood next to me, his hand around my waist. My mom looked between us and disappointment filled her features. "Oh, I see." Her eyes landed on Sam. "Can you read me more of that book?" She plopped down on the couch looking bored.

Chase cleared his throat. "I'm going to start unloading the truck."

I sat next to my mom and grabbed her hand. "Do you remember me?"

My mother studied me intently. "I'm not sure. You look somewhat familiar but I don't remember your name. I'm sorry."

"It's Emmy."

"That's a pretty name. Not ringing any bells though."

Those simple words were like a knife to the heart. "I'm your daughter."

Audrey's eyebrows rose and she let out a loud laugh. "Oh, honey. I think I'd remember if I had a child. "

I sighed and stood. Aunt Sam watched me carefully. I walked over to a closet and dug through until I found an old photo. Aunt Sam stood and held up her hand. "I don't think this is the time."

I stepped past her and sat down beside my mom. I gently offered her the photo. She stared down in wonder as she studied herself, Aaron and myself within the frame. "Who's the boy?"

"Your son, Aaron."

"Good looking fella, isn't he?" She looked at me quickly. "You're a pretty girl, I did good." Confusion took over. "If I have kids, how come I don't remember you? Where's my husband?"

I stole a glance at Aunt Sam. She sent me a look of disapproval and left to help Chase. I looked back at my mom. "Dad left when we were very young; I have no memories of him."

"Oh, that's disappointing. Why don't I remember any of this?"

I squeezed her hand gently. "You're sick. Sometimes your mind disappears. It's almost like a computer that goes in for re-programming; the slate gets wiped clean. You temporarily forget us."

My mother started shaking her head. She looked at the photo again. "No, no, no."

"Do you know where you are? Do you recognize it?"

My mother looked around urgently. "No." She stood up suddenly and her arms began to twitch slightly. She looked at me wide eyed. "What kind of cruel trickery is this?"

I stood up and tried to comfort her. "Mom, I'm not trying to trick you. I'm trying to help you remember." I pointed to a corner of the living room. "That's where Aaron took his first steps. And over in the corner by the window is where the Christmas tree always goes."

Audrey covered her ears. "Get out! Stranger! Stranger! Get OUT!"

Her words shell shocked me. In the past, even when her mind went away, she took comfort in my presence. This was the polar opposite.

Audrey's voice went shrill. "Sam! Sam! Help me!"

"Sam? Mom, it's okay, I won't hurt you." I took a step closer.

My mother lunged for the phone and whipped it in my direction. I ducked in time as it crashed against the wall. Chase and Sam rushed in at the commotion.

"Stranger!" Audrey began chanting.

Aunt Sam swooped in. "It's okay. Focus on your breathing. Listen to my words 'For I know the plans I have for you, plans to prosper you and not harm you, plans to give you a hope and a future' Jeremiah 29:11"

"Stop with the Bible bullshit!" I hollered.

Chase scooped me up by the waist and placed me outside. My eyes were wide in disbelief. "What just happened? It's gotten so much worse so quickly, how did this happen?"

"I think we should go until things calm down."

"Did you unload the truck?" I asked blankly, staring at nothing in particular.

"Yeah, your aunt is going to set everything up."

"She brain washed her." I glared at the house.

"Em-let's go."

"Not yet." I darted around him and ran inside. The suddenness of my entry startled the women inside.

Sam's hand flew to her chest. "Emmy, you surprised me." She sent a look of reassurance to my mom and rose to meet me. She nodded for me to follow. "I think it's best if you leave. I'm sorry; I thought having you here would be best for her. I didn't think she would react the way she did."

"What have you done to her?" I cried.

"Excuse me? What have *I done to her?* Besides dropping my life and coming at a moments notice?"

Guilt gnawed at my bones. *I'm an asshole. A royal asshole.* "God damnit!" I picked up a glass and tossed it at the sink. Glass shards shattered everywhere. Aunt Sam flinched and closed her eyes, pinching the bridge of her nose. "Do you feel better?"

Chase scrambled inside and took a quick evaluation of the mess I had created. "Right. We're done here for today." He clasped my hand and led me outside without protest. Chase practically carried me to the truck and plopped me inside. He hopped in and slammed the door, staring at the house.

"What the fuck happened in there? Was that really necessary?"

I pressed my lips together and crossed my arms. "God's presence was not felt by all apparently."

"Amen," Chase muttered and started the truck.

⌘

"I have to go to work for a bit. Can I trust you to behave here?"

I smiled. "You bet. This is my escape, remember?"

"Let Ace give you wings."

"That's the plan." I hopped out. "When will you be back?"

"I'll pick you up in about two hours."

"See you then." I marched to the barn with purpose. Calmness flooded over me as soon as the familiar scent wafted in my lungs. My steps suddenly faltered as a laugh floated through the barn. My shoulders slumped in weariness. *Today is not my day.*

Miranda Brooks tossed her shiny hair over her shoulder. Her smile faded once she saw me. "What are *you* doing here?" she nearly growled.

"Seeing my horse."

"You board your horse *here?*"

"Unfortunately," I muttered.

A stable hand interrupted. "Sorry, the horses are in the field today. We were doing some maintenance on the barn and the noises were upsetting them. We figured they would be happier outside. I can help you bring your horse in if you'd like."

I smiled. "No thanks, I can get Ace myself. Thanks though."

The stable hand looked toward Miranda. She glared at me. "No," she said tightly. "I can do it too."

I grabbed the bridle and reins from my hook and grudgingly followed Miranda. We entered the field together and her eyes landed on her horse. "Trigger," she clucked. "Come here." Miranda took a few steps closer to Trigger and he snorted. He kicked up his heels and cheekily took off, feeling frisky in the winter air.

I cupped my hands around my mouth and hollered. "Ace! Come here buddy!"

Miranda snorted in disgust. "He's not a dog." Her eyes widened as my boy came loping over.

I held my hands out to slow him. "Good boy. Wanna go for a ride?" I tossed the reins over his neck and slid the bridle on. I mounted in a single leap and settled onto his bareback. I patted his neck. "Good boy." I glanced at Miranda. "I had a lot of years with this horse. We've put in our time figuring each other out." I bit my lip and continued. "Give it time with yours. It will get easier."

Miranda glowered. "I don't need advice from you."

I chose not to respond. I clucked to Ace and led him to the gate. I leaned forward, opened the gate and Ace side stepped through. I clicked the latch on the gate and set him at an easy walk to the trails. The silence of the woods eased my tension. As Ace increased his pace, I let my worries and fears temporarily fall away. I settled into his smooth transitions and my mind went quiet. The thickness of the treed trails melted away and we found ourselves in an open field. Ace began to dance beneath me, begging me to let him have his head.

I smiled and leaned forward. "Let 'er fly."

And just like that, we were flying. The scenery blurred into one and without the saddle separating us I could feel Ace's heart race against my leg. The heat from his body took away the coolness of my own. We became the perfect team. We slowed to a walk and made our way back to the barn where I took my time brushing him out and tucking him in for the night.

"I'm so glad to see you two reunited. Chase did really good."

I turned in surprise toward Elayna. "Hey! What are you doing here?"

Ace swung his head over the stall door, chomping on a mouthful of hay. He stared big eyed at Elayna and extended his nose to her. She laughed and gave him a pat. "He's still a big child I see."

I smiled affectionately. "Wouldn't have it any other way."

"Chase called, he's going to be later than he thought. So, I'm here to pick you up."

"Sorry you have to taxi me around."

"I don't mind." Elayna's eyes danced. "Chase says for you to be ready by 7:30 tonight."

"Oh?"

"He's performing tonight. He's going to pick you up."

"Oh."

Elayna nudged my side. "We'll meet you at the pub. I think he's going to take you out for dinner first."

"So, this is a date."

"Yup!"

I found myself smiling as Elayna clapped her hands together. "Everything seems to be coming together nicely. Well, almost." She gave me a sympathy squeeze.

Almost.

CHAPTER FOURTEEN

I have nothing to wear. My god, I feel like I'm sixteen years old again. I sighed in frustration at the reflection that stood before me. My hair was twisted into a tousled low bun, and I wore black slacks with a dark blue sweater with buttons down the back. "Whatever, good enough."

I headed downstairs, grabbed my jacket and pulled on my bootie heels. The ticking of the clock seemed loud and incessant. The nerves began to twitch in my stomach and my heart picked up speed. A loud knock at the door caused me to jump a mile high.

"Pull it together, woman." I chided myself. I straightened my posture and swung the door open.

Chase gave his lazy smile and let out a low whistle. "You look nice."

"Thank you. So do you."

Chase held out his hand. "C'mon, let's go. I hope you're hungry."

I wasn't. "Famished." I lied.

"Excellent. Kappa's it is."

⌘

The restaurant was packed. Chase had called ahead to make reservations so we got a seat immediately. *Pre-meditated, so unlike Chase.* We slid into the candlelit booth and I glanced at the gently falling snow outside. I turned away and faced Chase.

"Are you nervous for tonight?"

"Which part? The date or my performance."

I smiled wrly. "You choose."

Chase smirked. "The butterflies are present for both if you must know."

I perked up and laughed in triumph. "Good to know."

"How are you doing, Em?"

I sighed and put down my wineglass. "I wish people would stop asking me. I feel like everyone is expecting me to have a mental breakdown." I sighed in frustration. "I'm okay. Not good, not great. Just simply okay."

"Good to know."

Our meals arrived and we ate in comfortable silence. Chase paid the bill and we stood from our booths stiffly. "I'm so full," I moaned.

Chase gave his stomach a slap. "You and me both. C'mon, we have to head to the pub. I need to set up the stage."

The drive was quick. Chase grabbed his guitar from the back of the truck and metal suitcase that looked heavy. "Sound equipment," he stated. "Here." He held out the guitar for me to take. I followed Chase into the back entrance reserved for employees and entertainment. Chase introduced me to the band and I smiled shyly. Their curious glances were short lived as their attention refocused to the task at hand.

Chase hopped down from the stage and led me into a quiet corner. "Elayna and Jay will be here soon. Are you going to wish me luck?"

I scoffed. "You don't need it. The ladies will be falling left, right and center." I took a step closer and pressed my body next to his. "Good luck."

Chase wore a broad grin and shuffled even closer. "Thank you."

"Jay, I found her! We've been looking for you all over the place."

Chase sighed and pulled away. Disappointment temporarily fell over me. *So close!* I turned to face Elayna and Jay.

"Hey guys." I nodded to the bar. "Shall we?"

Elayna sidled up to me. "Sorry, our timing is impeccable, huh?"

I waved my hand. "Don't worry about it."

"Are you excited for tonight?"

The band began to warm up, lifting the already elevated mood in the room. "I am. I'm really looking forward to this. It's been so long."

We grabbed our cold drinks and found a seat with a good view. As the band began to play, I couldn't take my eyes off of Chase. His voice was whisky smooth with just the right amount of grit. He played the guitar like it was a part of him.

"I forgot how good he was."

Elayna leaned close and wriggled her eyebrows. "Look around you, Em. All the women here want a piece of him. You better put a claim on him soon."

"Elayna! What, you think I should smack a sign on him? 'Back off ladies. Taken.'"

She shrugged. "Or you could plant a big kiss on him. Either or works."

My cheeks burned red. Elayna chuckled. "Just like old times, best to remind everyone, you know?"

After a solid hour of playing, the band bid their adieu. Chase hopped down from the stage and his eyes locked on me. A group of woman grabbed his arm, stopping him in his tracks. His eyes pulled away from mine and turned to the women begging for attention. I watched as the ladies put on their best performance and spared no expense to stroke his arm. They tossed back their heads and let out twinkling laughter that did not sound natural. My eyes grew wide at the obvious feeding frenzy.

Chase's eyes began to dart toward us in a silent plea of help. I could tell he was doing his best to politely end the conversation but it was a lost cause. The women were high on the buzz of alcohol, their confidence elevated. The desire clear. Target acquired.

"Good grief," I muttered and stood up.

"Atta girl. Go get 'em," Elayna cheered.

I turned to shoot her a glare. *You can do this. No biggie. Just breathe.* I forced myself to march with a confidence I did not possess. I squirmed my way into the group of women and ignored the dirty looks. I stood in front of Chase and his face fell in relief. The look he gave me would have been enough. I would have been content to simply take his hand and lead him away, but I made the mistake of glancing at the glowering group behind me. They stared at me with their disapproving eyes and snorted. Their heavily made up eyes said "Really? Yeah right."

That was all I needed. I smiled and stood on my tiptoes and tossed my arms around Chase's neck. His eyes widened in surprise but he leaned toward me. Our eyes locked and for a split second we held the gaze. Chase broke the spell as his gaze fell to my lips. "Bout time," he whispered before our lips met. It was cautious at first, until the hunger of the passed years wanted more. I pulled back first, breathless. Chase smiled softly and wrapped his arm around my waist. I allowed myself to be led away and took one last glance at the disbelieved faces before me. I gave a quick wink and felt a rush of adrenaline course through me. *Long time coming.*

Once we got back to the table, Jay smiled coyly and for once, Elayna said nothing. Her facial expression said more than enough.

⌘

My phone rang before the sun was up. I awoke with a start and clumsily kicked off the heavy quilt. I grasped the bedside table until my hands clasped around my cold phone. I answered it quietly. "Hello?"

I tip toed out of the bedroom as to not wake Chase. "Emmy!" the voice was in near hysterics. "Your mom is gone. I don't know how this could have happened, I-"

"What do you mean she's gone? How long has she been missing for?"

"I don't know. She went to bed around midnight last night. I got up to use the washroom and noticed her room was empty. I've scoured every inch of this place. The car's still here which means she left on foot."

I glanced at the time, 4:45 am. Jesus, it was well below freezing outside. I forced the panic down and willed myself to keep it together. "Stay at home. I'll go look for her."

"I can't stay at home and do nothing!"

"Someone needs to be there in case she shows up. What state was she in?"

As Sam went on, I pulled on my boots, toque and attempted to shove my shaking limbs into my winter coat. Something Sam had said caught my attention. "Say the last part again."

"She said she's been away for too long. She needed to get her ducks in a row."

I'll be fine, Mom. All my ducks are in a row. "I know where she is," I gasped.

"That line means something to you?"

"It does. I'll call you as soon as I can." I hung up the phone and grabbed Chase's keys. Before heading out the door, I grabbed one of his winter jackets and took off running. "Crap," I skidded to a stop and turned back to the house. I scribbled on a piece of paper to Chase and secured it with a magnet on the fridge. Once I was in the truck I slammed the key in and turned the ignition with more force than required. The engine destroyed the silence. I stuck it in gear and began the lonely drive. *Please be okay, please be okay.* I was not a religious person, but I hoped someone, anyone could hear my prayer and let my mother be safe.

⌘

I came to a halt at the stop sign. The engine idled loudly, the exhaust smoke drifted like a cloud in the frozen air. *Delway St.* My breath caught and for a moment it was hard to breathe. The scar on my arm began to ache. *I can't do it.* I stared down the road to my left and blew past it. I took the long way to my destination and let my foot off the gas. My eyes darted carefully back and forth, praying, hoping I would see a silhouetted figure in the distance standing upright.

My eyes locked on something ahead. I pulled over to the side of the road, the headlights illuminating her. She did not flinch, she did not move. I killed the engine and grabbed the coat from the passenger seat. As much as it killed me, I did not run to her. I took my time as not to spook her if she didn't know who I was.

"Mo- er Audrey?" No response. I continued my walk until I stood beside her. "God, you must be freezing." I draped Chase's oversized jacket around her and began to run my hands up and down her arms. Audrey stood in her pyjamas, boots and a light cardigan. It was a wonder she was alive.

Her eyes flickered and she looked at me. "Emmy."

Relief flooded through me. "I'm here, Mom. Let's get you inside."

"I found him. I told him everything."

I kept my eyes on the truck. I didn't want to look where she pointed. "I'm glad." I helped her get inside the still warm truck. I turned it on and blasted the heat.

"Are you okay?"

"I'm cold." Audrey looked at the jacket. "Thanks for bringing this."

"You're welcome."

We drove in silence until Audrey cleared her throat. "Sam told me what I did."

I was surprised. "Did she?"

"Honey, I'm so sorry. You know I didn't mean it, right?"

"Of course I do. It's okay."

"But its not. Nothing about this is okay," she whispered.

I tightened my grip on the wheel. *I know.* "Do you remember leaving the house this morning?"

"Crystal clear."

"You weren't dressed properly."

"I know. I woke up needing to go. I knew Sam would make me wait until later and I just couldn't wait any longer. I needed to see him."

"I know."

"Have you been to visit?"

I shook my head. "No."

"It's comforting, I hope you try it sometime." Audrey let out a very tired sigh. "I don't know how much longer I will be here, truly present. What you saw....it was traumatizing. No one should ever have to go through what you did. I would like to see you heal, to truly move on. I want to be your mother for as long as I can." Audrey's voice broke. "It will never be long enough. I wanted forever."

Her words cut into places I didn't know existed. If I tried to speak, I would crumble. Instead, I reached out and grabbed her hand. She held on with everything she had in her.

CHAPTER FIFTEEN

"This isn't home."

"No, I'm not ready to take you back yet."

Audrey smiled and got out of the truck. "I'm game." Her eyes took in the quaint house. "Where are we?"

The porch light was on and the door swung open. Chase's eyes took us in and he ushered us inside quickly. He guided Audrey next to the roaring fire. The sweet smell of brewed coffee filled the house. He walked next to me as we entered the kitchen and gave me a quick hug. "You scared the shit out of me. How are you? How is she?"

"Cold. She's lucid right now. She's upset, about everything." I looked around the cozy home. "Thank you."

"I didn't do anything."

"You knew I'd bring her back. You got the fire ready for one, and the freshly brewed coffee? Nice touch."

"It's the least I could do. I was on pins and needles hoping I wouldn't get a phone call from you. That would mean…"

"I know." I jolted. "I need to call Sam."

Chase nodded. He grabbed a warm mug and sat beside my mom. I punched in my aunt's number and watched the two of them from afar. How did I get so lucky to have him in my life? Round two.

"Emmy, is she okay? Please, god, tell me you found her."

"I did. She's okay. She was quite cold but we have her with us now. She's by the fire with a warm coffee. She's safe."

"I promise you this will never happen again. I'll get coded locks for the inside doors, or an alarm system put in. Where are you? I can come pick her up."

I pinched the bridge of my nose."An alarm system might be a good idea." I paused and lowered my voice. "It's like she's a prisoner inside her own home, bloody hell."

"Emmy. it's for her own safety."

"I know. Don't worry about picking her up. I'll drop her off later. I want to get some food in her and hopefully she'll rest."

Silence filled the other end. I grimaced; I could sense aunt Sam's distain. "Aunt Sam I will watch her. I want to spend some time with *my* mom. "*While she's here.*

"Alright. I'll take the opportunity to run out and get errands done in the meantime. Emmy?"

"Yes?"

"I'm sorry I lost her."

"No one blames you for this, and you shouldn't blame yourself either. You're doing a good job with her. You're buying me time to breathe and wrap my head around all this. Thank you."

Aunt Sam's voice filled with emotion. "You're welcome. I will see you tonight, for dinner?"

"Sounds good. We'll see you at 6:00."

⌘

Six o'clock came all too soon. We spent the day reminiscing about the happier times, and I became all too aware of how precious and fleeting time truly was. The ticking of the clock marked every second that my mother was here, and I knew that within a single moment, a barely noticed mili-second could take her away in the blink of an eye. She knew it too. I saw a look beyond sadness within her eyes, a fear she was trying to contain. My mother began to stare at me like I was a long lost artefact, though I knew she was only trying to burn me into her mind and hope that the image remained strong. Chase broke out the camera and captured one of the last possible days my mother was here with me. And that was the damn kicker, the hardest part. The simply not knowing of how much time was left.

"We should go to see Sam. She's been working on dinner for us all day."

Audrey stood slowly and her eyes drank in Chase's quaint home. "Okay. She's been working over time for us, hey? I suppose we shouldn't be late."

Guilt again edged me. I shouldn't leave the burden on my aunt solely. I had been by my mother's side day in and day out since this all began. I had no right to bail out now, no matter how hard it was on me. "She's been a big help for sure. Chase, do you want to join us?"

Chase stole a glance between myself and my mom, looking for approval. He nodded. "Sure thing. I'll warm the truck up."

As Chase shut the door behind him, I zipped up my jacket and shoved my hands into my gloves. "Mom, can I ask you something?"

"Of course."

"When aunt Sam reads the Bible to you, how does it make you feel?"

My mother let out a twinkling laugh. "Believe it or not, I don't mind it. I give her a hard time for it, but I find comfort in the joy it brings her."

"Oh, that's a different way of looking at it."

"You know me, Em. I'm not 100% sold on this whole God business. If it is real then he really hasn't done much for me, has he? First Aaron, and now my disappearing mind?" Audrey let out a bark of bitter laughter. "He's a bit of a jerk."

Despite the hardness those words held, I couldn't help but laugh. I leaned close and gave my mom a quick hug. "I love you, Mom. Don't ever change."

"I'm trying."

We linked arms and headed into the bitter cold, making a run for the warm cab of Chase's truck. Chase flicked on the radio and my mom hummed along to the radio. We pulled up into the driveway of my childhood home and we all stumbled outside. Aunt Sam opened up the door quickly. Her eagle eyes quickly flew to my mother and her body visibly relaxed once she saw she was all in one piece.

Audrey sidled up next to Sam and swung her hip into hers. "Lighten up sister. I'm still here."

The stark contrast between the two siblings was night and day. Physically they were quite similar with their lithe builds, dark hair, and large eyes. However, Sam stood with a stiff grace and she played well within the lines. My mother was a stark contrast. Her free spirit shone down on her, lighting her up from the inside. The rules of the world were a mere suggestion, ones she often skirted around.

"Let's all go inside before we freeze to death," Aunt Sam muttered.

I shot Chase an apologetic look and nodded for us to follow. I couldn't help but notice the way Sam watched my mom with faint disapproval. An uneasy thought tore into my mind, and I wondered if aunt Sam preferred to be around my mom when she was vacant; it was then that Sam could speak freely about her faith without protest.

"Something smells amazing," Chase sighed in pleasure.

I rolled my eyes and nudged him in the ribs. "Food is the way to a man's heart."

Aunt Sam smiled in pride. "Please everyone sit down. Let's eat."

Chase placed his hand on the small of my back and led me to the kitchen table. I slid into my chair and he sat next to me. Audrey and Aunt Sam sat across from us. Audrey wore a big smile on her face and sighed. "It does my heart good to see the two of you together again."

I nearly choked on my water. My eyes tore into Chase's with slight alarm and he grinned. "Life is a funny thing," he mused.

Audrey nodded. "That it is."

Aunt Sam wrinkled her brows. "I know the world may think the way I live my life is dated, but I hope you two aren't planning to move in together unwed."

The room went silent. Chase stiffened and he shot me an incredulous look. *Did she just say that?* "Um…" I began then faltered. Truth be told, I had no idea what we were doing. We were just starting to get to know each other again.

Audrey cleared her throat. "I don't think that's any of our business. These two have known each other for a long time. They've been through thick and thin together."

I cringed inside and fought the urge to cover my face. *Through thick and thin.* Those words must have stabbed Chase in the gut. When our world crumbled like ruins, I ran. I left him behind. I stole a glance at Chase but he remained visibly unphased, until his eyes met mine. The hurt was there, for only a split second but I saw it.

Aunt Sam studied us very closely until we both began to squirm. "Dinner is getting cold. Let's eat."

We dished our plates and despite the thickness that was heavy in the air, I was hungry. Chase took an eager bite and I was about to follow suite until I caught the look of disapproval that Sam wore. My mom's eyes went wide and mouthed a silent *no* to the both of us. She put her hands together in a silent prayer.

"Oh," I said aloud.

Chase had followed the silent conversation and he set his fork down. "Ah, crap." As soon as the words were out, my mother and I let out a loud laugh.

Aunt Sam took a forced breath and attempted to dust the taboo under the rug. "I'll say a quick prayer and then we can eat." Aunt Sam clasped her hands together, lowered her head and closed her eyes. "Dear Heavenly Father, we thank you for this food…"

I looked away and found Chase's hand under the table. I gave it a firm squeeze and leaned into him. I pressed my lips to his ear. "I'm sorry."

He shook his head and a playful smile appeared. "I'm not on her list of invites back."

"Amen." Aunt Sam's voice cut the room.

"Amen," we mumbled quickly.

Aunt Sam settled her eyes upon Chase. "You may eat. Please enjoy."

The food was delicious; Sam's kitchen skills were incredible. The conversation fell into an easy rhythm and everyone seemed to breathe a silent relief. Once the wine came out, aunt Sam seemed to lighten up. Her and Audrey even managed to fall into a fit of laughter at times. I settled back into my chair and allowed warmth to take over in the pit of my stomach. This house almost began to feel like home again. The gripping panic that once tore through me and stole my breath had faded enough to let me relax. On instinct my eyes fell to an empty chair at the table and the old ill feelings began to stir ever so slightly. I forced my gaze away as quickly as I could.

I cleared my throat and stood."I'll be right back, I need to use the washroom."

I wandered through the familiar home. I peeked inside my old bedroom and smiled. It looked as though aunt Sam was staying here; a Bible sat on the night table. I strolled over to the window near the bed and traced my fingertips over the window ledge. I spent many nights crawling through the window to sneak out where Chase stood below, waiting to catch me. It became habit for him to boost me back inside before the sun rose. I quietly slipped out of the room and peeked inside my mom's room. The familiar scent of her perfume wafted softly in the air. After I washed my hands in the washroom, I splashed some cold water on my face and headed back into the hallway.

At the far end of the hall, a door was shut. My mind went fuzzy and my limbs took on a mind of their own as they led me to the closed door. I opened it and carefully stepped inside. My breath was sucked from me in an instant. *Aaron.* Nothing had changed. Everything remained where it was. A heavy layer of dust overtook the remains, marking the time that had passed. The bed was unkept, Aaron was never one to make his bed. Snowboard posters remained on the wall, his clothes hung in the closet, his favourite baseball cap still stood on his dresser along with spare change. Everything was still here. Well, almost everything. The light that brought these items to life had faded.

"I still can't bring myself to clean this room." My mother's voice caused me to jump. I let out a squeak of surprise.

Audrey smiled sadly and stood next to me. She squeezed my hand. "Look at you," she whispered. "You're in this house, in this room and you're still standing."

Tears welled in my eyes and I nodded shakily. "I am." My vision grew blurry and I forced myself to blink. "Do you come in here often?"

"As much as I can. I find its become more of a comfort than not."

"I'm not there yet. It feels so…empty."

"Not to me. I feel him in here. He's everywhere." Audrey's eyes fell to the bed. "Do you know how hard it is for me not to make that damn bed?" she laughed softly.

The cold emptiness began to stir from deep within. I felt the coolness creep over every inch of my skin and take hold of my heart. I needed to leave. I began to back out of the room slowly, careful not to disturb the past. "I shouldn't leave Chase alone too long with aunt Sam."

"Fair enough." My mom left the room and she shut the door with tender care. "Let's go save the boy, shall we?"

The rest of the evening remained fairly uneventful. We enjoyed dessert and some more laughs. I could see the tiredness that crept into both my mom and aunt. They walked us to the front door and we said our good-byes. Audrey hugged me longer than what most would consider to be a reasonable amount of time. I cherished it, for every good-bye we shared could very well be our last. I gave aunt Sam a quick hug and as we left, I noticed the alarm system that had been installed in the mudroom. Aunt Sam and I exchanged a quick glance. My eyes landed to my mom and she smiled unknowingly. I turned away and stepped into the cold. For the first time it did not catch my breath for my body had already begun to grow numb.

CHAPTER SIXTEEN

Red is more than just a color. It has a life form all in its own. *Not you. You were not supposed to find me. Don't look at me, please.* The deep crimson was all I could see. It stained the skin, took over the clothing and seeped into the pores of the sparkling white snow. Beyond the red, I remember the haunted scream that broke the silent night. I don't remember who let out the scream, but I think it came from me.

⌘

"Shhh, it's okay. It's okay."

I awoke to Chase's arms wrapped firmly around me. He gently rocked me back and forth, stroking my hair.

"It burns!" I cried. I scrambled out of bed as the scar on my forearm began to pulsate and throb. A hot searing pain took over the raised flesh and I wondered if this was how cattle felt while being branded. I bolted to the washroom and ran cold water over the old wound. My heart beat rapidly in my chest and my breath came out fast and garbled.

Chase followed quickly behind. "What can I do?"

"Water," I croaked.

He nodded and was gone and back within an instant. He offered me the cold glass and I gulped it gratefully. I turned off the tap and began to pat my arm dry with a towel. I pressed my back into the solid wall and let my feet slide out from under me. I sat on the cool tile floor and let my legs lie sprawled out.

Chase sat next to me and put his arm around me. "How long have you had the nightmares for?"

"They started a week after it happened."

"Me too," he whispered.

I looked at him eagerly. "You have them too?"

Chase buried his face in his hands. "I still hear you screaming. Him too." My heart faltered but he continued. "I remember when you got that," his eyes landed on my scar and he traced it carefully.

I swallowed hard. "That was me screaming, wasn't it?"

"Yes. I have never heard such a sound."

"When I think back to that night, what scared me the most was when the night went quiet. Everything became so still, all the noise just…stopped. That was the most terrifying thing of all."

Chase paled. "It never went quiet, Em. I was yelling at you to stay with me."

I squeezed my eyes closed and tried to fish through my memories of that night. Everything happened so fast, there was so much chaos things became muddled together. Memories became lost. "I don't remember you yelling at me."

"I was begging you not to go. To stay with me. I don't know how many times I said that to myself over and over. And then you let out a breath."

Chase began to tremble next to me. I sat up in alarm and watched as his face drifted away to that night. I crawled into his lap and took his face between my hands. I forced him to look at me. "Chase, it's okay. I'm here, I'm okay."

His eyes fogged over and they landed on my forearm. He studied the scar and raised it to his lips. He gave it a gentle kiss and then met my eyes. "Don't ever do that again to me. Do you hear me?"

"Yes. I promise."

He wrapped me up in a tight hug. I gathered my arms around his neck and we stayed like that for a long while. "C'mon lets go to bed, I'm exhausted." He plucked me up from the floor and I followed into the comfort bed promised. Chase pulled me next to his chest and intertwined our legs. I settled neatly against him and let the warmth from our bodies spill into each other.

"Do you think we'll always struggle to forget it?" I whispered.

"As hard as it was, I hope we never forget."

I sat up slightly. "What? Why would you want that?"

"It impacted our life so greatly, Em. It always will. It's forever a part of our story, a part of his. I hope the sting of the memory will leave, but its something I can never forget."

I settled my head on his chest. "I don't think I will ever forget it either." I let my eyes flutter close and hoped that a dreamless sleep would welcome the both of us.

⌘

My phone awoke me with a start. I groggily leaned over and grabbed the phone. "Hullo?" I croaked.

"Good morning my darling daughter. I'm still here."

I sat upright, fully alert. I glanced at the time 6:30 am. "Mom?"

"You betcha, kiddo. Want to go for breakfast?"

I glanced down at Chase who had begun to stir. "Uh, sure. I can get you."

"Excellent. Amy's Café will be open. I'd like to go there."

"Okay, I'll see you in twenty minutes." I ended the call and Chase propped himself up slightly. "I'm going to take my mom for breakfast."

Chase smiled sleepily. "Drive safe. Enjoy your breakfast."

I beamed and gave him a quick kiss. "I will. Go back to sleep." I gathered up some clothing and tossed them on. I ran out the door and dove into the vehicle. My car sputtered to life rather unhappily, it was used to a cozy garage life and it was now forced to bear the bitter winter outdoors. I pulled in front of my mom's place and met her on the front porch.

Audrey grinned. "2445"

"Excuse me?"

"2445 remember that. It's the alarm code."

"Ah, gotcha."

Audrey shrugged as she slid inside the car. "Sam figured I should know the code. If I can remember it, then I get to use it. Can you imagine?" My mom crossed her arms and huffed. "Treated like a child again. Though to be fair, I don't realize it when I have a lapse in the mind."

My face crumpled. "I'm really sorry, Mom. Life isn't fair."

"No, it's not. But you know what? Screw it."

"Excuse me?"

"You heard me. I said screw it. Life is short; I am determined to make the most of it while I can and that includes waking up my little girl before the sun comes up to take me out for breakfast."

"Wherever this peppy attitude came from, I like it."

Audrey gave a cocky grin. "It's from living with the Lord's shepherd."

I burst into a laugh. "Oh, Mom. That's awful."

"It's our little secret."

I pulled into the near empty café. The soft glow of lights from inside dimly lit the parking lot. "We're here." We scrambled into the warm café, took our seat and placed our order. I grasped the coffee mug close to my heart and enjoyed the heat from the warm brew.

"You look happy."

I looked at my mom. "Oh?"

"It's Chase isn't it," she bit her lip, "and being back here I think. I know why you, correction, *we* left. At the time it was the right thing to do but you never belonged in the city, and with that guy. This is where your heart lies and always has. You were wasting away in front of me and your eyes had begun to dim. I'm so glad to see the spark lit again. It does a mother good to see that her children are okay."

Audrey chuckled and continued on. "The day you cut your hair and changed its color, I knew you would come back swinging. How did he take it anyways?"

I leaned back into the booth and smiled. "He hated it. To be honest, I think it scared the crap out of him. I was doing something for myself and not asking for his permission, it was liberating."

"And?" Audrey wiggled her eyebrows. "How are you and Chase coming along?"

I rolled my eyes. "We're doing good, finding our way."

Audrey grinned. "I always knew he'd be my son in law one day."

"Ha, don't get ahead of yourself, Mom."

"A mother knows these things."

We stayed in the café until the sun rose. I watched as a peaceful look filled my mom's features. The sun danced off her clear skin making her appear almost child like. She let out a soft sigh. "It's so pretty, isn't it?"

I watched out the window as the sun's rays broke through the dim blackness. The shale sky was washed away as shades of orange and bright red cut through, kissing the tips of the nearby mountains. "It sure is."

My mom reached across the table and squeezed my hand. "I'm so glad we got to do this."

"Me too, Mom."

"Do you mind if we head home? I promised Sam we would go to church together."

"Did I hear you right? You're going to church?"

"Oh, hush. It won't hurt anything and I was thinking of volunteering with the kids or a music program there perhaps."

I stared at my mother, dumbfounded. She shoved me gently. "Don't give me that look. It might be good for me to get involved with something other than my own misery.."

"Maybe," I said slowly. "Just don't go quoting the Bible to me."

"Oh, honey. If I start doing that, I'm already gone."

CHAPTER SEVENTEEN

After I dropped my mom off I got lost in the radio. I was heading back to Chase's place when I realized I was driving down Delway Street. I slammed the vehicle to a sudden stop as the realization came over me. The tires locked up and began to squeal against the frozen road. The back end of my car began to turn in slow motion until the vehicle had come to a full on spin. *Shit shit shit.* The car came to crawl until finally, it went still. I pried my fearful hands off the steering wheel and looked out the windshield. The nose of my car faced the wrong direction but I could not move to correct it. The simple task of manoeuvring the steering wheel and using the gas pedal seemed overwhelming. My body trembled like a leaf and the only sound I could hear was the blood pulsing in my ears.

Move the damn car. Move! I fumbled with my clumsy hands to grasp the steering wheel but it was useless. A full on panic attack was brewing beneath the surface and I was about to lose control. A cold sweat began to trickle down the back of my neck, and my clothes suddenly felt too tight. I unzipped my jacket and peeled the scarf away from my neck in hopes breathing would become easier. Headlights came toward me and the oncoming truck let out a blast from the horn. Still I did not move. My eyes wildly took in the surroundings and I settled my gaze into the nearby ditch. *Red, so much red. Oh God, no. No, no, no.* My breath came out in gasps as I fought with the car door to open. Once my hands steadied enough to clasp the handle, I kicked the door open and fell out of the car. I scrambled to get upright amongst the snow and grabbed onto my car for support.

The oncoming truck came to a halt and the driver hopped out. "What the hell are you doing? Get off the damn road!"

"I-I'm s-s-sorry." I stammered.

"Jesus, Emmy is that you?"

I forced myself to look up at the angry voice before me. *Ah, crap.* "Craig Brooks," I muttered and let out a low groan. There was no way I could even pretend to be a confident human being at the moment. I was becoming unravelled at an alarming rate and it had to be in front of a damn Brooks.

"I can't be here." I cried. "I need to get out." I kept my head down and began to walk away, leaving my car running in the middle of the street. "I can't be here."

"What the hell are you doing? You can't just leave your car running and walk away. Hey! I'm talking to you!"

A door opened and slammed closed in the distance. In a single moment Miranda Brooks grasped onto my shoulders and stared at me with alarm.

I tried to break her grasp free. "Let go of me. I can't be here, I have to go now!"

"Emmy what are you doing?"

"I shouldn't be here. I can't do this. I can't see it again. Move out of my way!"

Recognition struck Miranda. "This is where it happened." She broke her stare for a split second and hollered at her brother. "Craig, get her in the truck now!"

"Tell her to move her damn car!"

Miranda gripped my shoulders hard. "Don't move, I'll be right back." Miranda ran for her brother and said something in a hushed tone. It didn't take long for Craig to pluck me up and help me into his truck. I watched as Miranda slid into my car and turn it around. She began driving slowly in the opposite direction.

"She's driving to Chase's. I assume we're to follow?"

I nodded and pressed my forehead against the glass. My limbs still trembled but my breathing had begun to slow as we moved away from the memory I couldn't escape.

Craig kept his eyes on the road for the most part; every once in awhile I felt his eyes linger over me for a little too long.

"Stop staring at me."

"Just making sure you're not going to jump out of a moving vehicle." Craig cleared his throat. "You're in a bad state, aren't ya?"

Clearly asshole. "I like to avoid that street."

"Yeah, I suppose you would. Shitty thing that happened, everyone talked about it for about a year or so."

"Lovely."

"So…I see you haven't let it go easily, huh?"

"Craig, thank you for the ride but can you please shut up?"

He held his hands off the steering wheel in mock surrender. "Fine, I don't need you freaking out on me."

The rest of the drive was in awkward silence. Craig pulled up behind Miranda and she stepped out of my car. She stared briefly at Chase's home and I couldn't help but notice the faint look of longing that crossed her pretty features. I sighed and stepped outside.

Miranda stood in front of me and handed me my keys. I let them fall into my hand. "Thank you. I never should have driven down that road. I don't know how I didn't notice it earlier." I sighed heavily. "I didn't think about it until it was to late. It was out of habit…" I forced my eyes to the ground.

"It's okay. Everyone knows what happened there. If our situations were reverse, I would have had the same reaction as you. Maybe worse." She forced a smile.

Miranda's eyes lingered to the house behind us. "I used to wish I could be you," her eyes fell back to me and took me in from head to toe. "Now I thank my lucky stars I'm not."

I winced at her words. Typical move of Miranda, a hint of kindness followed by her usual subtle blows. I opened my mouth to speak but nothing came out.

A door behind us slammed closed and Chase's voice cut through the silence. "What's going on? Em, you okay?"

Craig spoke first. "Your girl had a breakdown in her car. She abandoned it in the middle of the road."

Chase's grey eyes flew to me. Miranda cut in quickly. "She was on Delway Street."

I spoke meekly. "Thank you Craig and Miranda for helping me. I'm fine, you guys can go."

Craig seemed relieved. "C'mon. Miranda. Let's get out of here."

Miranda gazed at Chase and took in his tousled hair and beard. Her gaze drifted ever so slowly before she tossed her hair over her shoulder. Her eyes narrowed in on me. If she could shoot fire from them, she would have. The flames would be aimed directly at my head.

I crossed the yard to meet Chase. His eyes filled with worry and he began assessing me for injuries. "I'm fine." I waved him away.

"Let's go inside."

I followed him to the couch and we plopped down. I kept my eyes glued to the fire that roared in the fireplace. The flames licked greedily at the wood, which popped and snapped with defeat. "I had a good morning with my mom. I was on a high; the radio was playing good music. I wasn't thinking. It was an old habit. I was simply driving down a street. And then, I realized what street I was on. I saw that damn twisted tree and it hit me all over again. I saw it. I saw everything."

I took an angry breath as I replayed the scene all over again. "I didn't think. I slammed on the breaks, the tires locked up and I swung around. That awful, debilitating feeling took over and I lost control. I felt this overwhelming need to get away. It would have been faster to take the car, but my limbs wouldn't work. I needed to *run*. And then out of all the people in the world the damn Brooks had to be there. Not just one, but the both of them."

Chase shook his head slowly. "Em, I don't even know what to say. You could have hurt someone, *you* could have been hurt."

I buried my face in my hands. "I know, I know. Do you think I enjoy this? Hell, even I didn't even know I would react that way. I've never been down that road since it happened." I forced my gaze on him. "Can you drive down it?"

"Yes. I avoid it if I can, but yes, I can drive down it. I don't look around,

I keep my eyes forward and just get the hell out of there." He sighed and grabbed my arm. "I've had a lot of time to practice and heal. I've been here the whole time, you just got back."

I searched his eyes with mine, wondering if there was a hidden shot amongst his words. I found no trace of remorse, just genuine concern. I sat heavy against the back of the couch and sighed. "I'm exhausted," I muttered.

"Lie down, you should get some sleep."

I stretched out on the couch, and Chase draped a blanket over me. He sat on the single recliner across from me and picked up his guitar. He gently strummed one of my favourite songs and I closed my eyes. His gravelly voice filled the room as he lulled me into slumber.

⌘

"In order for you to move on, you're going to have to face what happened." Elayna spoke in a soft tone.

I blew out a frustrated breath. "Word travels fast I see."

"I wish you told me what happened, Em."

"I know, I'm sorry. I'm still trying to come to terms with it myself."

"If I can help in anyway, please let me know." Elayna glanced at the time. "Oh! It's almost time for your class. We better head in, we can't have the teacher being late."

I rolled my eyes and stood, stretching my back. I had taken on a gig at the local gym as a yoga instructor. It had been a long time since I had been through a good flow, and it seemed to help some of the unpleasantness that had plagued me lately. After the class was over my body felt limber, though my mind was still busy.

"You did so good!" Elayna crowed.

I couldn't help but grin at her infectious energy. "Thanks. I was a little nervous in the beginning but once I got into it I felt myself relax."

Elayna bumped me with her shoulder. "Nobody was the wiser."

We chatted and headed into the lounge for a warm beverage. I skidded to a stop as I saw Miranda Brooks with her gym bag. Her eyes locked with mine and she smirked. She tossed her gleaming waterfall of a mane over her shoulder and strolled toward me.

Elayna shuffled uncomfortably and stood in a protective manner. "What does she want?" she muttered.

"Hi ladies," her eyes glanced over me. "I'm seeing you everywhere these days."

"It appears that way," I mumbled.

Miranda smirked. "What brings you here?"

Elayna piped up. "She's one of the yoga instructors here. She taught her first class today, which was amazing if I do say so myself."

Miranda's face fell slightly. "Well, look at you go. I applaud you in your attempt to pick up the pieces. It's like old times, isn't it? Well, almost."

My face fell as her tone turned taunting. Miranda skirted widely around us to leave, as though we were a hacking cough.

Elayna glared and closed her hands into fists. "I can not stand her. What's her problem anyways?"

I sighed. "We've never seen eye to eye and she's always had a thing for Chase."

At the sound of his name Elayna brightened. "Things are going well between the two of you, hey?"

We placed our coffee order and sat with our steaming beverages. "Things seem to be going well. We know each other inside and out, and he knows what I-we've been through. It helps to have someone understand, y'know?"

"I can only imagine." Elayna tucked her hair behind her ear. "Are you moving in with him?"

Her question caught me off guard. "Oh, I don't think that's a good idea. It's too fast." I set my cup down and let out a long sigh. "I don't think it's fair that we fall back to where we left off. There needs to be a transitionary period for us."

Elayna nodded slowly. "I get it, I do. You do know he built that place for the both of you, right? And technically, you own half. You guys bought the land together, remember?"

"I know. I think its smart to take things slow, build up what I left to fall apart."

"You're too hard on yourself, Em. That's what I think."

"Perhaps." I bit my lip, a thought forming. "Elayna, do you still have living quarters above your garage?"

"Oh the carriage house? Yeah, why?"

"I was hoping I could rent it out from you."

Elayna's eyes grew wide. "Are you serious?"

I nodded. "It has a kitchen, a bathroom and heat, right?"

"Well, yeah of course."

"So, yay or nay?"

Elayna sighed. "I'm all for it but I foresee another option for you."

"I know but I'm trying to rebuild my life. Baby steps."

Elayna stood and grabbed me with her. "C'mon, I'll help you haul your things over."

⌘

It didn't take long for me to settle in, I didn't have much to begin with. Despite the cold, I left the window open a crack to allow fresh air to circulate. The heaters hadn't been used in awhile and the smell of burning dust filtrated the small space. I sat on the edge of the bed and stared at the white world outside. The crunching of tires stole my attention as Chase's truck pulled into the drive. I disappeared down the backstairs and met him below.

"Hi," I said brightly.

He slammed his truck door behind him and warily met me. "Hey." He looked at the garage behind me. "So, this is it."

I took his hand and led him inside, up the stairs. "It's not so bad."

He scanned the four hundred square foot space and winced. "Em, is this really necessary?"

"It is." I stepped into him and threw my arms around his waist. "Besides, I always did love a sleepover."

Chase rolled his eyes and embraced me. "The sleepovers you speak of will be at my place," he muttered.

"I'd hope so."

"Are you hungry?"

"Famished."

"Good, grab your coat. It's BBQ night at the pub tonight."

I gave Chase a light shove. "Be right back."

I tossed on a warm jacket, toque and gloves. I scrambled around the room looking for my purse. I strapped it over my shoulder and grabbed my cell. My eyes glanced at a pile of mail on the counter with a sticky note. *These came in the mail for you, Elayna.*

I rifled through the mail when familiar script writing caused my body to grow cold. I stared at the cursive writing and as usual, there was no return address. The color left my body. *How did they find me?*

CHAPTER EIGHTEEN

I tossed the envelope in my pocket and ran down to meet Chase in the warmth of his truck. I hopped in and he smiled. "All good? I'm starving."

I fumbled a smile. "Sounds good."

Chase began the drive and glanced at me curiously. "What's wrong? Regretting your decision to live in a box already?"

I found myself smiling a little. "No, I believe the term used is *cozy* and *quaint.*"

Chase wrinkled his nose. "It's a dog kennel."

I laughed. "Stop." I placed my hand in my pocket and grasped the envelope. I pulled it out and ripped it open. My eyes scanned the script wearily.

The day is almost here. As the years pass, this day always manages to sneak up on me. I don't know how that's possible. How could you forget the day your world changed? How is life treating you, Emmy? Does your scar still throb and possess a life of its own? Do you still wake up at night, screaming? I must say, you surprised me. I never thought in a million years you'd come home.

"Oh my god," I gasped. "Oh my god."

Chase tore his eyes off the road and glanced at my shaking hands. "What's that? Em, you alright?"

"Can you pull over?"

"Hang on." Chase pulled over quickly and leaned close. "What is that?"

"My yearly letter." I whispered and handed it over. "Whoever wrote this is watching me. How in the *hell* would they know that I came back home? "

Chase put the letter down. "How long has this been going on?"

130

"They started a month after that night. Every year since then, nearly to the day I've gotten one."

"I don't like this one bit. What kind of mind game is this? *Who* would do something like that?"

"I don't know. I've been trying to figure it out for awhile now. Whoever it is obviously knows what happened."

"That could be anybody…" Chase said slowly. "It could be someone from town, someone who saw it on the news…"

"It must be someone who knows me."

Chase looked at me sharply. "Why do you think that?"

"They know about my scar and my nightmares."

"That could be nothing more than an assumption." His voice sounded weak, unconvinced.

I shook my head. "No, someone knows."

Chase put the truck in drive and pulled a sharp turn. "I'm sorry, Em. I don't feel comfortable with you being on your own. Let's grab your stuff and go back to my place."

"Hey, wait a minute here. We had plans tonight."

"Plans change."

"No, turn around. Let's have a night out, please. *Please.*"

Chase gripped the steering wheel tightly and let out a frustrated breath. "Fine, but you're spending the night with me."

"Sounds like a deal." I settled back into my seat and my mind ran a million miles a minute. The letters had never been so personal before. They were usually short and to the point. *The day your world fell apart is approaching. It's also the day my world changed forever. I'm sorry.*

This one had an air of a threat intertwined in its words. Whoever this was had been watching me for quite some time. The question was, why? What did they want from me?

⌘

The pub was packed. We wriggled our way inside and found an empty seat, and placed our order quickly. Chase was wired on high alert and I placed a hand on his leg, patting him soothingly. "Lighten up."

He forced himself to smile. "Sorry, I'll do my best. The idea of this whole thing makes my skin crawl. I swear, if I find out who's been doing this…"

I gave him another comforting pat. "I know. It's okay. Everything will be okay."

The waitress arrived and placed our drinks before us. I sipped my whisky hungrily, while Chase swigged back his beer. Our eyes began to scan the crowd and I knew we were asking ourselves the same question. *Is it someone in this room?* A figure caught my eye. I recognized the frame and perfect posture. I squinted my eyes and leaned forward. The silhouette turned to the side and his profile came into view. I shot up like a rocket.

"Em?"

"Holy shit. He's here. What the *hell?*"

Chase stood beside me. "Who? Who's here?"

"Sean." I whispered.

Chase straightened up. "Your ex boyfriend, Sean? The rich asshole?"

"That's the one." *Is it a coincidence? It can't be him. It can't be. It doesn't make sense.*

The strength from my legs dissipated. I sank into my seat and covered my face with my hair. "Maybe we should head out." I was met with silence and quickly looked up. Chase was no longer beside me. I stood up quickly. "Chase?" I scanned the room hurriedly and saw him face to face with Sean. "Aw, crap!" I elbowed my way through the crowd, toward the heated voices that were quickly becoming the centre of attention.

"What is this? Do you own the town now?" Sean seethed.

"This doesn't look like the type of place you normally frequent. What are doing here?" Chase shot back.

"Passing through on business if it's any of your concern. I remember this was the only decent place in this hole of a town."

I stepped into view and Sean's eyes landed on me like an eagle spotting its prey. "I see you found yourself settling into old habits. Didn't take you long."

His words cut like knives. Hurt was present in his eyes as well as disgust. He studied me from head to toe. "What a waste of time."

Chase tossed the first blow and it connected with a jarring sound of flesh on flesh. Sean faltered backwards and steadied himself. Hoots and bellows broke out as the crowd fed on the energy. I got shoved backwards in a sea of people and desperately tried to fight my way to the center of the action. I begged Chase to walk away but my voice was lost amongst the noise. I scrambled out of the warm bodies that surrounded me, and ploughed my way to the outer edge. Sean ran toward Chase like a bull and tossed him back, followed by a quick shot of his fist. Chase recovered quickly and shook his head. A trickle of blood ran down his face as he stepped in for more.

"Stop!" I hollered. "Somebody stop them!" Again, I was ignored. The disgust I felt for humanity in that moment nearly blinded me. I ran toward the men and hoped I wouldn't be accidently pummelled as I slid between them. My back was to Chase and I pressed my hands against Sean's chest. "Stop!"

I felt Chase freeze behind me. I bored my gaze into Sean's bloody face and for a moment I thought he was going to hit me. His fist was raised and aimed my way. In a split second he reached for a nearby glass and tossed it at my feet. I jumped back in surprise and Chase plucked me up and scooted me behind him. I almost let out a sigh in relief until I realized Chase was pursing him. I gripped his arm and dug my nails into his skin.

"He's not worth it, Chase. Take me home, please. Let's go."

Sean snarled. "Listen to her, Chase. Walk away."

"Chase, please let's go."

Chase hesitated and glanced my way. His face softened and he nodded. He was about to turn on his heel, when like the coward Sean was, he sucker punched him. Chase stumbled and went down. I fell to my knees and cradled his head to soften the landing.

I glared up at Sean. "You fucking coward. How typical of you to take the cheap shot."

Sean straightened his jacket. "I always win, Em. Always."

Just before Sean broke into a triumphant grin, a fist came out of the crowd and knocked him sideways. Sean stumbled and fell to his knees.

"3,2,1. Knock out." Craig Brooks stood amongst the crowd, shaking his reddened fist. "We stand by our own in this town."

I stared up at him in disbelief. Craig bent over and helped me drag Chase to his feet. Chase groaned and I winced in sympathy. "I'm so sorry."

"Let's get him out in the fresh air."

As we stumbled toward the exit the police entered. They took one look at us and shook their heads. Craig pointed back toward Sean. "He started it."

"Mr. Brooks and Mr. Havens, why am I not surprised."

Craig pulled out his most charming smile. "I swear officers, I was in the right place at the wrong time, honest."

"That's not how the saying goes," I mumbled.

The officer looked my way. "Are you okay ma'am?"

"Fine, thanks."

They nodded and proceeded inside, letting us go. Craig nodded. "Keep going, lets get him in his truck. Can you drive?"

"Yes." I began to fish through Chase's pocket, finding his keys. I unlocked the passenger door and we positioned Chase inside. He flickered his eyes open and winced. "That fucker."

"Do you need to go to the hospital?"

Chase shook his head "no" and Craig laughed. "We've had worse. Are you okay getting him home?"

"Yeah. Thanks Craig, you're not such a bad guy after all."

Craig shrugged his shoulders. "It was a cheap shot, I hate when a fights not fair."

I smiled my thanks and squeezed his hand in passing. Who knew Craig Brooks had a human side to him. I hopped in the truck and started the engine, driving very cautiously home. I was careful to avoid the potholes as best as I could as to not jostle Chase's already shaken head. I pulled up in front of Chase's home, getting as close to the front porch as I could. I hurried over to the passenger side to help Chase, who was already groaning and holding his head.

"Come on, lean on me." Chase nearly fell out of the truck and dropped one of his arms around me. I unlocked the front door and guided him to the couch. I rummaged through the freezer and wrapped up a bag of frozen veggies with a dish towel. I kneeled in front of him and gently placed it on his swollen cheek. He winced but didn't pull away.

"Can you hold it up yourself?"

"Yeah."

"I'll be right back." I found a washcloth in a drawer and wet it with water. I balanced a bottle of whisky and a shot glass under my arm. I sat beside him and began to blot away the dried blood. His eyes watched me carefully. I set down the rag and tossed back a shot of whisky. I poured another and gave it to Chase. He tossed it back. "One more." I poured him another, which he drank quickly.

"Your ex is a son of a bitch."

"I know. You didn't have to hit him."

"I did. I don't regret it one bit."

I shook my head in disapproval. "Are you okay?" I leaned forward to study him. "Oh, Chase. This isn't high school." I touched his face gingerly, and to my surprise he leaned in toward my touch.

"I know, but he deserved every hit he got. The first hit was for you, and after that I got carried away."

I snuggled into him. "I shouldn't be touched by such a barbaric move, but thank you."

Chase stood up and held out his hand. "Can you take me to bed?"

I laughed and linked my fingers through his. "Of course."

I helped lie him down and placed the covers over him. He shifted onto his side and his breathing deepened and slowed as he settled to sleep. I brushed a lock of hair from his eyes. "Oh, Chase. What have you done to yourself?"

His left cheek was swollen, and his bottom lip had a slight split. His knuckles were red and bloody. I ran my finger over them gently and he didn't stir. "You're going to feel that tomorrow," I whispered.

I stood up and tip toed out of the bedroom, closing the door softly behind me. I added what was left of the wood to the fire and stood motionless as I let the rich heat seep into my bones. The temperatures would be dipping well below seasonable for the next few days. I rifled through one of the drawers until I found a headlamp and secured it on my forehead. I flicked on the porch light and stepped outside. I kept my head low from the whirling wind and blowing snow as I marched to the nearby woodshed. I pulled on the lamp string and a soft glow illuminated the near full wood shed. I filled an empty rubber maid bin full of wood and kindling then began the trek from the shed to the house, and got busy stacking the wood neatly under the covered porch by the front door.

As I began my second trip to the woodshed I took a moment to admire the near full moon half hidden behind the clouds. It shone brightly and partially illuminated a path. I began tossing wood inside the bin when the back of my neck hairs stood. I shot upright and peeked out of the shed, my eyes scanning the night. I could see nothing out of the ordinary but I got the distinct feeling I was being watched. I flicked off my headlamp and the shed light. The world went dim around me and I fought the sensation of claustrophobia that nipped at my heels. My mind began to imagine large spiders crawling from the confines of wood heading for me as I took away their home. *Breathe in. Breathe out.* I forced myself to concentrate as I continued to scan the landscape. Nothing was out of place in the open fields. The long treed driveway looked as it should. The east side of the property was heavily treed with forest and a trail system. I held my breath and continued my assessment. A loud crunch followed by a grunt sounded behind me. I held my breath and stood stalk still. Noisy, laboured like breathing continued along the side of the shed followed by heavy footsteps. I held my breath and forced a peek around the corner. *Oh, fuck.* A large shiny black coat appeared. The bear raised it's massive head and looked picture perfect under the silken moon. *Shouldn't you be in hibernation?* I began judging the distance from myself to the house and wondered if I could make it.

The bear lowered its long snout and began following a scent, coming closer to where I hid. *This is what I get. All I wanted was a warm house and this is how it will end.* I extended my arm behind me and felt along the darkness. I wrapped my hands around the firm handle of my prize; the axe and drew it close, praying I wouldn't need to use it.

The rumbling and bumping of tires forced my attention away from my fears. The bear looked up and leaned back on its well-muscled haunches, propelling itself into a run. I watched as the bear disappeared amongst the trees. With one concern out of the way I turned my attention back to the night visitor. It was a car, with its headlights off. It parked half way down the long driveway and the engine went quiet. A lone figure stepped out of the car and jogged quickly toward the house. My eyes went wide as I watched the silhouette scan the house and avoid the lighted areas. *What the hell is going on here?*

I tossed the axe over my shoulder and waited. Stupidity or curiosity got the best of me and I ran toward the car, careful to stay out of the open areas. Once I was near the car, I bent down in the bush and waited. The coast looked clear so I continued toward the car. It was nothing special, a black Honda. I didn't recognize it and I made a mental note of the license plate. I peered into the windows, hoping for a clue on the driver. Behind me, footsteps sounded followed by quickened breathing. I stood up slowly and saw the reflection of another behind me. I took a deep gulp and in one swift motion, I turned around and used the axe handle as a hammer into the intruder's stomach. I held onto the axe head and allowed the cool metal to burn into my hands.

"Who are you and what do you want?" I yelled.

The intruder was on their hands and knees, with one hand wrapped around the torso. "Emmy, it's me."

"Mom?"

"Yes," she croaked.

I dropped the axe. "Oh no! You scared the bejesus out of me. Are you okay? I'm so sorry."

"This is what I get for night creeping."

"Why didn't you just knock on the door?"

Audrey dusted the snow off herself. "I did. No one answered so I went around the back."

I held on to my mom. "Is your stomach okay?"

She shrugged me off. "It'll be fine. What was that anyways? A broom handle?"

"No, an axe handle."

Audrey's eyes grew wide. "Oh dear. This could have ended up a bloody mess."

I sighed in dismay and picked up the axe. "Come on, let's go inside."

We stomped our boots off and settled by the fire. I handed my mom a mug of tea. "So, are you going to tell me what you're doing here in the middle of the night? And driving might I add?"

"I know, I know. I shouldn't be driving. I just needed to see you."

"What's wrong?"

"I don't know, to be quite honest." Audrey sighed. "I know my memory is a fumbly thing but something doesn't feel right."

Concern took over. "Do you need to see a doctor?"

Audrey waved the thought away. "No, no nothing like that. I feel like someone has been watching the house, watching *us.*"

My blood ran cold. "What?"

"You know that feeling you get when someone's watching you? I've been having that sensation lately. I told Sam and she shooed the idea away but I think she feels it too. She's been quite jumpy, and seems distracted. She's been talking to Jesus more too."

I fought a smile at the last part. I bit my lip, pondering. "Have you received anything unusual lately?"

Audrey's eyes burned into mine. "Unusual…as in a letter, perhaps?"

My face paled. "Yes."

Audrey put down the mug and leaned close. "I thought it was just me."

"How long have you received letters, Mom?"

Audrey closed her eyes, thinking hard. "They started shortly after Aaron. They've been very vague, simply acting as a reminder that the day was drawing near. They almost sounded like an apology until the most recent one." Audrey looked up and grabbed my hand. "It mentioned you. Something along the lines of the prodigal daughter has returned home. It went on to blast our choice for coming back."

Fear choked me. "Where's the letter?"

Audrey looked apologetic. "I burned it. It frightened me and I didn't want Sam to see."

"Oh, Mom."

"I know, I'm so sorry. I just needed to know you were okay."

"Mine was similar," I mused.

"It doesn't make sense. Who would watch us, who would care?"

"I don't know."

Audrey clasped her hands together. "A part of my brain is reaching for something. There's something I'm forgetting. I keep seeing a face, but it's out of focus like I don't have my glasses on."

I leaned forward and reached for her. "It's okay, Mom. We'll figure this out."

Audrey smiled and suddenly looked sheepish. "Promise you won't judge me if I tell you something."

"I promise."

"I've been talking to one of the preacher's at the church about, well, everything."

"Ohhh, Mom."

"You promised you wouldn't judge!"

I held up my hands. "Sorry. Why?"

"They have a way of making me feel better, and though I don't always understand the quotes they say, it feels like they help. It offers me some forgiveness."

"Forgiveness? For what?

Audrey raised a brow. "I don't know. There's something I can't quite remember, like I've said, but I know I didn't mean to do it." She paused, then smiled. "The music they play in church is rather good."

I tried to decipher my mother's words and forced a laughed. "Oh, Lord have mercy. You're converting on me."

Audrey barked a laugh. "Not at all. Trust me, honey they couldn't handle me."

I glanced at the time. "I don't feel comfortable with you driving yourself this late. How about you stay here tonight?"

"That sounds lovely."

I stood up and locked the front door. "This way to the guest room."

Once Audrey was settled in, I checked the house one more time before retreating to the bedroom. I put in a quick call to my aunt and updated her on my mother's whereabouts. My eyes wandered to the bed where Chase lied flat on his back, out like a light. I smiled and settled next to his warmth. My mind wandered to the letters and the purpose of them. Who felt the need to send a constant reminder of something we could never forget? And who would care that we returned to where it all began?

CHAPTER NINETEEN

I awoke to an empty bed. Voices carried from downstairs, jarring me awake. I kicked on my slippers and went downstairs. The smell of bacon and coffee filled my lungs.

"Good morning!"

I smiled at Audrey who looked giddy. "Morning, Mom."

She tilted her head toward Chase and lowered her voice. "I hear he got into a tussle defending his loyalty for you."

I rolled my eyes. "Hush."

"You're going to have such beautiful children."

I sent my mom a mock glare and met Chase by the oven as he scrambled eggs. "Morning, sunshine." I peeked at his face. "Oh, hun."

Chase tried to grin. "I know. I look awful."

"How did you sleep?"

"Apparently very well. It sounds like you had quite the eventful evening." He raised a brow.

"Hm."

"Uh-huh."

I placed my hands on his chest. "How about you have a seat. I'll take it from here." I grabbed his coffee mug and handed it to him. "Go, relax."

He gave me a kiss on the top of my head. "Thanks, babe." He turned and stopped. "Oh, by the way there's no way you're living in that carriage house. Especially after everything your Mom told me."

My jaw dropped and I shot Audrey a look of betrayal. She shrugged her shoulders and gave a feeble grin. "I guess we can pick my things up after we drop off my Mom."

Chase smirked. "Yes, dear."

I rolled my eyes and focused on getting breakfast ready. After we ate, we dropped Audrey off. I met Sam at the front door. "Aunt Sam?"

"Yes?"

"Is everything okay here with you guys? Have you felt uneasy at all?"

Sam tsked. "Your mother 's been going on I see."

"Aunt Sam-"

"It's nothing to worry about. I haven't noticed anything unusual. Your mom keeps bringing it up; it's like when you watch a scary movie and you get the initial jitters is all."

"Okay," I said slowly. "Well, if you need me you know where I am."

"Thank you. Have a good day."

"You too."

Chase and I swung by Elayna's and I packed up what was left of my belongings. We placed everything in Chase's truck and I surrendered my keys.

Elayna opened her hand and smirked. "Well, that was the shortest rental opportunity ever."

I winced. "I'm sorry, I—"

Elayna held up her hand. "I'm happy for you. Go. Go enjoy that home of yours."

I grinned. "I will. See you soon."

Chase walked me to my car. "I'll see you in a bit?"

"Give me a couple of hours. I need to take Ace out for a good run."

He grinned and gave me a soft kiss. "See you at home."

Home. My stomach danced. "You will, see ya later."

As Chase's truck bounced away, I unlocked my car. My hand froze in mid motion; the car was already unlocked. I thought back and could have sworn I locked it. Yes, I *know* I did. I opened the door hesitantly and scoured inside. Nothing seemed out of place, though the air was slightly off. I slid inside hesitantly and opened the glove box. A white envelope with the familiar cursive fell out. I watched the envelope fall to the floor and my heart deflated.

They've been in my car. I took a deep gulp of air and reached for the envelope. I gingerly opened it and pulled out the letter.

"Why would you come back? I don't want to remember, and now I see the both of you. You shouldn't be here. Leave, I don't want to see you. Don't make me remember. She needs to forget."

My breath came out in gasps. "I don't understand," I whispered. My mind rattled on thinking of a possible explanation. It found nothing. I shakily started the car and tested the brakes before heading to the main road. Everything seemed to work. I parked in front of the barn and headed for the field.

"Ace! Come here buddy."

A joyous sound broke the still afternoon. Hoof beats tore my way and my heart set fire. "Hey, handsome. Wanna go for a ride?"

I clucked to Ace and slipped the halter over his head. I led him to the barn and clipped him in the crossties. I busied myself giving him a quick groom and once over. "Be right back bud. We need your saddle today."

I entered the tack room and swung his bridle over my shoulder. Movement caught the corner of my eye and I turned. Miranda Brooks stood in the room, lost in space. Her fingers fiddled with a cross on her necklace.

"You're religious?" Miranda turned quickly to face me and I wish I kept my mouth shut. "Oh, sorry," I stuttered. "I didn't mean for it to sound that way."

"Like an accusation?" she snapped.

"Sorry, you just don't strike me as the religious type."

Miranda raised a brow. "What makes you say that?"

"To be blunt, you've never been that nice of a person. Especially when it comes to me."

Miranda's face flushed. "You always take things from me," she growled. "You deserve everything that's come your way. You and your family." With that, she shoved past me.

I watched her stalk down the aisle in shock. I grabbed Ace's saddle and swung it on him. Once he was tacked up, I placed my foot into the stirrup and swung myself up. "Let's go bud. I need you to help me with something."

I chose our usual trail in the beginning, but instead of heading deeper into the woods, I took a cut in the path that led us along the back roads of town. I made sure Ace stuck to the side of the road and kept him to a walk. Ace tipped his ears forward, breathing in the new smells. His head danced left to right, taking in the new route. I leaned forward and gave his neck a pat. "Good boy. I'm throwing you out of your routine, I know. Sorry."

As we began to approach Delway Street my pulse quickened and a cold sweat began to trickle down my back. Ace's pace faltered as he sensed the tension in me. He began to toss his head and dance nervously. "It's okay," I muttered. "Good boy, easy does it."

I tried to calm myself, knowing I was sending danger signals to my horse. Ace was normally unflappable but he was feeding on my fears. I pulled him to a halt and stared at the quiet road before me. It was straight and flat with a single twisted tree next to the ditch on the sides. *It's so straight. So flat. What happened, Aaron?*

I placed a hand against Ace's neck to steady him. I began to look at the road with a new set of eyes. I clucked for him to walk on and he took choppy steps forward. As we came closer to the tree, I saw it; my mind flashbacked to that night releasing a memory. There were two sets of skid marks that night. Not one, but two. I closed my eyes and began to dig through the depths of my mind. *We pulled up behind him. Something's not right. What am I missing?* My eyes flew open. I looked around and Ace stood where it happened. The realization hit me like a ton of bricks.

I pressed my heels to Ace's side and leaned forward. "Let 'er fly," I yelled.

Ace pulled back, then shot forward like a bullet. His hooves kicked up snow as we took off. He ran at break neck speed; I didn't even notice the car that watched us from a careful distance.

⌘

Once Ace was groomed and tucked in for the night I began to pack up my things for the drive home. My cell rang and I answered. "Hello?"

"Hi, do you have plans this evening?"

"Hey, Mom. Nothing in particular, I was going to head home."

"Would you and Chase like to join us this evening for church?"

"Come again?"

"You heard me. It's a yes or no."

"Er, I'm going to have to get back to you on that. I'm not sure we're church people."

"We leave in one hour. I hope to see you there."

I hung up the phone and drove home. I met Chase in the garage as he tinkered away. I relayed him on the invitation. He laughed at my tone and shrugged. "Sure, why not. Let's go check it out."

My jaw dropped. "Really?"

"Yeah, it seems to be important to your mom, we should at least check it out."

"Oh, I suppose."

Chase wrapped his arms around me and pulled me close. He nibbled at my neck. "I need a shower, care to join me?"

"You mean commit a sin before church?"

Chase smiled and gave me a slow kiss. "Mm, sounds good to me. We'll ask for forgiveness later."

I laughed and allowed myself to be dragged away. Once we were freshened up and changed we made our way to church. I stared up at the concrete building with the chapel roof. "Huh," I mused. "We're here."

Chase took my hand in his. "Let's go find your mom and aunt."

He led me into the building and we entered a large lobby. Tables hosting food and beverages were on display while a crowd mingled about. Curious eyes glanced our way, and I wanted to bolt. Chase sensed my uneasiness and he gave me a reassuring squeeze.

"Well, well. Is that Miranda?"

I followed Chase's gaze and my face dropped. "We should go."

Miranda's face fell in surprise as she stared back at us. When she glanced at Chase she gave an alluring smile. Once her eyes landed on me, she darkened. A man stood behind her and placed a hand on her shoulder. It took her by surprise as she turned. Her features fell into recognition as they broke into a conversation. Miranda walked toward us and the man followed. He was in his mid sixties, had greying hair and pale blue eyes.

The man held out his hand and shook Chase's first. "Welcome, I haven't seen your faces here before."

Chase gave an apologetic grin. "No, we don't come here very often."

"Not to worry. We welcome newcomers all the time, the more the merrier." His blue eyes squinted as he studied Chase's marred face, still fresh from his fight. Chase pulled his hand back and looked away. The man didn't say a word as he continued his study. His eyes turned to me and he smiled softly, taking my hand gently. "Welcome."

I forced myself to make small talk. "Thank you, and you are?"

"Reverend Brooks."

Chase and I looked at each other in surprise. His eyes fell onto Miranda and she smirked. Chase shut his eyes tightly and looked uncomfortable. I cleared my throat. "Miranda's your daughter?"

"She is. I take it you all know each other." Reverend Brook's eyes landed on Chase. "Some more than others."

My mouth opened to protest but nothing came out. I wondered how many strikes that would be against us if I back talked a Reverend. In that moment my mom and aunt walked into view.

Audrey did a double take and hopped toward us. "Oh, I'm so glad to see you kids!" She looked back to the Reverend. "This is my daughter."

He smiled warmly. "Ah yes, the famous Emmy. We just met."

Audrey placed her hands on her hips and tilted her head. She chuckled. "You two look uncomfortable being here. Don't worry, you'll do fine."

The Reverend spoke up. "Make yourselves at home, please have some food."

Audrey glanced toward the table. "You should add wine to the beverage list."

Chase burst out in laughter as I grew smaller. "C'mon," he said. "Let's go find our seats."

As Chase led me away, I grabbed my mom's elbow for her to follow. I caught aunt Sam's eyes and she bustled after us. We found our seats in the pew and I shivered. "It's freezing in here. They must do this on purpose so you don't fall asleep."

"Emmy, shh." Aunt Sam scolded. "Please behave."

I crossed my legs and leaned in to Chase. "You broke the heart of a Reverend's daughter. That's got to be a big sin somewhere."

He shot me a look. "I had no idea. Did you see the way he looked at me? I thought I was going to get struck down by lightning."

I patted his leg reassuringly. "I'll pray for you," I teased.

Chase glared but before he could protest the Reverend went up and began his sermon. As he drawled on, my mind and eyes began to wander. I glanced across the row and Miranda sent death glares my way. Chase looked bored. Aunt Sam was completely enthralled. My eyes settled on my mom and my heart sank. Confusion was heavy in her features as she looked around, unsure of where she was. She tried to focus on what the Reverend said but her eyes kept darting around the room. Her eyes landed on mine and she studied me. Her head tilted left to right, trying to place me in her mind. I offered her a small smile.

I nudged Aunt Sam and leaned close. "Mom's gone."

Aunt Sam jumped in surprise and studied her sister. Sadness filled her eyes and she quickly leaned in, whispering in my mom's ear. Whatever she said seemed to ease her and she relaxed in her seat. I sighed angrily and leaned my head against Chase's shoulder.

The Reverend's voice faded away until he asked, "are there any questions?"

I raised my voice without a second thought. "At what point is enough, enough? How much loss can one person take in their lifetime?"

The Reverend smiled. "Ah, good question. God will never throw you things in life you can't handle. He always has a plan. What may seem like a loss to you is a lesson. Listen and learn from it."

I glanced at Chase. "That tells me nothing."

Once the Reverend stepped down, Aunt Sam took my mom by the hand and hurried to him. Chase and I followed out of curiosity. "Can you spare us some time to talk, Reverend? It's happened again."

He took one look at Audrey who was rather subdued as she gazed around. "Yes, of course. Come to my office." He halted for a second and met my gaze. "You are more than welcome to join."

I nodded firmly. "I will." I grabbed Chase and yanked him in with us, giving him no choice in the matter.

⌘

The Reverend sat in his leather chair that creaked in protest. He clasped his hands together and leaned forward. His eyes bored into me. "Emmy, was it?"

"Yes."

"I assume your question this evening was directed toward your mother."

"Amongst other things, yes. What kind of lesson is this? How is this fair?"

The Reverend sat deep in his chair. "Perhaps it's a consequence; those are the hardest teachings of all but they possess a powerful lesson to be learned from."

I stiffened. "A consequence? I thought God was supposed to be forgiving and kind." It was a statement, not a question.

The Reverend's eyes sparkled. "There is much to be learned."

My mouth gaped as I stared back. The man was a riddle, he provided me with no absolute concrete words of wisdom.

Aunt Sam leaned forward and gripped my hand. "Your Mom has been talking to the Reverend a lot lately, it helps her. I think we should give them some privacy."

I looked toward my mom who seemed at ease. She was actively taking in our words. I sighed and stood. "Thanks for your time, Reverend."

"Of course. We hope to see you back soon."

Chase took my hand in his and gave a reassuring squeeze. I gave him a look that said "there's no way in hell we will be back here." He nodded in agreement. We left the church at a brisk pace and came to a sudden halt as Miranda leaned against Chase's truck. I shot him an uneasy glance.

"Get in the truck, Em."

I nodded and did as asked. I left my door open a crack to hear what she had to say. Miranda stepped back from the drivers side and offered an apologetic smile. "I'm sorry if my dad made you uncomfortable, he's a little over protective."

"You couldn't have told me your dad was a Reverend?"

"If I did, you wouldn't have come near me."

Chase sighed heavily and ran a hand over his scruff. "No, I wouldn't. I don't want to get mixed up in things like that."

Miranda hardened and glanced my way. "It doesn't matter anyways. As long as your dear Emmy is around there's not much hope for you and I."

Chase softened his voice. "Miranda…we never stood a chance from the start. I'm sorry. You deserve to be with someone wh-"

Miranda cut him off. "Don't give me the pity speech. You can tell Emmy that she and I have much more in common than she knows."

Chase furrowed his brow. "I'm not sure what you mean."

Miranda glared and stormed away without a word. Chase slid in the truck and I spoke. "What was that all about?"

"Beats me." He stared at the church. "I don't know why people enjoy coming here. I don't know about you, but I don't feel comforted at all."

I stared at the concrete building and chills crept up my spine. "Me either."

CHAPTER TWENTY

"You haven't been by to see me."

I shook my head. "I can't."

"Why not?"

"I just can't. You're not there anymore."

"Technically, I am."

"Aaron, hush. You're not."

"I know you went to where it happened. I'm proud of you. Are you learning anything yet?"

"Not yet. I haven't figured it out but something's not right."

Sadness spilled across Aaron's face. "No, it wasn't right." He leaned back and looked at the sky. "I wasn't done yet, y'know? Dammit. I wasn't ready."

I leaned forward and wrapped my arms around him. "I wasn't either."

"Watch out for Mom, okay?"

"Always."

"No, really. Watch out for her. She's vulnerable."

"I know, I'll take care of her."

Aaron stood up and brushed the seat of his jeans. He took a step forward and grabbed on to my shoulders. "Dig in her mind, the answer is there. She knows."

My eyes widened. "What do you mean?"

"Dig, Em. Really dig. She knows."

⌘

"Mornin' pretty girl."

Lips pressed against my shoulder and I rolled over, smiling. "Morning handsome."

"How did you sleep?"

"Okay."

"Just okay?"

I smiled. "I slept great."

Chase leaned down and pressed his lips against mine. "Good, you needed it. How about you and I go out for breakfast this morning?"

I wrapped my arms around his neck, pulling him closer. "We're in no hurry this morning, right?"

Chase smirked. "Nope."

"Excellent, let's take our time."

Half an hour later we were on the road. We pulled into the café and walked inside hand in hand. We slid into a corner booth and placed our order. I took a sip of strong coffee when Chase's face suddenly fell. I shot him a curious look and someone slid next to me. I stared in surprise as Sean's shoulder connected with mine.

Sean spoke quickly. "I don't want any trouble."

My eyes were wide. "What are you doing here?"

"I came to apologize. I really am just passing through for work. I'm heading home this afternoon."

Chase fought to keep his voice calm. "What do you want?"

Sean shot him a look of silence. "I didn't come to apologize to *you*. I came to apologize to *her.*" Sean sent me a desperate look. "Last chance, Em. Are you sure you want to waste away in this hole? Come back with me."

I fought to keep my jaw from dropping. Sean took my hand in his and I tore it away. "You need to leave." I said coldly.

Sean's eyes cast to Chase and his face crumpled. He stood up as though he were tossed with cold water. He shook his head slowly. "I thought I'd give you one last chance, one more out. Be smart, use your brain. Take it."

"I'd be an idiot to accept your offer. You were never there, Sean. Never in my life had I been so alone than when I was with you. I can't do that again. I won't. I'm happy here. Please leave."

Anger took a firm hold of Sean. "There really is no helping you. Such a waste."

I flinched at his words and spoke before Chase could. "And that's why we would never work. When something doesn't go your way, you are so quick to toss someone under the bus."

Chase stood. "I can show you where the door is if you'd like."

Sean glared and said nothing. I could only imagine how hard it must have been for him to keep his mouth shut. I watched him storm out and tear out of the parking lot.

Chase slid in the booth next to me and placed his arm around me. "You okay?"

I leaned into him. "Yes. Thank you for being there."

"Anytime. Let's brush that off and salvage what's left of the day."

I patted his lap. "Sounds like a plan."

⌘

After breakfast we strolled through town and enjoyed the local shops. Chase got called in to work and he dropped me off at home. I decided to take a nice hot bath and slid deep into the soapy bubbles. The aroma of vanilla and spice filled the room and I sighed in bliss. I lounged in the tub until the water turned cold. I got changed into some leggings and an over sized sweater, scooped my hair into a loose topknot and snuggled into slippers. I began to dig through my boxes and found what I was looking for; old photos. Through the mess, I found an empty photo album and began to make an album for my mom. I wanted her to remember our life whenever she disappeared. Once I was satisfied with it, I set it aside.

Thoughts turned to Aaron and my mind began to turn recent events over. Something wasn't right between the letters, and the newfound memories. An uneasy feeling clawed within my gut. I felt like I was so close to finding an answer, yet so far. A knock at the door pulled my attention. I peeked outside and froze as I spotted an unfamiliar car.

I hesitated before answering the door. The Reverend stood outside, looking rather cold as he jostled side to side. "Good morning, Emmy. May I come inside?"

I looked around uneasily. "Uh, sure. What brings you here?"

The Reverend's face lit up as he spotted the roaring fire. "Thank goodness, its toasty in here." I said nothing and waited for him to answer me. He smiled apologetically. "I hoped the two of us could have a chat about your mom."

My stomach dropped, as it usually did when it came to my mom. "Please, have a seat." I gestured to the kitchen bar.

He hopped onto a stool. "Thank you. Would it be to much trouble to ask for a coffee?"

"Not at all." I began our brew and placed the mug in front of him.

"Ah, thank you." He took a cautious sip and nodded. "This is good." His eyes took in his surroundings quickly before settling back to me. "As you know your mother has been coming to see me regularly."

I nodded. "So I've heard."

The Reverend continued. "We often talk when she is having an episode. Her mind is grasping at straws, it's sometimes hard to follow but I can gather enough information from her to make some sense of it." He paused and cleared his throat. "She also comes to me when she is fully lucid. A lot of our conversations come back to your brother, Aaron."

The dreaded cold sweat appeared. My breathing quickened and I grew fidgety. "What does she say?"

"She comes to me for comfort and forgiveness."

"Forgiveness?" I whispered. "For what?"

"For what happened to your brother. What we say is in confidence, but I feel it is my duty to come forward, at least with you. You are her family and because of your mother's condition, well, I feel it is the right thing to do."

My mind crashed and it brought me back to that night. Flashbacks filled my vision followed by a searing pain in my forearm. I remembered the deep shard of glass that tore through my flesh as if I were made of paper. The feeling of the warm red liquid that oozed from me followed quickly. Out of habit, I began to rub my forearm rapidly.

"Emmy, are you alright?"

The Reverend's voice brought me back. "What about Aaron? What does she say?"

He paused before continuing. "She told me there was an incident when she was driving. She drove into a pole but she doesn't remember how she got there."

I paled. "It only happened the one time. She stopped driving after that, and then she was diagnosed."

"Is there a chance symptoms could have started earlier?"

"What are you trying to say?"

The Reverend held up his hands in a calming matter. "I'm not accusing anyone of anything. It's just that…well, your mother is having doubts. She appears to be having nightmares, or flashbacks that are causing her some concern. She is having difficulty making sense of everything and that's why she comes to me."

The Reverend softened his voice. "She is worried that her condition is a punishment for what she's done."

I jumped off the stool. "It sounds to me like your accusing my mom of something awful. How dare you?" My thoughts scrambled to absorb the words he said. "Have you gone to anyone with this information?"

He shook his head. "What we say is in confidence. Your mother is going through enough in her life, no need to make things worse."

"You need to leave. Please leave."

The Reverend stood. "Emmy, God offers everyone forgiveness. I am doing my best to comfort her in her time of need."

I held the door open wide. "Please go."

He stepped outside and offered a small smile. "Your mother is not lost. God is always close by."

I slammed the door in his face and locked it quickly for good measure. I covered my face with my hands and sank to the floor. His words couldn't hold any truth. They just couldn't. The dream from my morning flitted through my head. *She knows. Dig deeper, Em. She knows.* My eyes widened and I let out an angry yell. I sprang to my feet and tossed the coffee mug against the wall. The mug exploded into tiny fragments and I watched as the black liquid oozed across the floor. My anger quickly dissipated and I began to sob.

CHAPTER TWENTY-ONE

Thunderous hooves beat into my eardrums. Ace held a steady pace as we tore through the field. His speed blew away the tears that escaped my ducts. I leaned forward and asked him to go faster. Once Ace had enough, he slowed and I let him. His breath blew out in quick snorts. White plumes filtered from his nostrils as the heat from his breath mixed with the frigid air. I let him gather his breath and adjusted my tuque. The hazy sky above had begun to spit snow. I watched as the first few flakes twirled down from above, only to be lost amongst the already white ground.

I gave Ace a quick pat and pointed him toward the road. We ambled along at a relaxed pace. I kicked my feet free from the stirrups and let them hang loosely at Ace's side. It was time to see Aaron.

I took an unsteady breath and kept Ace marching forward. The cemetery came into view and I let out a sob. I choked it back and kept moving forward. I maneuvered Ace carefully around the grave sites and dismounted. I ground tied him and weaved myself until I stood in front of Aaron's resting spot.

My vision blurred and I reached out to touch his stone. *Aaron Jacobs. Forever loved, forever missed. Taken much too soon.* I hung my head and closed my eyes. This spot felt foreign, it felt final. I had never set foot in this place. I didn't even attend the funeral. I had seen enough. I had watched the life slip out of him. I held him until his body went hard and cold. It would forever haunt me. I did not need to watch him be lowered in the ground while the community and loved ones cried for the loss of a young life.

I sank to my knees and placed my hands on his stone. "I miss you, so much. I'm sorry its taken me so long to visit. Not a day goes by that I don't miss you." I bit my lip and chewed it thoughtfully. "Somebody came by today and told me something awful about mom. Please tell me it isn't true. It can't be. I promise I will sift through her mind. I will find out the truth."

Ace snorted loudly in the distance. I stood up stiffly and threw my arms around my horse. The smell of leather and the sweet scent of horse sweat filled my nostrils. I breathed in deep and slow, trying to make sense of the world. I pulled away and mounted in a fluid motion. We made our way back to the road when a familiar rumble sounded behind. I pulled Ace to a stop as Chase pulled up beside us.

He rolled his window down and his voice softened. "You went to see Aaron?"

I nodded and wiped away the last of my tears. "I did."

Chase's eyes filled with pride and emotion. "I'm so proud of you. Are you okay?"

I smiled weakly. "I'm not sure to be honest. I think so."

"Do you want me to meet you at the barn?"

"No, that's okay. I need some time to pull myself together."

"Be safe. I'll see you at home."

Chase drove away and I guided Ace back to the barn. I gave him a thorough grooming and led him back to his clean stall. I filled his hay net full and said my good night. I crossed my arms and leaned over his stall door, watching him pull eagerly at his hay. His brown eyes watched me softly and I smiled. Though he couldn't speak, his eyes said so much. Life is a funny thing. Timing is everything, whether it leads to good or bad. Selling Ace had broken my heart, but now, here he was. He was and always will be my lifeline, forever willing to take me away from the madness and heartbreak of the world.

"He's a good looking horse."

I jumped at the sound of Craig Brook's voice. "Oh, Craig. You scared me. Thanks." I eyed him suspiciously. "What are you doing here? This isn't exactly your scene."

"It's not. Miranda needed a ride, her cars giving her trouble. I'm just waiting for her to finish up."

"Oh."

"How's Chase doing?"

"He's good, thanks. His swelling has settled down."

Craig nodded. "That's good." He eyed me carefully. "You sure everything's okay between the two of you? You look upset."

Heat crept into my cheeks and I looked away. "I went to see Aaron."

Craig whistled. "That's a big move for you. What brought that on?"

Miranda's shrill voice followed. "You went to see him? *You?*"

Her tone sent my defenses up. "He is my brother," I snapped.

"I know that," she retorted. "Why would you see him?"

"Miranda," Craig scolded. "Wait for me in the truck."

She glowered at him then twirled away. I shot Craig a look. "Why does she care?"

"She has a lot going on. Don't take it personally."

"Hey, Craig. Can I ask you something?"

"Shoot."

"I didn't know your dad was a Reverend. Are you religious?"

His face darkened. "I don't buy into all that. Some people take it to seriously. They get warped by it."

"What do you mean?"

"They can't tell the difference between right and wrong. In their mind they're fulfilling some sort of prophecy or something. Miranda took after dad."

I barked a laugh. "Yeah right. She doesn't strike me as the forgiving, warm type."

Craig grimaced. "Like I said, there's a dark side. Some people take it too far." He glanced at the time. "I should go. See you around."

"Bye." I watched him walk away and pushed myself off Ace's stall. "See you tomorrow, bud. Sweet dreams."

I slid into my car and my phone rang. I glanced at the screen and saw it was Chase. I smiled and answered the call. "Hey, you."

"Hey. Are you on your way back here soon?"

I tensed at the stiff tone of his voice. "I'm leaving the barn now, why?

What's wrong? I hear it in your voice."

"I was chopping wood in the shed. I found a letter as I was stacking wood on the porch. It's for you."

"Did you open it, what does it say?"

"Em, I want you to come home, k?"

"I'm on my way. Chase, what does it say?"

He paused before speaking. *"Don't trust those you keep close. Someone is lying. You need to leave."*

My blood went cold. "I'm on my way."

⌘

Chase and I sat at the kitchen table and I shared the Reverend's house call with him. His eyes widened and he ran his hand through his hair. He blew out a breath. 'This is bigger than you, Em. I don't like where this is going."

"I don't either. But it can't be true about my mom. Somebody knows something, and I intend to find out answers." I grabbed the letter on the table. "Who in the hell is sending me these damn things? They know something."

"I don't like the idea of you digging around, I don't want you to get hurt." He stood and began to pace. "Look, I'll try to help as best as I can. Promise me you won't do anything stupid. Don't go jumping into something without thinking it through, okay? We don't know who's doing this. It could escalate into more."

His words made me uneasy. He was right; it *could* escalate into more. Of what, I wasn't sure, but I certainly didn't want to find out. "I promise. I'll tread lightly."

Chase sat down and stared at the letters. "Whoever this is has been watching you for awhile. They knew where you lived before, and they know you're back. I don't like it. I don't like it at all."

I shivered. "I don't either. I wish it would end already."

"Let's see what we can dig up. If this escalates, we're going to the police. Do you understand me?"

I nodded. "Yes."

Chase frowned. "If I find out who did this, they're going to be sorry. Man or woman."

I stood up and rummaged through the fridge, grabbed a bottle of wine and unscrewed the top. "Care for a glass?"

"Fill me up." He stood in front of me and we clinked our glasses together. "Drink up."

I laughed and lifted my glass before taking a long swig. "Care to get drunk with me tonight?"

"Hell yes." He paused. "I think its mandatory this evening."

I tilted my head back and let the strong liquid pour into me. His words were an understatement.

⌘

I wish I could say there was something remarkably different that night than any other. But there wasn't. Chase and I were heading back from a trip in town. It was mid November. By 4:30 pm the roads were dark. I remember the way the road sparkled and glittered like diamonds. Nick Cunningham was on the radio and we sang along to 'California.' Chase's voice cut through the cab inside the truck; his silken voice sent goose bumps down my spine. I remember the way my eyes drifted to his stature until that moment pulled my gaze away. The lone twisted tree illuminated from the flickering taillights ahead. It was hard to see in the dark, but I remember the way I squinted desperately trying to make out the scene before me. Chase flicked on his high beams and drove with a quickened speed.

A black Jeep teetered at an awkward angle. It's back wheels still spun in mid air. Smoke rose like a slow dance in the cold air. The front end was crushed in; the tree now bore the Jeeps scar. "This doesn't look good," Chase muttered to himself.

I dug through my pocket until I found my phone. I began to dial 9-11. "Emergency, what would you like to report?" The voice spoke like a loudspeaker in my ear. "There was an accident. We're on…" my voice faded as a sticker on the back window stopped my heart. I knew that logo anywhere. *Aaron.*

"Oh God," I cried. My body went weak. My fingers released their grip and the phone clattered to the floor below. I tossed the door open and took off running on unsteady legs.

"Aaron!" My scream echoed amongst the silent night. I slipped twice but somehow managed to scramble upright and broke into a breathless run. I reached the teetered Jeep and slid into the ditch. I laid onto my stomach and peered into the dark vehicle.

"Aaron, can you hear me?" My eyes pleaded to see. My heart beat wildy in my chest and my limbs began to tremble. "Aaron? Can you hear me?" Again, I was met by silence. "Oh God, please no. Aaron say something!"

An inaudible moan caught my attention. I adjusted my position into a seated one and pressed myself against the drivers window. My eyes frantically took in the crumpled Jeep and knew I couldn't open his mangled door. "Hang on Aaron. Stay with me."

I ran toward the passenger side and took in the damage. The hood of the Jeep was pressed into the tree, the hot steam from the warm liquids hissed into the night. The drivers side was on its side, pressed into the unforgiving ground. I placed my trembling hands into my hair and had never felt so helpless in my life.

A beam of light broke my dismay. Chase jogged toward me, and god bless him, he had a flashlight. "An ambulance is on the way. Put this on."

I stared at his outstretched hand; he offered a headlamp. I shakily placed it around my head and flicked on the light. "Chase, it's A-"

"I know babe. Let's see what we can do."

A scream tore into the night and I felt the sickness burning the back of my throat. Chase paled and I saw his hope evaporate. His eyes pierced into my soul. "Let's get him out." His left hand dangled at his side and turned white from gripping the first aid kit with everything he had.

"Chase, what if-"

Chase gripped my hand with a breakable force and we ran toward the Jeep. Chase shone the light into the cab and I let out a gasp. Aaron was slumped over the steering wheel. Blood ran down his head in a steady stream. Aaron turned his head ever so slowly toward the light. His eyes found mine and relief temporarily replaced the fear.

My hands worked the driver door desperately, but it wouldn't budge. The ground acted like a vice, keeping a life in its hands.

160

"Chase, try the passenger door!"

"It's locked!" Chase's frantic eyes assessed the situation. "Em, the windshield!" I ran toward Chase, my frantic mind not being able to make sense of anything. Chase gave me a boost onto the hood and I scrambled toward the opening. "I'm right here Aaron. I'm coming."

Broken glass cut into my clothes. I felt the sting as they diced into my flesh. I adjusted my headlamp and continued on. "Cover your face Aaron. I'm coming in."

Headlights cut through the darkness and Chase went out to meet them. I assumed it was the ambulance and kept moving forward with my mission. The windshield was cracked and weakened. It was the only way in. I aimed my foot upward and with all my might I let it connect with the glass. It took three good stomps and an area shattered. The sound of Chase's voice followed by another arguing caught my attention briefly. I tried to find their voices in the dark but then Aaron let out a yell. My heart leaped into my throat and I dove toward the entrance I had made. I reached my arms into the vehicle and wriggled onto the front seat, careful not to jostle Aaron.

"Em, I made a mistake. I think I screwed up."

"Shh, Aaron. It's going to be okay. I'm here."

My hands worked methodically. My brain was moving at a million miles an hour, I couldn't keep up to its thoughts. I unclicked the seat beat from Aaron, and quickly assessed the damage. "What hurts?"

"Everything," he moaned.

Shit. "Can you move?"

Aaron nodded. "I think so."

"Good. Let's try to get out through the windshield."

Aaron looked up dubiously but he nodded fiercely. "Okay."

I grabbed one of Aaron's arms and placed it around my neck. He used his free arm to pry himself up as I began to lift. The yell he let out no longer sounded human.

"Stop, Em. Stop!"

"Oh my God. Aaron, what hurts?"

His face paled and he fell back onto the seat. Tears began to blur my vision. I kneeled over him and my hands began to work gently and quickly. The thick blood trickled down his face and knotted his hair. I tore open the first aid kit and found what I needed; gauze. I gingerly wrapped the bandage around his head and kept going. I worked at his sides and he flinched.

Aaron grabbed my forearm and pleaded with his eyes. "Em, don't look. Please. I can tell its bad."

His grip was meant to be strong but it was weak. His skin had paled considerably and his temperature had grown cold. My teeth began to chatter as I lifted his shirt. A dark bruise the size of a large book had taken over his stomach; the deep colors spread over healthy flesh like a cancer. My eyes flew to his and the tears fell from his eyes.

"That bad, huh?" He smiled weakly. He tried to sit up but it was too much. His rebel yell filled the night and deafened my ears. He began to cough violently. He tossed his head to the side and I saw with a sickening jolt the amount of blood he spit out.

I yelled out into the night. "Chase! Where are you? Where is the fucking ambulance?"

"Em. It's getting cold."

I tore off my jacket and wrapped Aaron tightly. "I'm getting you out, do you hear me?"

Aaron smiled softly and closed his eyes. "I'm not worried." Aaron fought to open his eyes and clasped onto my hand. "Where is she?"

"Who?" My eyes scanned the crammed confines. "It's just you and me. No one else is here."

"She got out?" Aaron let his head fall heavy and peace seemed to find him. "Good."

Delusions are setting in. My breath came out shattered and my heart slammed against my tender chest. A rush of adrenaline tore through my freezing body and the world began to swim. I stared into the softly lit night and watched as the ice began to take over the shattered glass. A womens muffled cries filled the night and I remember thinking they sounded like my mother.

It's moments like this they say the world stops turning. The noise deafens and things go clear. That's not how I remember it. I remember the terror that took over my every fibre. I remember the way my teeth chattered and my heart felt like it was going to explode. I remember the fear that threatened to crush me. But most of all, I remember the way that life fades from another. The skin drains of color, slowly, but it seeps out of the body enough that you notice. A grey film takes over the flushed reds and signs of life. I will never forget the way Aaron looked at me like he knew. He smiled so softly as his grip weakened until he could no longer hold on to me.

The way a body stills once the soul slips away is something I will never forget. It's that exact moment that replays in my mind on a terrible loop; Aaron's hand slipping from mine and falling to the floor. How I pounced to his chest and desperately listened for a heartbeat and heard nothing, The way his breath stilled and his eyes grew vacant.

Flashes of red and white from the ambulance interrupted the icy night. Everything seemed to move in slow motion. My breath blew white smoke. Snowflakes drifted inside the broken window. I watched as they twirled and landed softly on the broken body. In that moment my heart blew into a million tiny particles and I released an agonized scream that tore through the night, if not the town. A loud thud pulled my attention to the passenger window and I saw Chase's wild eyes. He violently pried at the door trying to reef it open. My swollen eyes fell back to Aaron and an angry rush tore through me. I ignored the ambulance attendants who shouted at each other over the firemen. I grabbed Aaron and tried to pull him away toward the broken window.

"Emmy, no!" Chase's sob cut into me. He was sprawled onto the hood of the Jeep and stared at the sight before him in horror.

"We have to get him out, Chase. Help me!"

Chase let out another sob. "Emmy, leave him."

"Get her out of the vehicle. What are you waiting for?" An unknown voice hollered the order to Chase. He shook his head and a shudder coursed over his body. His gray eyes pierced into mine. He wrapped his arms around my waist and pulled me into the night air. I fought him; I kicked and screamed like a stubborn child. In a last ditch effort I reached out and grabbed onto Aaron's arm.

Chase breathed hot breath into my ear. "Please let him go. I can't do this."

"Let me go!" I scrambled out of his grasp and dove my torso back into the cab. My legs dangled uselessly on the crumpled hood. I gave Aaron a hard tug. "Wake up damn you! Come back God dammit!"

A tight pressure grew around my waist and an unknown voice filled my ears. "Let him go. You can't be here."

"Get off of me!"

The pressure grew and began to tug me out. As I thrashed a flicker of light caught my eye. It glittered from under the passenger seat. My eyes locked onto the shine and registered it as a gold chain. The brief moment of my lapse in attention was enough for the stranger to win. Aaron began to grow distant as I was pulled back. I outstretched my arm one more time and that's when the shard of windshield met my exposed skin. The stranger yanked back and I felt the point go deep into my tender flesh. The crimson liquid was warm as it oozed freely. It temporarily warmed my freezing skin.

"Dammit. I need a paramedic!" The firefighter scooped me up and set me into the snow. "Can you hear me?"

I held my severed arm close to my body, enjoying the warmth the wound brought. My gaze grew unsteady as I stared at the stranger. He snapped his fingers in front of my face. "Can you hear me?"

I forced my eyes away and took one last look at the ravaged Jeep as the crew cut open the door. A paramedic ran toward me in slow motion. Chase was right at her side. The paramedic gripped me securely and led me toward the ambulance. Chase's skin took on an unhealthy glisten. He reached out toward my back carefully. "Em."

I will never forget how I reacted to his worry and grief. Rage flowed through me like I had sprung a leak. It washed over me until I could feel nothing but the burning heat. "Don't touch me," I spat.

Chase recoiled and the hurt sprung to his eyes. "Em, don't. Please."

Tears blinded my vision as I struggled to breathe. "You took me from him. I could have gotten him out. I could have saved him."

We both knew that was a lie, but he kept his mouth shut. Chase stood silently as he watched me get loaded into the ambulance. I lied down on the stretcher and held my arm close. The pain had begun to grow and I let it fester. I needed to feel something; anything other than the loneliness I knew was waiting for me. I stole one last glance at Chase. His gray eyes were already filled with an emptiness that would later hit me hard. This was the beginning of the end and we both knew it.

CHAPTER TWENTY-TWO

I swirled the wine in my glass before taking another long sip. I closed my eyes as the liquid warmed my throat. I glanced at Chase who gave me a lazy smile. I grinned back before I fired the shot. "Chase?"

"Yeah?"

"Do you remember that night with Aaron?"

Chase froze and nodded slowly. "I could never forget it. Why?"

"I've been thinking about it a lot lately, I'm not sure why." I paused and furrowed my brows. "I don't remember everything clearly, there's a few parts that are hazy."

"That's understandable. There was a lot going on that night..."

I nodded quickly. "Where were you when I was in the Jeep with Aaron?"

Chase moved his eyes to his wine glass. He stroked the stem with his thumb and stared into the liquid. "I had my hands full."

"With what?"

Chase sighed loudly and closed his eyes, pinching the bridge of his nose as he did so. "Your mom showed up. It was all I could do to keep her from looking into the Jeep herself."

My heart dropped into my stomach. "My mom was there?" I whispered. "How did she know?"

The color drained from my skin and the world began to spin ever so slightly. I pulled my gaze to Chase. He read the assumption in my eyes and took my hands in his. "Don't go there. There wasn't a dent on her car, believe me I looked."

"The letter…"

Chase shook his head. "Don't go down that road. We don't even know who is sending those letters. For all we know it could be a low life looking for the high. Your mom's an easy target."

"I know she is but there's always that chance. Her mind was starting to get fuzzy around that time…"

Chase pushed back his chair and stood. He pulled me up and nestled me into his chest. "Your mom loves you and Aaron more than anything in this world, even the days she can't remember. If she was somehow there when Aaron's Jeep went off the road, she would never have forgot that, let alone kept it a secret. You know that."

I sighed heavily and wished I could quiet the small voice of doubt that had begun to grow. "I know." I glanced at the clock and the dying fire. "Can we go to bed?"

"Yeah. Let's put this day to rest."

Chase slipped his hand in mine and led us to bed. I settled into the warm crook of his arms and felt the effects of the wine kick in. I closed my eyes and let my mind wander freely into the depths of the memories I wanted to forget.

⌘

The night should have been pitch black, but it wasn't. The sky was clear and the full moon transformed the snow into glittering diamonds. Within the thick forest I wasn't alone. I marched with nervous determination as I longed to find the clearing amongst the trees. Tire tracks caught my attention and I ran into their path. A deep urgency fuelled me to keep running, though the cold winter air burned my lungs. The tracks began to descend as I quickened my pace. A snow covered tree root clawed at my foot and sent me tumbling into the white powder. I scrambled upright and held my breath, listening for the thing that hunted me. The hairs on the back of my neck stood on high alert as I felt the hidden gaze watch my every move. The cracking of a branch in the distance sent me lurching forward once again.

I ran until I could run no more. I stopped to gather my breath and calm my trembling limbs. A few feet ahead of me, the dark shape moved between the trees. Its shadow was quick and lithe despite the bulkiness it showed. My heart began to bang within my chest and my eyes scanned the forest rapidly. My gaze stopped as it spotted solace. I lunged forward toward the familiar mangled Jeep and reached for the cold handle. Before I could force the door open, a heavy, blunt force sent me flying. I stayed on my belly and crawled underneath the Jeep. Heavy black paws ambled past me. They paused and I heard the beast smell for my scent. It lowered its black snout to the snow and I knew it found me.

I said a silent prayer and stared at the undercarriage of the Jeep. A gold chain swung from the brake line and I clasped it toward me. The chain swung lazily in my fingers and I studied it carefully.

"Don't move."

I fought the urge to yell as the once familiar voice rang loud in my ear. "Aaron, where are we?'

"Always watch out for the bear."

"I'm scared. I want to go home."

"I know you are. Em? Keep your eyes open, tread lightly but pay attention to everything."

I shook my head and tightened my grip on the chain. "I don't understand what's happening."

"You're remembering."

"Maybe I don't want to remember."

"Watch for the bear."

"This doesn't make any sense, what do y-"

A cold blast of air assaulted my face. I forced my eyes upwards and found myself staring into a large brown eye. The black, wet nose trembled and it's lip curled back revealing a row of sharp teeth. The thick paw came at me before I could even scream.

⌘

I awoke in a cold sweat. I reached for Chase but the bed was empty. I glanced at the clock and knew he would be starting his shift. I tossed the covers off and started a steaming hot shower. As I stepped into the near scalding water,

I felt unnerved. Something had shifted, something was coming but I had no idea what.

I scoured the internet for hours, reviewing Aaron's accident and the photos taken at the scene. Nothing triggered any new memories, nothing set off warning bells. I closed my laptop in frustration and slipped on my riding boots. A trip to the barn was needed to clear the cobwebs. As I made my way to the car, a white envelope sat underneath a wiper blade. My heart faltered as I reached for the paper. I slid into the drivers seat and stared at it. "Are you kidding me right now?" I muttered angrily. I slipped my thumb under the crease and tore it open.

There is no need to go backwards. Don't go looking into the past. You won't like what you find.

I scanned the script angrily and tossed it into the backseat. "Fuck you. Whoever you are."

I turned the key and began the drive to my sanctuary. I pulled into an empty spot and stepped into the well lit barn. The horses dozed contently in their stalls and gazed at me curiously. I was almost at Ace's stall when a voice stopped me.

"Good morning, Emmy."

I let out a silent groan and turned to face the voice. "Good morning, Reverend. What brings you here?"

"I'm looking for Miranda. Have you seen her?'"

"Nope."

The Reverend nodded and fiddled with his glasses. "That's too bad. I need to speak with her but she's not answering her cell."

I shrugged my shoulders. "I'm sure she's busy."

"I suppose so." The Reverend studied me for a moment. "How is your mom doing?"

"She's doing alright. She has good days and bad days. Like all of us." I felt the need to emphasize the last part.

"She hasn't been to church in awhile."

"My mom was never really the religious type. I wouldn't take it personally."

"I just worry she might be letting regret get to her. I hope she comes by soon."

My back went up and my jaw tensed. *Stay away from her.* "Reverend, I want to make this clear to you. She is not some brain to pick apart and mess with. She's vulnerable in her current state and I'm not sure that I feel comfortable with your private 'chats'."

The Reverend's eyebrows shot up and he held his hands out as if offering a truce. "Emmy, I do not intend to cause ill harm to your mother. I only aim to help and offer her the comfort of God."

"Reverend, if you and God are so close, tell him he's being a bit of an asshole will ya?" With that, I turned on my heel and headed for my horse. I saddled Ace up in record time and we were soon on the trails. The muffled sound of Ace's sure hooves didn't hold the relaxation I hoped for. Ace sensed my tension and he pranced unsurely. I was nervous in the trails as I constantly scanned the woods for a black bear that haunted my dream.

I leaned forward and stroked Ace's neck soothingly. "I'm sorry bud. I'm just not myself today. C'mon, let's head for the road."

Soon enough we were out of the trails and ambling down the quiet, open back roads. I settled into Ace's rhythmic walk and felt a bit of the weight dissipate. My serenity was momentarily disturbed as Ace stumbled beneath me. I pulled back on his reins, signalling him to stop. I dismounted and after a quick glance I found the problem. Snow had bunched up in one of his hooves, causing him to walk on an unsteady snowball. I reached for the hoof pick in my back pocket and cleaned out the mess.

"Good as gold," I clucked. I swung myself into the saddle and settled into my seat. Ace's head shot up and his ears flicked back and forth. I glanced at my surroundings and saw nothing out of the ordinary. I held my breath to listen and made out a very faint muffle. I paid close attention to my horse for signs of danger. He didn't seem frightened, just curious. Up ahead, before the road curved a horse and rider heading our way. I gave Ace a light nudge with my heel to urge him forward.

"What are the chances?" I murmured to myself.

Miranda Brooks rode toward me. I held up my hand in a feeble wave. She did not return the gesture. As she got closer, I could see that her eyes were red and slightly swollen as if she'd been crying.

"Hi Miranda. Nice day for a ride, huh?"

She glared at me and pulled her horse to a stop. "What do you want?"

"Nothing. Your dad was looking for you at the barn."

Her eyes grew large. "What did he want?"

"I'm not sure. He didn't say, just that he was looking for you."

I studied Miranda as she got lost in thought. "Miranda, are you okay?"

My voice broke her out of her trance. She met my gaze, and her eyes hardened. "Why are you back here?"

Her question threw me off. "It's none of your business, to be honest. Why does it matter, anyways?"

Miranda sighed. "It doesn't. I just don't know why you would come back to a place that holds nothing but such bad memories." Her lips twisted into a smirk. "Well, I guess not all is bad here."

I gathered my reins. "I'm not in the mood to argue with you. Have a good ride."

I clucked Ace into a walk until Miranda's voice stopped me. "I would never have come back, not after what you saw. I don't know how you keep going to be honest."

I turned in the saddle to face her. "I don't know either."

She nodded solemnly. "You have a scar, right? From that night?"

Her words sent a tingle down my forearm. Right on cue it began to throb and pulse as though it were alive. "I do."

Miranda bit her lip. "We all have our scars. Not everyone wears them as a physical reminder."

I nodded slowly. "I suppose that's true."

Miranda tilted an eyebrow up. "Do you like to read?"

"I do. You?"

She shook her head vehemently. "No. I can't stand stories." With that, Miranda urged her horse into a fast walk, heading in the opposite direction as me. I watched until she disappeared into the distance.

I sent Ace on the path to the barn and replayed the brief conversation. The sadness in Miranda's eyes and the jumbled words we shared held meaning. I just had to find the connecting dots.

CHAPTER TWENTY-THREE

"I'm telling you, Chase it was weird."

Chase smiled tiredly and wrapped his arms around me. "At least she didn't bite your head off."

I leaned against the kitchen counter and crossed my arms. "I suppose." I studied Chase and frowned slightly. "What's wrong?"

Chase sighed and sat heavily into a chair. "The boss called. One of the senior guys at work is going to be off work for awhile. Since I'm next in the rank, I'm the guy to take over."

"Oh no. He's got the night shifts right?" I strode over to him and wrapped my arms around his neck. "You haven't done nights in years."

He yawned. "I'll be alright. It won't be fun but I can do it."

I kissed him on the cheek. "I'll swing by around dinner and bring you some food."

"I'd appreciate that. Please bring coffee...strong coffee." Chase glanced out the window. "More snow is coming in tonight. I'll help you bring in firewood before I try to sneak in a quick nap."

"Okay, thanks." I straightened up and we put on our gear. Chase handed me a head lamp and I secured it against my forehead. We stepped out into the dusk and marched through the snow toward the woodshed. I glanced around nervously as my last encounter involved hiding from a bear.

"The bear has been back."

Chase's voice snapped me into reality. "What?" I followed his finger as he pointed to tracks. "Shouldn't they be hibernating?"

Chase looked around and shrugged. He flicked on the light to the shed and began filling the bin. "They should but sometimes they get disturbed. I want you to be careful when you go outside alone. Take the bear spray with you."

I nodded eagerly and helped fill the bin. "I will."

We both carried our full bins and stacked the wood neatly on the covered porch next to the front door. I held out my arms and Chase began to stack wood in my arm cradle until I could hold no more. I followed him into the warmth of the home and to the fireplace. He opened the door and stoked the fire. I brushed off wood debris from my coat and watched as the flames licked the dry wood, engulfing them rapidly.

Chase stood and sighed. "I should head to bed for a bit."

"Good idea." I raised on my tip toes to give him a kiss. "Want me to wake you in an hour?"

He smiled. "Yes, please."

"K. Off you go."

He rolled his eyes. "Yes, mom."

I stuck out my tongue playfully then wandered into the kitchen. There was ample time to kill, so I gathered ingredients to set them in the slow cooker and plugged it in. I found myself passing the time curled up on the couch with a book before the alarm I set for myself began to chime. I turned it off and made my way toward the bedroom. I pressed myself lightly against Chase's chest and shook him softly. "Wakey wakey."

Chase moaned. "Already?""

"Unfortunately so."

He groaned and tossed the covers off. He stood grudgingly and threw on his work clothes. I met him at the front door with a to go mug of coffee and sympathetic smile. "I'll bring you food as soon as its ready."

Chase leaned in and gave me a long kiss. "Thanks, babe. Have a good night and drive careful."

"You too. Be safe."

As the hours passed, the savoury aroma of the slow cooker flitted through the air. I gathered my things and packed a cooler with food and beverages to get Chase through the night. Before I left I decided to stoke the fire. I bundled up and opened the front door. The night was quiet but the hairs on the back of my neck rose. I flicked on the porch light and scanned the nearby landscape. Nothing was out of place but the feeling of unease stayed with me. I quickly piled my arms full of wood and filled the fire. I turned the damper on low to allow for a slow burn. I grabbed my cooler and locked the door behind me. I marched purposefully for my car and slid inside quickly. For good measure I locked the doors.

The car started unhappily in the cold. My headlights lit the night and illuminated the quickly falling snow. As I began the drive down the long treed drive, I thought I saw the glow of eyes. I pressed on the gas a little harder and was on the main roads in no time. I drove carefully and pulled in next to Chase's truck. Working quickly, I gathered my things and ran for the warmth of the building. I stepped inside and stomped the snow off my boots.

"There she is."

Chase rounded the corner toward me with a warm smile. I wiggled the cooler teasingly."I got you reinforcements."

"You're an Angel." He grabbed my hand and led me to an empty room. "Did you bring enough dinner for yourself?"

"You bet."

Chase pulled out a chair and we ate dinner together. "What are you going to do for the rest of your evening?" He inquired.

"I'm going to pop in and visit mom while I'm out and about."

"Good idea."

"If the roads get too bad I'll probably stay there for the night. I'll call you to let you know."

"Okay. Are they getting bad?"

"A little slick. My cars not made for this climate."

Chase grinned slyly. "No its not. We need to trade that thing in. You'll get a pretty penny for it."

"Yeah that's probably a good idea." I stood and stretched my back. "I should let you get back to it. Have a good night, enjoy the goodies."

Chase tapped on the cooler lightly. "Oh I will. Drive safe."

"I will. You too. I'll see you tomorrow then." My feet weren't quite ready to leave. I stopped and pressed myself into his chest. "It feels like we've stepped back in time and just started dating again."

He shook his head. "It does. Can't say I miss this night shift crap though."

"I know. It's just temporary, right?"

"So they tell me. Trust me, I'll make sure this doesn't become permanent."

A chuckle escaped my lips. "I bet you will. I really should go though."

Chase linked his fingers in mine. "I'll walk you to your car."

"Look at you courting me."

"What can I say? I was raised right."

"That you were." I unlocked my car and slipped in. With a wave, Chase shut my door and I drove away. I weaved the familiar roads and pulled in front of my mom's softly lit home. Aunt Sam's car was already covered with snow. I killed the engine and ran for the porch. I stomped my feet on the front mat and rapped at the door.

The door opened and Aunt Sam's cautious look fell as she saw me. "Emmy! Come in, come in. What brings you here?"

I pulled off my toque and unravelled my scarf. "Chase is on nights and I could use the company."

Audrey rounded the corner. "Oh, the poor guy."

"Hi, Mom."

"Hello my darling girl." She wrapped me in a tight embrace.

Aunt Sam interrupted. "Is anyone in the mood for tea?"

I nodded eagerly. "Yes, thanks."

"Okay, I'll get it started."

"Thanks Aunt Sam."

Audrey nodded for me to follow to the couch. She studied me closely. "How are you?"

"I'm okay. How are you?"

"As far as I know I'm good." Audrey frowned slightly. "What's up? I can tell you're hiding something."

I bit my lip. "Not necessarily. I've just been thinking about Aaron a lot and the letters. I also had a run in with the Reverend. He tells me you haven't seen him for awhile."

Audrey stiffened. "No, I have not. I was clear with Sam that I needed a break. I made her promise me, even when I have one of my lapses, that I do not want to go."

"Why? I thought you enjoyed it. What changed?"

"I'm not sure. I feel like I'm talking too much about things I don't want to discuss. It has made unwelcome feelings resurface. The lines are getting muddled between when I can remember and when I can't. He's wanted me to elaborate on a few things that apparently I said but as you know, I have no recollection of it at all."

"Do you go in alone, or does Aunt Sam go with you?"

"It's just me. Silly, I know." Audrey patted my hand reassuringly. "He's only trying to help but I need a break."

I nodded slowly. "Okay, if you say so."

Aunt Sam entered the room balancing a tray of hot mugs and snacks. She placed it on the table carefully and smiled. "There we go."

I grabbed at a cookie eagerly and smiled. "Thank you. This looks good."

"Enjoy." Aunt Sam raised a mug to her lips and took a careful sip. Her eyes darted to the window and she frowned. "It's really coming down out there. I don't know that I want you driving in this."

I turned to the window. "I had a feeling it was going to pick up. Do you mind if I stay the night?"

Audrey smiled. "Ah, a girls night. I like it!"

Aunt Sam grinned. "I think that's a good idea. Better safe than sorry. I can make up one of the bedrooms for you."

A flutter of panic shot through my gut at the thought of being stuck in one of the rooms. I wasn't ready. "Um, actually would you mind if I sleep on the couch?"

A knowing look crossed my aunt's face. "Not at all."

"I'm going to give Chase a call and let him know I'll be here." I stood quickly and stepped into the hall. I dialled his number and while I waited for his answer, my body gravitated toward Aaron's closed door. I stood in front of it, almost mesmerized.

"Hey, babe. I take it you're spending the night?"

His voice brought me back. I quickly stepped away from the door and cleared my throat. "Yeah, I don't trust the roads. They should be cleared somewhat by the time you're off."

"Most likely." He yawned loudly.

Sympathy filled my voice. "How are you making out?"

"The food helps. I'll have a better sleep tomorrow it will help me get through tomorrow night with ease." He sighed. "I should get back to it. Have a good night. Say hi to everyone for me."

"I will. Have a good night. Be safe."

The call ended and I plopped back onto the couch. We continued with light conversation until the yawns took over. We said our goodnights and I crawled under the covers wearily. The house was silent aside from the popping fire and the ticking of the clock. My chest felt tight as my surroundings sank in. Despite the warmness of the décor, this house didn't feel like home anymore. While my mom sought comfort in this place, I felt the opposite. Memories of what used to be ran deep in every inch of this place, I found it almost suffocating.

I peeked over the comforter gingerly and almost expected to see Aaron leaning against a doorframe. Nothing remained but the blackness of the night. I closed my eyes and let the ticking of the clock lull me to sleep.

⌘

A loud thud outside sounded. I sprang off the couch, temporarily unsure of my surroundings. The motion light shone dimly through the closed curtain. I pulled back a corner and scanned outside. My heart stilled as a black bear rummaged through a knocked over garbage can. The animal must have sensed me for its head snapped upright. Its trained eyes found me. We stared at each other, motionless. The blackness of its coat shone in contrast with the white snow. I watched as the beast moved swiftly, shaking loose the collecting snow from its coat. Once it determined I was no threat, it lowered its nose back to the contents scattered about.

"He's back again."

I nearly jumped out of my skin from the low voice. Audrey peered over my shoulder. "You just about gave me a heart attack," I gasped.

"I'm sorry." Audrey studied me closely and pressed a hand to her forehead. "I know you. I think I do."

My heart dropped, as I knew her mind had turned fuzzy. My mom turned on her heel and set a brisk pace for her bedroom. I followed cautiously, yet curiously. Audrey sat on the edge of her bed and flipped frantically through a blue photo album. My heart ached as I realized it was the album I made for her to remember.

Audrey glanced up at me with me of a familiarity. She tapped a page in the book and held it toward me. "This is you."

I focused on the photo of my mother and myself on the page. "Yes. That's me. I'm your daughter, Emmy."

"So the book says. I'm sorry, I don't remember you that well." Audrey looked at me in earnest. "Can I show you something?"

"Of course."

Audrey set the book aside and went down the hall. She opened Aaron's door like it was nothing at all. My feet faltered as some invisible force stopped me from entering. Audrey bustled around the room like she'd been doing so her whole life. She looked over her shoulder and with slight impatience she gestured me inside.

I grudgingly entered the forbidden barrier and focused on slowing my heart. Audrey seemed to notice my uneasiness. "What's wrong?"

"I-uh." I took a deep breath and willed my words to co-operate. "It's this room to be honest."

Audrey clucked. "He's everywhere, isn't he?"

My jaw dropped. "Do you remember Aaron?"

Audrey looked deep in thought. "He's the young man in the album, right?"

"Yes."

Audrey blew out a low snort. "I dream about him all the time but I don't know that I remember him entirely." She lowered her voice. "He comes to me in my dreams."

Goosebumps took over my skin. "He comes to me, too."

Audrey went down on her knees and pulled a notebook from under the bed. She held it toward me. I took the book carefully and opened it curiously. My breath cut short as sketches of a bear were scribbled about. I flipped through the pages quickly and the sketches ranged from life like detail to tribal. "Where did you get this?" I breathed.

"I drew them." Audrey placed her shoulders back. "Do you know the spiritual meaning of a bear?"

"No," I said slowly. "I don't."

Audrey nodded eagerly. "The bear as a spirit animal is believed to be a powerful guide to emotional support and healing." Audrey lowered her voice. "It's also feared and admired for its strength."

The room grew cold. My eyes frantically worked the room, looking for a dark figure. Audrey stepped beside me and grabbed my arm. "He's not here. You don't need to fear him."

I shook her arm off. "Excuse me?"

"You and I both know who I'm talking about. He's not the one to fear."

"What do you mean? Who should we fear?"

"I don't know."

My thoughts began to turn as I took a step closer to my mom and grabbed her by the forearms. "I think you know something. Think. Who should I fear?"

Audrey glanced at my tightened hands unsurely. "I don't know. I can't make out a face."

Frustration tore through me. "Do you remember the night of the accident? Were you there?"

Audrey's eyes widened. "I don't know."

My hands shook her. "Think, Mom, think! Were you there? What aren't you telling me?"

Fear replaced Audrey's confusion. "Let me go, let me go!" Audrey shook me off and shoved me hard. I hit the ground with a thud and I saw her feet shuffle away.

Dammit. Good job, Em. Real smooth. I sat motionless on the cool ground until something caught my eye from the corner of the bed. My body moved stiffly as I raised myself to my hands and knees and crawled toward the mark. *Clever boy.* My fingertip traced the roughness of the floor into a square. I bit my lip and scanned the room for a thin, strong object to help me pry. I grabbed one of Aaron's thin screwdrivers he used to adjust the bindings on his board. The flat blade sank into the crevice and I pried up a portion of the floor. I couldn't help but smile at the clever vandalism. *Mom would have freaked out on you.*

I reached into the hole and pulled out a Ziploc bag. My eyes studied the bag in the dim room light and let out a laugh. Two joints lay in the bottom, along with a lighter. I set the bag aside and felt the presence of Aaron. For once, it didn't feel lonely. I pulled out a handful of change, random candies, and a small wooden box. My hands grabbed the wooden box tenderly and I scooted into a comfortable position. I flipped open the lid and stifled a surprised yelp.

My trembling fingers clasped the golden chain as I held it up. Flashbacks to Aaron's accident knocked the breath out of me as I remembered this chain catching the light before being pulled from the wreckage. "What the hell," I gasped.

My eyes hungrily peered into the remains of the box as I opened the folded letters. *"It's okay. We don't need to worry. He will never know. Trust me. I love you."* I let the paper drop as I scanned a few of the handwritten scrawls, all draped in love tones. I shook my head trying to make sense of this. Near the bottom of the box was a faded strip of photographs. Aaron was next to someone but the face was hidden. My fingers frantically opened the last letter with a trembling hand. My eyes read it hesitantly and as the words sank in, I felt ill. The sickness began to grow as the anger set in and I began to weep.

"Again, when a righteous man turns away from his righteousness and commits iniquity, and I place an obstacle before him, he will die; since you have not warned him, he shall die in his sin, and his righteous deeds which he has done shall not be remembered; but his blood I will require at your hand. Ezekial 3:20"

CHAPTER TWENTY-FOUR

"Are you okay, Emmy? You've been very quiet this morning."

I forced a smile. "I'm okay. I had a restless sleep, I'm not used to the noises in this house." The bear flashed through my mind. "Plus you had a bear wandering your yard."

Aunt Sam scowled. "Again? I thought they should be hibernating."

"It seems to be a restless winter for all." I stood and pushed back my chair. "I'm going to get head out. Thank you for letting me stay over." I glanced at my mom, who pushed around the food on her plate mindlessly. Audrey met my gaze and stared blankly. I let out a sigh and Aunt Sam walked me to the door.

Aunt Sam gave me a reassuring squeeze. "I'm glad you came over. It was nice to see you."

A weak smile formed and I shuffled anxiously. "I'll try to come around more often. It's hard for me to be here."

"I know it is." Aunt Sam opened the door and I stepped out into the day. My boots crunched methodically over the hardened snow. The sun bounced off the white landscape, nearly blinding me. I shielded my eyes and slid into the car. My ignition coaxed the engine to life and I began the drive home. I idled at a stop sign, and the pocket in which I shoved Aaron's box began to throb. Without hesitation, I took a left instead of right and drove for the church.

The car coasted into the nearly vacant lot and I stared at the building, my mind battling what I was about to do. I had no proof but an old letter and a gut instinct. *Shit. Here I go.* The car door swung open heavily and I marched with force to the building. The door was unlocked and my legs did not hesitate; they carried me purposely to the office that I sought. I raised my knuckles to the door and rapped loudly.

"Come in."

I stepped inside cautiously and stared at the Reverend at his desk. His glasses were lowered to the bridge of his nose, his graying hair was tidy, and his eyes meaningful. As I studied him, some of the venom I possessed drained away. He looked harmless. My eyes broke his stare and they began to wander the office. *God is everywhere.*

"Emmy. What a surprise. Please, have a seat. What can I do for you?"

My gaze took in his open arm that gestured me to sit. I did so, rigidly, cautiously. The Reverend waited for me to speak. I slipped my hand into my deep coat pocket. My fingers traced the box, willing it to give me the strength I so needed. I cleared my throat. "You knew my brother?"

The Reverend nodded solemnly. "Of course."

"How well did you know him?"

The Reverend frowned and leaned back into his plush leather chair. "I can't say I knew him particularly well. Why do you ask?"

"I've been thinking about him a lot these days."

"Being home must bring a lot of memories back to life."

"Yes." I paused and forced my gaze to burn into his. "And I think I've missed something. Something important."

The Reverend furrowed his brows. "I'm sorry, I don't follow."

"He shall die in his sin, and his righteous deeds which he has done shall not be remembered; but his blood I will require at your hand."

The Reverends arm twitched slightly. "Emmy, I still don't follow. I'm sorry."

"Do you know the verse?"

"Of course. It's a powerful statement. Revenge is a strong emotion."

My gaze darkened and the anger crept into my veins. "I need you to hear me. Stay away from my mom. Stay away from us." I pushed the chair back loudly. "I'm on to you."

The Reverend stood abruptly. "I think there has been some sort of a mistake."

I backed out slowly. "Stay away from us. I don't know why you did it, but I intend to find out."

I slammed the door closed and marched down the hall. My heart hammered in my chest unevenly and my limbs began to shake as the adrenaline coursed through. *What have I done?* I hopped in my car and drove for home, replaying the accusation in my head over and over. The drive home was a blur. I parked in the driveway and made my way into the home quietly. It was not the warm embrace I had hoped for; there was a damp chill in the air. I opened the fireplace and used the fire poker to stir the dying embers. The cool air rushed in and reignited the orange glow. I tossed some kindling in and watched as the last remains of life transformed into a hot flame. The fire grew, devouring the dry kindle with a snap and crackle. When the new flame was ready, I fed it some logs and latched the door closed.

With Chase fast asleep I rummaged through the fridge mindlessly. It was nearly empty. I bundled up and headed to the grocery store and wandered the aisles, filling the cart. As I headed to the check out I nearly collided into a familiar face.

"Craig!"

Craig looked amused. "I sure hope you don't drive like that."

My posture relaxed. "Funny guy." I studied him briefly. "Sorry, I was distracted. There's a chance I may have over stepped my boundaries with your dad."

Craig raised a brow. "Oh, how so?"

Uneasiness stirred in my gut. I bit my lip, unsure of how much to tell him. "Um, I may have accused him of being responsible for Aaron's crash."

Craig's smirk dropped and he lowered his voice. "What in the hell makes you think that? Look, its no secret my dad and I don't see eye to eye, but that's a little far fetched. Don't you think?"

The blood rushed to my face as the heat of embarrassment set in. "Look, I'm sorry. I am. It's just that….well, I found a box hidden with some of Aaron's things. There was this letter that was along the lines of threatening and biblical. I just thought…"

Craig's glowered darkened. "You can't just go around accusing people of murder." My face paled and I said nothing. Craig took a step closer. "That is what you're saying, isn't it? *Murder.*"

My eyes remained glued to the floor. "I may have jumped the gun a little bit. But something was missed at the accident. I can *feel* it. Aaron wasn't the only one in the Jeep that night."

Craig stopped mid step and turned to face me, confusion heavy in his features. "Why would you think that?"

"I was there, Craig. Don't you remember? I was there with Aaron until his last damn breath. He told me so himself."

Craig shook his head. "Leave my family alone."

Craig turned on his heel and stormed away. *Leave my family alone.* His words echoed in my head. How ironic, that was the last thing I said to his father. I paid for the groceries and placed them in my trunk. A sharp breeze swept through, causing me to shiver. The hairs on the back of my neck stood on edge. The parking lot was vacant, but my nerves were on edge. I shook my head and sat in the car. Instead of heading for home, I headed to my mom's. As I pulled in to her driveway, disbelief set in at the sight of a familiar vehicle. I stuck the car in park and ran to the front door. Without knocking, I stepped inside and rounded the corner that led me to the kitchen. My feet came to a halt. My eyes widened as I stared at my mom, aunt Sam and the Reverend. He looked at me sheepishly and stood quickly.

"What are you doing here?" I scowled.

Audrey stood and held her hands out calmly. "Emmy, it's okay. He's just worried about you," she soothed.

The Reverend tipped his head. "I'll see myself out."

I followed him, despite the protests behind me. "I told you to stay away."

The Reverend straightened his shoulders. "I'm worried about you and I felt the need to share my worries. I know how hard this must be for you, for your entire family. There are many stages to the grieving process. There is no time limit."

Words left me as I stared at him. He slipped out the front door and shut it quietly behind him. Audrey cleared her throat behind me. "Emmy, can we talk?"

"Sure, why not."

She took me by the hand and led me to the couch. She softened her voice. "I know how hard Aaron's death has been on you, for me as well. There is something I need to tell you about that night."

My heart shuddered as I met her eyes. *Please don't say you were there. Please don't say it.* Audrey blew out a breath. "I was there."

Tears began to build. "What do you mean?" I whispered.

"I saw the aftermath. I heard you screaming," her voice broke and she paused for a moment. "I can not tell you the pain in which my heart felt. Chase held me back and convinced me to leave. Honey, it took everything he had in him to keep me away."

"So it was you. I heard you calling my name, I thought I was going mad."

Audrey shook her head. "I briefly recall the month leading up to the accident. My symptoms had only just begun."

"I know," I whispered.

"That's why this is hard for me to share this with you. I don't know if I can trust my mind to remember things clearly."

I met my mom's faraway eyes. "What do you mean?"

"What if I did it? What if it was me that caused the accident?"

My throat went dry. My brain clicked slowly but no response came. Audrey shook her head and raised her large eyes to mine and began to cry. "He won't last much longer. Now is the time to say good-bye. I remember the people at the scene repeating it over and over." Audrey paused. "They also asked me for my keys."

After I gathered my composure, I gathered my things and left. I stepped into the darkening day and walked to my car in a zombie like fashion. As I neared, the flapping envelope under my wiper blade gathered my full attention. I reached for it numbly and opened the letter.

All those you love are easily lost, some more than others. Stop digging.

I shoved the letter into my purse and flopped into the drivers seat. There was only one person here who could have given me the letter. My only question was why.

CHAPTER TWENTY-FIVE

Chase gathered his things for the night. I watched, battling an internal struggle of sharing recent events. In the end I decided against it. He had enough on his plate. Chase shoved the last of his meals into a bag and stood.

"That's everything," he forced a smile.

"Not thrilled to go to work, huh?"

"Not even a little bit." He glanced out the window. "Another storms blowing in. I packed extra clothes in case I have to sleep at work. Are you going to be alright?"

"I'll be fine. We have plenty of firewood and food."

"Okay." He bent down and gave me a kiss on the forehead. "Have a good night."

"You too."

I leaned against the doorframe and watched him leave. Emptiness filled the room as soon as he was gone. A sigh escaped and I wandered the darkened house, replaying everything from today. My mind was fogged with confusion; there wasn't much to go on. I pulled back the curtain and looked at the threatening sky. There was some time before the brunt of the storm broke loose. I gathered my keys and drove to the barn. The soothing scent of sweet hay met me, temporarily masking the heaviness I carried.

Ace swung his head over the door and nickered an eager greeting. I cupped his nose between my hands and smiled. "You're going stir crazy from being cooped up, aren't ya buddy?"

Ace blinked his chocolate eyes. "Want to go for a ride?"

We were saddled up in no time. I contemplated for a millisecond about riding in the warm arena, but my heart tugged for the trails. I guided Ace outside and he began to prance eagerly. He knew the route by heart as I rode with a loose rein. We weaved our way between the trees as Ace's hooves eagerly ate up the path. I focused on deep breathing and allowed my mind to clear. The gold chain entered my thoughts; I needed to find the owner. It would give me one more clue toward the puzzle. *Don't let it be my mom. Please. Don't let it be her.*

Ace suddenly tensed. He began to dance nervously and I sat deeper in the saddle. "It's okay bud, we're okay." I soothed and ran a hand down his stiff neck.

The loud cracking of a branch caused Ace to spook. He jumped forward with an awkward thrust. I swayed to the left and had to gather myself quickly before I went over. I held the reins tighter than normal and urged Ace to circle so he didn't bolt. Even though a saddle separated myself from Ace, I could feel his muscles bunch into tight knots. His breath blew out in quick snorts as he began to dance unsurely. As I fought to keep him under control my eyes caught the black figure, the source of the stress.

The bear stood motionless as it watched the chaos it created. I stared at its glossy coat in wonder and fear. The bear met my eyes and stood swiftly on its hind legs. *Fuck.* I could keep Ace reined in no longer. With a tug, he tore the reins from my grasp and bolted. I leaned as low as I could over his neck, fighting to stay on. As I struggled with my seat, I reached desperately for the swinging reins. I managed to get a clumsy grasp of them and attempted to pull Ace to a stop.

"Whoa, Ace. Whoa!" My words were useless as the wind tore my voice away. The bitter breeze whipped and broke my hair loose from its ponytail. *Shit.* I glanced warily at the fast moving ground before us. My stomach dropped as I realized Ace was a runaway horse. All I could do at this point was fight to stay on. The snow covered ground below us was dangerous at these speeds as it masked the terrain and hidden obstacles. With a firm grip I desperately tried to pull Ace to another stop.

"Ace, whoa! Stop!" I yelled as loudly as I could and leaned back deeper into the saddle.

He did not slow. He carried on with a renewed sense of urgency. I stole a look behind me, and to my relief, the bear was nowhere to be seen. With the threat of being followed by a hungry bear off the list, my attention was again focused to stopping my horse. Ace lunged forward and the ground below us gave way. The cracking ice nearly split my ear drums. I gasped as the cold water pooled up to my waist and my teeth began to chatter wildly. Ace snorted repeatedly as his legs kicked below me. I hung on for dear life and begged for my legs to move at Ace's side to help guide him out. *Turn around, Ace. Go to shore. Turn around.* I thought it over and over, hoping he would read my mind.

The water rose to Ace's chest and I felt the panic course through him. "I-i'it's o-o-o-okay," I chattered.

As the water deepened, my body went weak and I toppled out of the saddle. The sheer shock of the cold stole my breath. I kicked my legs and arms furiously in an attempt to swim. I didn't know how deep the water was, and I didn't want to find out. The water thrashed around me from my horse's body and the world went temporarily dark. Aaron's image flashed through my mind. My vision came black in a blinding flash. I tore my eyes to the white shore and I could swear he was there. *Fight Emmy, don't let go. Don't let me go.*

I let out a scream of rage and kicked my legs. "Ace!"

The splashes of water sent the broken ice dancing as Ace thrashed in a panic. My eyes locked on to him as the whites of his eyes took over the brown. He snorted wildly as he fought to keep his head above the water. I swam toward him as fast as I could. My brain worked slowly as I made my way to him. His primitive eyes followed my every move, as I grew close. Finally I reached him. His breathing slowed and his legs quieted as fatigue set in. Worry and uncertainty kicked at me. "Swim Ace, swim. Why aren't you moving?"

Out of frustration I slapped his rear end. He shuddered and tried to lunge forward. He was abruptly pulled back and the fear in his expression was undeniable. My heart dropped into my stomach in defeat. And then it clicked. I reached my arm into the dark waters and felt for the problem. His stirrup was snagged on a fallen tree under the murky water. I desperately tried to free the stirrup but I was sloppy as the cold took over. My legs grew tired trying to keep me afloat and I began to sink. With a desperate kick, I managed to keep my head above water as my hands felt for the cinch. My frozen fingers worked as quickly as they could to loosen the saddle off Ace completely. He felt the pressure release and his legs worked rapidly. He found his way out of the icy waters and stood unsurely in the snow.

He snorted like a dragon and paced the shore frantically. *Swim. Keep moving, swim.* I kept my gaze glued to the shore and my horse. I forced myself to swim until I reached the shallows. I urged my body to walk, but my legs were useless. I sank to my hands and knees into the mud and crawled on the shore. I fell on my stomach and somehow forced myself to flip onto my back. Ace stood next to me and shuddered from the cold. My body shook beyond control as I fought to gather my voice. "Go Ace. Go to the barn. To the barn, go!"

He hesitated. "Go!" I screamed.

He jumped from the harshness of my tone and took off. I let my head fall into the snow and begged he would make it back. I squeezed my eyes shut and desperately tried to envision heat. Fire, the embers of burning wood, anything that could erase the suffocating chill. My teeth trembled so hard I feared they would crack in half.

"Emmy, stay with me."

"It's so cold."

"I know, but stay with me. Don't fall asleep."

Sleep. Oh, how I want too. "It's so cold," I complained.

"Stay with me."

I blinked my eyes open and the world appeared white and hazy. My breath came out choppy, and I shivered from head to toe. My body had begun to grow numb from the cold. "I don't feel anything anymore."

I was met by silence. I blinked my eyes rapidly and hoped the world would clear. It was useless. It was though I was looking through a set of drunken goggles. "Aaron? Where did you go? Aaron?" My voice was taken by the falling snow.

"Watch for the bear. It's coming."

I yelped from the closeness of the voice though no one was there. "Aaron? Aaron don't leave me," I sobbed.

A strong male voice cut through my sobs. "I found her!" Warm hands gripped my limp body. "I've got you Emmy, it's okay. Hang in there."

The world began to move ever so slowly, I realized I was being carried. "Here, let me take her." My vision began to come into focus. I gasped suddenly as the image of a black bear appeared.

"Watch for the bear." Aarons voice rang loud in my ear.

I began to squirm. "No, no. Put me down. Let me go!"

"Shh, shh. It's okay, Em. We got you. Quick, open the truck door."

The arms were warm and strong. My body was useless and slow. A truck door swung open and I was nestled carefully into the warm cab. A blanket was draped over me. Two voices shouted at each other but they began to fade as the ringing in my ears took over. The warmth from the truck nipped at my skin and began to burn. *Look at them, Emmy. look at them.* I willed my brain to connect to my body. *Look up. Just look up.* I focused my gaze on the driver.

My heart caught in my throat as Chase gripped the wheel in a ghostly form. His worried eyes flicked from me to the road before us. He forced a smile. "Stay with us, Em. Do you hear me? Stay with us. Stay with me."

My brain began to click to life, but it wasn't firing on all cylinders. The truck jostled violently from left to right as the ruts in the road gripped the wheels.

"Shit," Chase cursed.

My body bounced into the passenger. My head sank into the firm chest with a gentle thud. The passenger wrapped his arms around me and tugged the blanket tighter around my sopping body. "I've got you, it's okay. Once we saw Ace running wild, I gave Chase a call. We knew something was wrong. I'm glad we found you."

I craned my head and looked up. Craig Brooks smiled back at me. My heart dropped to my stomach. My eyes fell to his tattooed forearm. *It's a bear.* "Oh God." I did my best to push him away. My body did not cooperate but my voice could. "Don't you touch me! Get off of me!"

"Jesus Christ, Emmy. Calm down."

"Don't touch me!"

Chase's voice cut through the cab. "Keep her still she's not thinking clearly."

Craig clasped his arms around me in a vice like grip. "Stay still and calm down." He looked from me to Chase. "Are we almost there?"

Chase's voice was clipped. "Soon. Hold on to her."

I didn't fight his grip; I knew I was outmatched. The only thing I could move was my eyes. I met Craig's crisp blue eyes with a fierce glare. His stare locked into mine and I saw the linger of realization. I glared more darkly.

"We're here." Chase jumped out of the truck and took me from Craig.

"Get her inside, quickly."

"Aunt Sam?" I moaned.

"It's okay, honey. Your Mom and I are right here."

"Where do you want her?"

"The bathroom."

Images passed by in a quick blur. My head spun as my brain worked overtime trying to make the figures fit. *Aunt Sam. Mom. I'm home.*

Aunt Sam shooed Chase out of the room and shut the door. Audrey and Sam worked quickly as the wet clothes were stripped off. They fell to the floor with a heavy plop.

"Do you have her Audrey?"

"Yes."

"Help me lower her in the tub. Gently, not too fast."

The warm water bit my skin like a rabid dog. "Stop," I cried. "It hurts, please stop."

Audrey's voice shook gently. "It's okay, honey. It's going to help you. Shh, shh."

My Jell-O like limbs were no match for their gentle strength. My body lowered into the warm water. I let out another whimper until I was submerged to my neck.

Audrey leaned over the edge of the tub and gripped my hand tightly. "I'm right here, honey. You're safe now."

I let my mom's soothing words fill my ears. The burning began to subside as my skin adjusted to the heat. My clacking teeth eventually halted.

"We can take her out now."

Audrey hesitated. "Leave her in for a moment. I'll give her some warm clothes to put on."

Aunt Sam nodded. She stroked my hair and smiled wearily. The door creaked open and Audrey and Chase stepped inside. Audrey nodded toward Sam. "I think Chase can handle it from here."

Aunt Sam nodded and rose stiffly. "I'll put some tea on."

Chase shut the door carefully behind as the women exited the room. He lowered himself onto the cool floor. His gray eyes locked with mine. "Don't you ever do that to me again. You scared the living shit out of me."

My lips trembled into a weak smile. "I'm sorry. I thought it was solid ground, it all happened so fast." A brief flashback of Ace's terrified rolling eyes flashed into view. "Oh no. What about Ace? Is he okay?"

Chase gripped onto my forearms. "He's okay. He ran into the barn and caused quite the fuss. Miranda took really good care of him. He's tucked in and was given warm mash."

A sob broke. "My poor boy. I can't believe I put him through that."

"Hey, shh. He's going to be fine. It's over now." Chase stood up and helped me rise. He wrapped a towel around me and brought me to his chest. His arms wrapped me in a vice like grip as he rested his chin on the top of my head. "Please don't ever do that to me again. Em, you were blue."

I fought my arms to wrap around his torso. "I'm still here."

"Let's get you dressed."

The towel slipped away and I lifted my arms into the air as Chase lowered the oversized sweater over my head. I stepped into the pyjama pants. I looked down at the familiar shirt and my heart fluttered. It once belonged to Aaron. A hand flew to my chest as the realization hit.

"Are you okay?"

Chase's voice tore me away. "Yeah, I'm fine. Can we go see Ace?"

"Of course. Are you sure you want to leave right away?"

"Yes, why do you ask?"

Chase hesitated slightly. "Please don't tear my head off for this, Em. I've just noticed that you haven't been spending a lot of time with your mom."

My anger sparked but fizzled like the end of a shooting star. I sighed heavily and leaned against the bathroom counter. "I'm scared to be around her. I hate it when she's "here" because instead of enjoying the moment, all I can think is how long will it last this time? And I hate it when she disappears because I wonder if she'll ever come back to us, or is that it? Is she gone forever? I'm so tired of the back and forth," I took a gulp of air and continued. "Does that make me a terrible person?"

Chase softened his voice. "No, Em. It makes you human. I don't think there's a right or a wrong way to deal with it. These situations don't come with a playbook. However, I think you'll regret not spending as much time with your mom as possible. I don't want to see you regret anything later on. Get to know her, in any mental state she's in."

I stole a glance at the reflection staring back at me. *Coward.* I turned away and nodded. "Can we go?"

"Yeah."

I followed Chase into the kitchen. Without speaking to me, Aunt Sam knew what I was thinking. A flicker of disappointment passed through her face. I took a deep breath and walked to my mom. I gave her a tight hug and let the warmth of her body spread to mine. "I'm okay, Mom. But I need to see Ace."

Audrey returned the squeeze. "Please be safe."

"I will. I love you."

Audrey let go and took a step back. She studied me and smiled. "I love you too, honey. So much."

I kept my eyes low to avoid Aunt Sam's gaze. Craig waited wordlessly by the front door, clearly eager to leave. Chase took my hand in his and we ran for the truck. We hopped in and Chase fired up the engine and began the drive to the barn. I sat in the middle, sandwiched between Craig and Chase. My eyes stayed locked on his now covered forearm. "I didn't know you had a tattoo."

Craig gave me a sidelong glance and a cheeky smile. "It's not the only one I have."

Chase groaned. "Behave yourself or you're walkin'."

Craig grinned and gave a silent shrug. I persisted. "What does the bear symbolize?"

"Strength."

"I see."

Craig snorted. "What does it matter to you anyways?"

"I'm not sure yet."

Craig's smile fell. He tore his eyes away and focused on staring out the window. We pulled into the barn lot and scooted stiffly out of the cab. We entered the barn quickly and Craig disappeared around a corner. I stopped for a second before my concern for my horse took over. I walked down the alleyway to the familiar stall.

Ace stood in the corner with his thick winter blanket on. He pulled hay from his slow feeder. My limbs relaxed at once. "Hey, buddy."

I unlatched the stall door and stepped inside. Ace tipped his ears forward and took a single step toward me. I wrapped my arms around his neck tightly. "I'm so glad you're okay. I don't know what I would do without you."

Ace stood quietly until he got bored of the situation. He shuffled back and I let my arms drop. He began pulling at the hay eagerly. I smiled and quickly began looking him over for damage.

"He's okay."

I turned quickly at the sound of Miranda's voice. "Oh?"

Miranda's sharp eyes sized me up in a matter of seconds. Her features hardened slightly and she began to fidget with her necklace. "Nice clothes."

I looked down at the oversized pj's and shrugged. "They're warm and dry. I can't complain to much."

"I suppose not, given the situation you were in."

"Were you the one who looked after Ace?"

Her hand began to fidget at the necklace once more. "Yes. I was nearing the end of my lesson when Ace barrelled into the barn. Everyone went into a panic. One of the girls saw you head out for a ride earlier. When a riderless horse comes back, it means nothing but trouble. He let me get close to him, so I dried him off and got him settled."

I took a step toward Miranda. "I don't know how to thank you."

Miranda stepped backwards, putting a noticeable gap between us. "It's not necessary. I know you would have done the same for me."

I nodded slowly, taking in her busy hands. I studied closer and felt the tingling of realization hit. Her fingertips clasped onto the cross on her necklace firmly. She pulled it left to right, right to left. Craig stepped in behind his sister and watched me wearily. His eyebrows pulled together and his gaze was heavy in caution. "I think we should head home, Miranda."

Miranda dropped her hands and nodded. "Okay. For what it's worth, Emmy, I'm glad you're okay."

I nodded wordlessly and watched the siblings walk away. Craig stole one last glance my way before they disappeared from my sight. My brain began working at warp speed, clumsily putting the missing pieces together. They weren't quite clicking in a smooth motion, but I was getting closer to something. I could feel it.

Chase laid his hand on the small of my back. "I think we should get you home."

I looked up and smiled. "Okay."

I followed wordlessly and hopped into the vehicle. We pulled into the driveway and stepped inside the warm house. The fire was almost out. Chase hurried to feed it more wood. I excused myself briefly and rummaged in the closet for Aaron's hidden box. I found what I was looking for; the torn photos of Aaron's smiling face and the faceless woman he was next too. I traced the ripped photo and studied it closely. The missing women's face offered me nothing but there was a trace of her hair. The silky mocha coloured hair. I sat in the corner of the closet and stared at the torn photos. *It could be her. It very well could be her.* With a grunt of frustration, I placed the photos back inside the box and put them away. I stood stiffly and closed the door softly behind me. I walked into the living room and fell heavily on the couch. My eyes closed instantaneously, and I let the beating from the day take me into the dark. My last thoughts were of the Brooks. I had some digging to do.

CHAPTER TWENTY SIX

I held my breath anxiously as Elayna pulled her features together seriously. "Well," I began. "Am I crazy?"

"No," she began slowly then stopped. Her perfectly manicured brows pulled together. "If Aaron and Miranda were together, I never knew about it." Elayna paused. "So what are you going to do? Ask her point blank? I think we both know how that will turn out."

"I don't know. I haven't decided yet."

"Well, if you need my help I'm all for it. Whatever you decide."

"Thanks, Elayna."

"No problem." Elayna wrapped her hands around the coffee mug and pulled it close. "How are you feeling? How's your mom?"

"I'm fine. My mom seems okay, I guess."

"Em, what's wrong?"

I let out a heavy sigh. "It was different before when she was in the care home. I felt like I had backup if she wasn't herself, you know? Now...being back home, seeing her in that house. I don't know, it feels like everything could break loose at any given moment and I don't know how to handle it."

Elayna offered a sad smile. "I'm really sorry you guys are going through this but I think you should spend time with your mom. Give your aunt a break. I bet your mom would love it. I can go with you if you'd like."

"Thanks, but this is something I should do on my own." My mind drifted to Aaron's box locked away in the closet. I pushed the chair back and stood. "I want to show you something."

Elayna stood and followed curiously. I opened the closet door, and stood on my tip toes reaching for the old shoe box. I opened the old cardboard and fished out Aaron's box. I grabbed the photos and handed them to Elayna. She took them carefully and studied the pictures. "It's not much to go on, but that could be Miranda's hair for sure. It's flawless."

I rolled my eyes. "As per usual."

Elayna's eyes fell to the box. "Do you mind?"

I surrendered it to her. "No."

Elayna sat cross legged on the floor and rummaged through the contents carefully. She read the letters quickly and frowned. "I don't like these."

I sat beside her. "Me either. Nothing is making sense. I could be crazy, Elayna. I could be obsessing about absolutely nothing. There was nothing suspicious about the accident. I could be projecting on an idea that drags me away from what I'm avoiding."

"Sure, I completely agree. But on the other hand, your gut instincts are usually pretty good and why else would Aaron hide these things away?"

"I remembered the accident vividly about a week ago. For years I blocked it out, but I finally allowed myself to remember. There was this moment, right before Aaron passed out. He asked me 'Did she get out?' Everyone assumed he was alone. But what if he wasn't? I also remember a necklace under the passenger seat as I was pulled out."

"Oh, Em. What does Chase think about all this?"

I focused my gaze to the floor. "I haven't told him."

Elayna's voice rose. "Why not?"

"He has enough on his plate right now."

Elayna tsked. "You should tell him."

"I will, eventually."

Elayna studied the box again and she gave a wry smile. She picked up the baggie with the joint. "What do you say, Em? Care to de-stress a bit?"

My eyebrows rose. "What are you, sixteen?"

Elayna stood and stretched her back. "C'mon, let's go outside and unwind."

I studied her dubiously and put Aaron's box away in the shadows. Elayna wandered to the kitchen and fished out her toque from her purse. "Bundle up buttercup. Let's go outside for a quick toke, shall we?"

I murmured curses silently but did as told. We sat on the outdoor couch under the covered porch and said nothing. The hazy sky once again spat snow. I watched it swirl every which way covering up the already white landscape. Elayna placed the joint between her lips and lit the end. She took a long drag and blew the smoke out slowly. The skunky sweet smell lingered between us as she handed the joint to me. I studied the white paper hesitantly before I grasped it between my fingers and placed it between my lips. I took a long inhale. As the sweet smoke filled my lungs I began to cough.

Elayna chuckled and took it from me. "Inhale slowly. You went too fast."

She took another drag and handed it to me once more. I inhaled slowly and held the smoke in my lungs for a moment before releasing. I watched as the frigid air lapped at the sweet haze greedily. We leaned back in the chair as the numbing rush hit our heads and fell over our bodies.

"You look more relaxed already."

"Where did you get that?"

Chase's loud voice caused us both to jump from our seat. "Chase! You scared the bejesus out of me."

Chase stepped forward and grabbed the paper from Elayna's fingers. "Where did this come from?"

"Aaron," I admitted sheepishly.

Chase rose his eyebrows. "Excuse me? How much of this have you had?"

Elayna took the paper back and sat on the couch, folding her legs in a neat tuck. She motioned at me with her eyes. I held my head down and took Chase's hand in mine. "Follow me, I'll show you."

Chase looked between us accusingly but followed wordlessly. I gave him the box and filled him in on my thoughts. Chase handed it back to me very carefully. "Em, I don't know what to say to you right now."

I lowered my gaze to the floor. "Chase, I remembered the accident. Aaron wasn't alone. He asked me if she got out, and I saw a necklace under the passenger seat."

"Then you should ask her, point blank. Don't torture yourself over an assumption." Chase stood and pulled me with him. "C'mon let's get it over with."

"What, now?"

"I'll drive you girls."

"Chase, you've got to be kidding me."

"Nope. You need to stop worrying over everything you can't control. Take the box with you."

I tore my hand from his and placed my hands upon my hips. He sighed and crossed his arms, waiting. I stomped my foot like a child but obliged. I grabbed the box, tucked it under my arm and marched passed him. "I am not happy about this."

"Take another inhale on that joint, it might get you there."

Elayna stepped inside and widened her eyes. "Uh, you guys okay?"

I glared at Chase as he grabbed his keys. "We're going to end this once and for all. C'mon, Elayna, you're coming too."

I grabbed Elayna's hand and towed her along. We hopped in the truck and sat in silence as Chase drove to Miranda's house. He pulled in the driveway and cut the engine. "I'll wait here. You girls go on."

I stared at the front door and Miranda's car piled high with untouched snow. "I don't want to do this. I have no idea what to say."

"Pull the trigger and get it over with. Go on."

Elayna shoved me to move. "Let's get this over with," she muttered.

We unwillingly stepped outside and slammed the truck door closed with a glare. Elayna and I walked in silence, shoulder to shoulder as she knocked loudly against the door. Footsteps sounded and the door swung open. A blast of heat met our cool skin. Miranda stood in front of us, looking put together, the poster child of a magazine. *Dammit. Why couldn't we have caught her in sweatpants and looking dishevelled for once in her life?* Miranda stepped outside quickly and shut the door behind her. Elayna and I stepped back in surprise.

"What are you two doing here?" she hissed.

The harshness of her tone made my tongue go numb. "Um, well you see…" I glanced at Elayna for some help.

Elayna stumbled over her words just as I had and she clasped her mouth shut. "I don't how to do this," she whispered.

Miranda crossed her arms and glanced quickly at Chase's truck. "I'll say it again, what are you two doing here?"

I straightened my shoulders back and met her glare. I held Aaron's box up to my chest. "Do you recognize this?"

Miranda's eyes fell to the box and she paled. "Where…"

In that moment her door opened and Audrey stood behind her. "I finished the verse but I'm still confused."

My jaw dropped and Miranda sent me a plea. "Mom, what are you doing here?" I breathed.

Audrey looked at me, confusion etched in her features. My heart hammered in my chest as I knew that look. She wasn't there. I pulled my gaze away from my mom and focused the brunt of it on Miranda, whose anger had dwindled away. "What is my Mom doing here?"

The door of a vehicle slammed closed behind me. I knew it was Chase coming to investigate. "Care to invite us in?" I propped.

Miranda looked at us like a frightened rabbit. She let out a heavy breath and nodded. "Fine, come in."

I had never set foot in Miranda's house before. As I looked around, my stomach grew uneasy. God was everywhere. I took in my surroundings briefly and stared at Miranda in question. The image of her and the contents of her home didn't fit. Miranda motioned for Audrey to sit. "Read the next page, Audrey. I'll be back to help you finish."

Audrey studied us curiously but disappeared into the kitchen. Chase cleared his throat and watched me carefully. He stood next to me and clasped his fingers in mine. "Miranda, what's going on?"

"I'm giving your mom private Bible study. She does better one on one than in a group." Miranda lowered her eyes. "She comes to me for comfort."

My heart skipped a beat. "Comfort? For what?"

Miranda's face paled. "I think you already know the answer to that."

"No I don't. Care to enlighten me?" I spat.

Chase tightened my hand. "Miranda, tread carefully here."

Miranda's tone became clipped. "This is my house. What are you all doing here ganging up on me? Who do you think you are?"

Elayna held up her hands. "Whoa, whoa, whoa. We came to ask you a question and we're all a little taken back at the fact Audrey is here."

Miranda placed her hands on her hips. "Your mom has been seeking solace at church. She came to me one day and asked me to go through some verses with her to find comfort. I'm helping your mom, unlike you."

Her words were a slap in the face. Guilt fell heavy over my body. I looked away and tightened my lips. Chase spoke for me. "How long were you and Aaron together for?"

I glanced quickly at Chase in surprise and stepped closer to him. He gave my hand a squeeze but kept his eyes locked on Miranda. Her eyes widened as she gazed back at us like we were snakes. Her mouth fell open. "Excuse me?" she breathed.

I worked quickly and my hand slipped from Chase's to open the box. I fished out the photos and held them up to her. "I think this is you."

Her eyes stared at the photos. I watched her closely but she gave nothing away. Her mouth closed and her eyes grew vacant. "Please leave."

"Miranda, it's a simple yes or no. Is this you?"

"Leave my house, all of you or I will call the police."

Chase muttered under his breath but he ushered us toward the door. He opened it widely and Elayna stepped out first. I turned to face Miranda once more. "There was a necklace under the passenger seat of Aaron's Jeep. He asked me if 'she got out.'"

The hardness in Miranda's eyes wavered. "Get out."

Chase gave a gentle shove to the small of my back and Elayna took the cue to grab my hand. She yanked me toward her as Chase shut the door. We climbed into the truck and sat in silence. Chase spoke first. "I think you got your answer and a helluva lot more questions."

⌘

Over the next few days, I kept my distance. I did not see Miranda at the barn, I did not run into Craig in town. I paced the house restlessly, still in my yoga gear from the morning's class. I was mindful to keep noise to a minimum as

Chase napped in preparation for his night shift. I paused at the window and stared at the blue sky. For once, it wasn't snowing. The sky was blindingly blue, not a cloud to be seen. I tapped my fingers impatiently on the sill and made up my mind. I slammed a tuque over my dishevelled braid and left a quick note for Chase on the counter. I slid into my car and drove to my mom's. I parked in the driveway and made my way carefully to the front door. My knuckled tapped on the door three times before it swung open.

Audrey stood in the doorway, her hair was swept up on the top of her head and she smiled brightly. "What a pleasant surprise, come in!"

I smiled back and stepped inside, stripping off my coat. I placed it on the wall rack and the familiar scent of cinnamon and dough tempted me. "Oh! Do I smell cinnamon buns?"

Audrey winked and nodded for me to follow. "My special recipe. They just came out of the oven, do you want one?"

"Do you even have to ask?"

Audrey reached for a plate and placed a steaming, gooey bun in front of me. She sat beside me and handed me a fork.

I took my first bite and grinned dreamily. "These are amazing. I haven't had one of these in years."

"I'm glad you like it. I'm also glad the recipe is still in here." She tapped the side of her head.

Immediately I grew uneasy and offered a small smile. I placed another piece of bun in my mouth. Audrey smiled and looked out the window. Her smile faded and she focused her eyes on her fingernails. "Mom, what's wrong?"

"Its days like these that I miss driving the most; the freedom of it, the open road, music playing on the radio, the smell of gasoline." She sighed. "When you kids were little summer was the best time for road trips. I would bank my holidays so I could have three weeks off every July."

I set the fork down and grasped my mom's hand. "Of course I remember. They were the best."

Audrey squeezed back and stood quickly, putting away the ingredients. She kept her back to me, and an overwhelming amount of sadness gnawed at my heart. My mother was a strong, proud woman. She had raised Aaron and I on her own, got a good job, and she always found a way to keep her kids happy and safe. I realized that I had failed her. Instead of rising to the plate, I was retreating into the shadows.

"Where's aunt Sam?"

Audrey waved her hand. "Church."

My back went up. "And you didn't want to go?"

Audrey turned to me and wrinkled her nose. "I don't enjoy it very much."

A part of you does; you just don't remember. I placed my plate in the sink and scribbled a note to aunt Sam and placed it on the fridge. "Get some warm clothes on, Mom. We're going for a drive."

Audrey raised her eyebrows. "Really?"

"You bet. Now go, dress warm. The sun may be out but it's freezing outside."

Audrey smiled and rushed to her room. She came back moments later, grinning. We slid into my car and I turned the key. I backed out of the driveway and took the exit out of town. Audrey flicked on the radio and began swaying to an old familiar song. Her eyes were glued to the passing landscape and she laughed from pure joy. I settled into the driver seat and allowed my heart to swell with the contagious happiness. It was so nice to hear my mom laugh and see her eyes twinkle. I loosened my grip on the wheel and bopped to the rhythm floating from the speakers. Chase's voice echoed in my thoughts. *Spend time with your mom. Cherish the moments. Get to know her, every version of her.*

I stole a quick glance at my mom. "Well, where too?"

She didn't even hesitate. "Grande Lake."

I smiled wide; it was one of our favourite places to go as a family in the summer. "Make yourself cozy, we have a long drive ahead of us."

Audrey leaned forward and turned up the radio. She winked and began singing as loudly as she could.

CHAPTER TWENTY-SEVEN

"It looks quite different in the winter."

I zipped my coat as high as it could go and took a sip of the steaming coffee. I peered at the ice-covered lake before us; the trees were coated in white and the summer cabins looked deserted near the shore. "It's still beautiful though," I breathed.

"It's amazing. Thanks for bringing me here, Emmy."

"You're welcome." I glanced briefly at my mom before I spoke. "Why did you stop dancing?"

Audrey stiffened. "What did you say?"

"When you were at the care home you performed the most beautiful dance. I've never seen anyone so graceful. At the end of the dance, you asked if you got in."

Audrey let out a twinkling laugh. "That was a lifetime ago. Before you kids." She leaned against the car and sighed. "I had hoped to be a professional dancer, and for a while I was. That's where I met your father, actually."

"Did you stop because of us?"

"It was no longer my path. After your dad left we all had to change our lives."

I stared at the crisp snow. "If it brings you happiness don't ever stop, Mom."

Audrey smirked. "This speech sounds familiar."

"It is." I straightened my posture and leaned inside the car. I turned the key in the ignition to flick on the radio. As I searched through the stations, an upbeat tune filtered through the speakers. I held out my hand and winked. "C'mon, Mom. Show me what you got."

Audrey stared at my extended hand and laughed. "Keep up with me kiddo."

We let the beat and rhythm sway our bodies. Our feet moved side to side until the ground gently shook beneath us. Audrey took my hand and twirled me until I couldn't see straight. "Enough," I gasped. "I'm done."

Audrey tossed her hair and shook her finger at me. "I'm not." And with that, the silliness fell away from her and the swan took over. I watched mesmerized as her body moved like fluid silk. There were simply no words.

My hands came together in applause. "Bravo! Mom, that was beautiful."

Audrey came down from the tip of her toes, her face flushed. "Oh, Emmy. This has been one of the best days I've had in a very, very long time." She lowered her voice. "I don't want to forget this, ever."

Audrey linked her arm into mine and we leaned against the hood of the car and stared into the horizon.

⌘

The light began to fade as the sun lowered itself in the sky. The chilly breeze grew volatile. Audrey shuddered and tightened her scarf. "I think we better head back. The roads will be icy."

"Good idea." The phone jingled in my pocket and I fished it out. "Hello?"

"Hey, babe. Are you still with your mom?"

"I am. We're about to head home. Did you just get to work?"

"Yeah. Can you detect the thrill in my voice?"

I grinned. "You're practically bursting."

"How did your classes go today?"

I unlocked the car doors and we quickly slid inside. "They went really well, it was an early start. The first class was at 5:00 am. I'm exhausted."

"I'll let you go. You drive safe, okay?"

"I will. Love you."

"Love you too."

I turned the engine on and flicked on the heat. Audrey sat silently, grinning. "What?"

Audrey shrugged. "You two make a cute couple. Any plans for kids?"

"Mom," I groaned. "The topic hasn't come up."

"It will. Just remember one thing," Audrey turned to face me. "A parent loves their children, no matter what. They always will. *I* always will, no matter where I am. It's a love that goes so deep it becomes apart of you. Please, don't ever forget that." Audrey let out a shuddery sigh. "Don't ever forget me."

I swallowed the lump that grew in my throat. "That's impossible, Mom. You are unforgettable."

Audrey smirked. "Good. Forget me not then."

With a quick flick of the headlights we began the long, dark drive home. The radio played softly in the background and Audrey hummed to the tunes. There was a sense of tranquility in the car; I hoped it would last. As the roads became familiar, my mind got lost. Audrey reached over and squeezed my arm. "Are you okay, Em?"

I looked toward her for a split second before focusing on the road again. "I'm just thinking."

"Care to fill me in?"

"I'm afraid if I do, it will ruin the day."

"There's only one way to find out. Lay it on me."

"Did you know that Aaron hid a box in the floorboards?"

Audrey sat rigid in her seat. "No, I had no idea."

"I found it the night I stayed over."

"What was in it?'

"Some letters, photos of him and a girl. Only, the photos were torn in half. The girls face is missing."

"Interesting. I wasn't aware that Aaron had a girlfriend. He was a very social guy, everyone loved him. It could have been a friend?"

I could tell by my mom's tone, even she didn't believe her words. "Mom?"

"Yes?"

"Do you know that you go to church and have one on one Bible studies with Miranda Brooks at her home?'

Audrey burst out in laughter. She fell silent once she realized I didn't join in. "You're not kidding, are you?"

"No."

"That doesn't sound like me. I'm glad I can't remember to be honest."

"You don't remember any of it?"

"I know I've been to the church a few times. I only agreed to go because I know how important it is to Sam. I remember I stopped going because it began to give me an uneasy feeling. Perhaps my sub-conscious was aware of the things I seem to have forgotten." Audrey turned. "Where is this going?"

I gripped the steering wheel harder than necessary. "Someone knows something about Aaron's accident, and they're keeping quiet. I can feel it." I exhaled a frustrated breath and filled Audrey in on everything; from the things she shared with me when she wasn't lucid, to the clarity in which I reminisced about the accident.

"The bear's a tattoo," Audrey murmured.

"Do you remember drawing the bears?"

"I wish I did, but no. I found the notepad but couldn't make any sense of it." Audrey lowered her voice. "Follow your instincts, but be careful. It won't change anything in the end. Aaron isn't coming back."

The hardness of her words surprised me. "I know. I feel there is unfinished business. I can't let him go until I know what happened. I feel like he is here, waiting for me to see the truth. Mom, I couldn't even attend the funeral. I didn't want to be there, I didn't want to see the town cry for him. There's a part of me that's glad I was with him until the end. He didn't deserve to die alone. I can't shake the nagging feeling that someone left him there all alone. I need to know why. I need him to stop haunting my dreams."

Audrey remained quiet. She cleared her throat and spoke in a near whisper. "What if it was me?"

I shook my head violently. "It's not you. Why would you think that?"

"I feel responsible. There's a tiny voice in my head that whispers it over and over." Audrey's eyes grew dim. "I don't remember driving into that pole; I could have easily been a part of Aaron's accident. I remember driving the night it happened…what if I killed my own child?"

"Chase was there that night too. You showed up after the accident. He checked your car; there wasn't a dent on it. Somebody knows something. I will find out who. It's not you."

"I hope you're right. Sometimes I feel like this thing that's happening to me is destroying my brain as punishment for what I have done. Or perhaps, protection."

"Oh, Mom. It's not you. Please, listen to my words. It's not you." *But what if it is?* I squeezed my eyes closed for a split second. *It can't be her. It's not her.* We drove the rest of the way in silence. I pulled into the driveway and walked my mom to the front door. She gave me a fierce hug. "Thank you for today. It meant the world to me."

"Anytime, Mom. We'll do this more often."

She pulled back and opened the front door. "Go home and get some sleep. You look tired."

I fought back a yawn and smiled. "Have a good night."

"You too." She closed the door softly. I stared at the door for a moment before the full wave of tiredness hit me like a ton of bricks. I walked to the car slowly and felt ill with the burden my mother carried in her thoughts. Instead of going home, I went to the nearest drive thru and ordered two large coffees. I pulled into the lot where Chase worked and stepped inside the industrial building.

"Chase?"

"Em? Is that you?"

He strode into view and I held up the coffee as a gesture of peace. His face broke into a smile and he pressed his lips to mine. "This is by far the highlight of my day."

I smiled sympathetically. "I'm glad I could help."

"What brings you here?"

"I missed you. I just dropped my mom off and wasn't ready to go home."

"Did you two have a good day?"

"For the most part, yeah."

"What's up?"

My voice broke as I told Chase my mother's darkest fear. He set his cup down and cradled me against his chest carefully. "I was there, it wasn't her."

"I hope you're right."

"Hey, we'll figure it out, okay? My money is on whoever is sending you those damn letters."

I tilted my head up to him and offered a feeble smile. "You're probably right."

Chase tucked a lock of hair behind my ear. "Go home, stay warm and get some sleep. I'll be home before you know it."

I sighed wearily. "Okay. Have a good night."

"You too."

⌘

"Am I getting close?"

"You're on the right path, sis."

"It's so dark, I can't see you."

"I can't stay long, you know that."

"I know. Aaron?"

"Yeah?"

"I need to know, did somebody leave you that night?" I broke into a sob. "Who could do that to you? Who could leave you alone in the dark like that? Somebody should have been there trying to save you, holding your hand. You didn't deserve that."

"I wasn't alone, you were there."

"It shouldn't have been me."

"No, it shouldn't have. I'm sorry."

"Don't be. I wouldn't let you go into the dark alone."

"Wake up, Em."

"Excuse me?"

"Wake up, someone's coming."

A loud thud woke me. I bolted upright and held my breath. The loud clang sounded again from downstairs. I glanced at the time, 3:30 am. *Oh shit.* Chase would still be at work. I fumbled around the dark room until my hands landed on what I wanted; a baseball bat. I tip toed into the hall and hesitated at the top of the stairs. The thud sounded again, this time closer. My knees began to tremble and I forced myself to take a calming breath. The noise sounded again and I yelped. *Crap. Here I go. You got this, Em. Just move your feet and swing if you need too. Swing hard.* I gripped the bat harder and began my descent down the stairs carefully. I tip toed to the nearest window and peeked outside.

The sensor light was on; something had triggered it. I narrowed my eyes and peered outside. There were tracks in the snow leading to the house. We hadn't had any fresh snow within the past day; I couldn't tell if the tracks were old or fresh. I scanned the yard and noticed the garbage cans were tipped over. Trash was scattered about and I felt myself go weak with relief. *It must have been the bear.* I fell heavy into the couch and felt the release of adrenaline course through my veins. My body went limp and my eyes fell closed. The piercing scream of my car alarm sent me on my feet. I ran to the door to search for my keys. I found them and pressed the alarm button, hoping it would read the signal through the window. It did. The car fell silent.

I pressed my face against the glass and tried to ignore my heart jumping in my chest. A muffled voice cursed from outside, followed by a *boom* as something, or someone fell. I jumped toward the bat, held it tight and opened the front door. *Don't do it dummy. This is how people die.* I ignored my common sense and stood on the deck. I scanned the area quickly and found that I was alone. I felt dizzy with fear and lowered the bat slightly. Just as I did, a dark figure came around the corner. I didn't even hesitate. I picked up the bat and gave a mighty swing. It connected and a loud yell split through the night.

The figure fell to their knees and held an arm around their torso. The other hand shot straight outward as if waving a white flag. I raised the bat again and the voice hollered wildly. "Please no, it's me dammit. It's Craig!"

I lowered the bat at once and leaned forward. "Oh christ."

"I think you broke a rib, what the hell were you doing?"

"Me?" I hollered incredulously. "What the hell are you doing stalking my place in the early hours of the morning? What is wrong with you?"

"Help me up."

I bent over and helped Craig scramble to his feet. He tossed an arm over me and used my body as a crutch. We hobbled inside and I set him down on the couch. "Well," I began. "Do I need to take you to the hospital?"

He inspected himself tenderly and winced. "I think I'll make it."

I locked the door behind me and set the bat in the corner. "Well, do you mind telling me what you were doing out there? Besides scaring me half to death."

"I didn't mean to scare you."

I glowered and leaned closer, smacking him on the backside of the head. "Hey!" he yelled.

I stepped back and wrinkled my nose. "Oh, there's my answer. You reek of alcohol."

"I didn't know what time it was. I just came to tell you to back off my sister."

"Pff, what about your sister?"

"She said you ambushed her at home the other day. You really upset her. What's the deal?"

"Your sister is a liar, that's what. Who does she think she is, taking my mom in when she's not fully there and brainwashing her with Bible verses and god knows what else? I'll bet it's her who has been leaving me the notes. Well, at least one set of notes. There are a few that are in a different script. I mean, really. Who's dumb enough to hand write them anyways?"

Craig lowered his face into his hands. "You're not making any sense right now."

I glowered and stormed to the kitchen. I yanked open a drawer and pulled out a pad and a pen. I dropped them on Craig's lap. "Write me something. Now."

He stared up at me like I had gone mad. "Excuse me?"

"Write me something. I am not kidding, Craig. Write me something now before I swing the bat again."

"Fine, fine. Give me a second." Craig scrawled something on the paper and handed it to me. I picked up the paper and he watched me cautiously. *I don't know why you're making me do this.* I scanned the paper and groaned. I let it fall from my hands to the floor.

"I take it that's not what you wanted."

"Is this you're actual writing?"

"Yeah. Is it not neat enough for you or what?"

I glared. "It doesn't match."

Craig threw his hands in the air. "Doesn't match what?"

"The notes I've been getting," I growled. I stared at him angrily. "How did you get here?"

Craig looked away. "I drove," he mumbled.

"What did you say?'

"I drove here, alright. There, happy?"

"Of course I'm not happy you moron! My brother died in a car accident. You could have killed someone!"

"I know, I know. I'm sorry. I've never done it before, honest."

My eyes landed on his arms. I towered over him and rolled up his sleeve. "What does this mean?"

Craig pulled his arm away and his eyebrows pulled together. "I told you. It stands for strength."

"Why did you get it?"

"Because I liked it. And because it was hard growing up the black sheep of the family, alright? I'm the only one who didn't fall into the loving arms of God. It acts as a symbol to myself that I'm going to be just fine. What's it to you?"

I sighed the fight fell out of me. "Nothing. It means nothing. You can sleep on the couch until you sober up."

"Thanks. Emmy?"

"What?"

"What do you have against my sister?"

"She's hiding something about Aaron."

Craig sat up straighter. "She's had a rough go. Back off her. God can't fix everything."

I stared at him until my vision went fuzzy from sleep. "I don't think God can fix anything."

CHAPTER TWENTY-EIGHT

"Em. Wake up. Wake up."

"Mmm."

"Em? Why is Craig Brooks asleep on the couch?"

I opened my eyes and sat up quickly. "He's still here?" I rolled over to look at the clock, 7:30 am.

Chase stood unsurely. "Should I be worried?"

"Oh, God no. He came over drunk as a skunk to warn me to stay away from his sister."

"Did he hurt you?"

"No, but I may have broken one of his ribs. I'm not to sure on that."

"What, how?"

I shrugged sheepishly. "With a baseball bat."

Shock crossed Chase's features, and then he broke into a grin. "Well done."

"Mm, yes and no. Babe, you should get some sleep. You've had a long night. I'll give Craig some coffee and send him on his way."

Chase hesitated. "Are you sure? Do I need to talk to him?"

"No, I'll be fine. Please, go to sleep."

Chase yawned and stripped off his shirt. My eyes lingered over him for a minute to long. Chase met my eyes and grinned. I rolled my eyes. "Get some sleep, Mr. I'll tend to the guy on the couch."

Chase flopped onto the bed. "I hate night shifts. Holler if you need me."

"I will." I closed the bedroom door behind me and made a strong cup of coffee. I gave Craig a gentle shove. "Wake up."

Craig peeled one eye open and stared at the mug. "Coffee?"

"Yes, for you. Now wake up."

Craig sat up slowly and groaned. I winced in sympathy. "Is it broken?"

He reached for the mug and took a sip. "No, but if anyone asks what happened I fell on the ice."

I smiled. "Done."

Craig took a long sip and leaned back against the couch. "You said someone was sending you letters?"

"Two people, yes."

"What do they say?"

"Most of them are apologetic in regards to Aaron. The others are Bible verses and small threats mostly."

Craig's eye twitched ever so slightly. "That's messed up."

"You're preaching to the choir."

Craig set down the mug and stood. "I'm sorry about last night. I should get a move on."

"Are you okay to drive?"

"Yeah, I'm good. Thanks." Craig's hand paused on the doorknob. "There's something I need to know."

My voice grew hesitant. "What's that?"

"What's with the fascination of the bear tattoo?"

I crossed my arms and spoke carefully. "It was a forewarning."

"By who?"

"The brain has many faucets. They don't all forget, though it seems like someone may be trying to take advantage of that."

Craig watched me carefully. He nodded slowly and stepped outside. He kept his back toward me. "Em?"

"Yeah?"

"Take it up with God."

⌘

"We're going to church."

Elayna's jaw dropped. "'Scuse me?"

"You heard me, I need your help with something."

"Oh?"

My hands worked quickly as I plaited my hair into a braid. I filled Elayna in on Craig's late night visit and our brief conversation in the morning. "Okay, but how does church fit in on this?"

"The Reverend and I don't exactly see eye to eye. I need you to distract him while I sneak into his office."

Elayna held up her hands. "Uhh, I don't know about this, Em. This feels like we could burst into flames or something."

I made a face. "How so?"

Elayna looked around and lowered her voice. "Are you accusing the Reverend of something?"

"I don't know yet. It's just a hunch."

Elayna blew out a breath. "May God forgive us." She sighed heavily. "Fine, let's get this over with."

Elayna drove to the church and parked. She hesitated opening her door. "Are you sure about this?"

"Absolutely. Now come on, let's hurry. He should still be giving a sermon. If we're lucky we can do this without even having to look at him."

"Jesus. The things I do for you."

We walked briskly down the dim hall. Elayna wrinkled her nose. "Why do all churches smell musty?"

I forced a smile. "Most of them are old."

"I know they are, but why can't they at least make them more cheery, y'know? It's supposed to be a place of comfort but I always feel jittery in them."

The Reverends voice echoed the halls. His voice rose and fell as he delivered his speech with passion. The hairs on the back of my neck stood on edge. We marched down the hall and came to an abrupt stop as we reached his office. "Stay on guard, Elayna. Don't let anyone come in here if you can help it."

"Why me?" She squeaked.

"Please," I begged.

"Fine, but I'm not happy about this. You owe me a bottle of wine. An expensive bottle of wine."

"Done."

I placed my hand on the doorknob and turned. Nothing, it was locked. Elayna piped up. 'It's a sign. We tried, let's go."

"Why does he feel the need to lock it?" I turned to Elayna and studied her. "Oh! Give me your bobby pin."

"That makes me an accomplice." Elayna fished through her hair and gave me the pin unwillingly.

"I love you."

Elayna smiled nervously. "Who wouldn't?"

I nodded to her briefly, and then turned my attention to the door. I straightened the bobby pin out and fished it in the lock. I wriggled it this way and that until I heard the faint *click*.

"Got it," I muttered. "Please keep watch."

"How do you even know how to do that?"

"Aaron. He also taught me how to hot wire cars."

Elayna's jaw dropped and I slid inside. His office was cool, almost damp. His certificates hung on the wall followed by religious portraits. I scanned the bookshelf briefly, but nothing called to me. I walked up to the desk and sat in his chair slowly. The leather was cold; it cut through my clothing and sent goose bumps down my spine. The desk was tidy and orderly, everything had its place. I shuffled through the papers, but found nothing of importance. I tried to open the desk drawers, but they were locked. "Why is everything locked, Reverend?"

Elayna's voice rose in the hallway. "Oh! Excuse me? Maybe you can help me. I'm looking for the washroom."

"It's down the hall and to the left."

Chills ravaged my body, it was him. *Crap, crap, crap. Get him away from the door, Elayna. Please.* The door opened slightly and I hid under the desk. I tucked my knees to my chest and held my breath.

"Wait! Um, would you mind walking me to the washroom? I'm terrible with directions."

"It's down that hall, to the left."

"What hall?"

"That one, right there."

"I'm sorry, I don't know which one you're referring too."

The Reverend sighed loudly. "The one behind you."

I forced my breathing to remain quiet and prayed that Elayna could lure him away. I kept my eyes glued to the floor and tried to come up with an excuse, in case this whole thing backfired.

Elayana's voice rang loud with annoyance. "You know, this would be a lot faster if you just showed me."

The Reverend sighed. "Fine. Follow me." The door shut behind him. I counted to five and scrambled up. I bolted for the door when a picture pulled at my attention. My eyes widened as I stared at the photo. The Reverend smiled back from within the frame, as he posed by a dead bear. The Reverend smiled proudly, leaning against his rifle. My heart caught in my throat and I stumbled for a brief second. *Get out.* I slipped out the door and into the hall. I shut the door tightly and half jogged to put distance between the office and myself.

"Whoa there, slow down."

I skidded to a stop and felt the color drain from my face. The Reverend stood before me and looked surprised. "Emmy, what brings you here?"

"Oh, I uh thought I'd give this whole thing another try. I spoke to my mom the other day and she mentioned she felt comfort here."

"Ah," the Reverends face softened. "I'm glad. How does it feel to you?"

"Oh, you know," my eyes searched wildly for an escape. Out of the corner of my gaze Elayna stood. She looked dumbstricken at the sight of me conversing with him. I read her mouth *get away*. I nodded quickly but was side-tracked by the book he held to his chest. Scribbled cursive was sprawled across the pages. The blood drained from my face as the loopy letters sank in. "Oh, God."

"Excuse me?'

I shook my head and tore my eyes away. "Do you write the sermons yourself?" I could see Elayna shake her head and mouth *what are you doing?* I looked away and met the Reverends eyes.

"Absolutely. Why do you ask?"

"No reason. I can tell there's a lot of passion when you speak. I was just curious." I looked at the clock. "I better be going." I stepped out of his way and hustled toward the exit.

Elayna followed at my heels. "Why were you talking to him?"

I kept my eyes forward and quickened my pace. "Let's get to the car."

Elayna matched my pace and we hightailed it to the vehicle. We slid inside and I immediately locked the doors. I let my head fall heavy against the headrest. "Elayna," I breathed. "It's him. It's him."

Elayna furrowed her brows. "What do you mean?"

"There was a picture of him in his office with a bear carcass. He killed it himself."

"Okay…that doesn't mean it's him, Em."

I pinched the bridge of my nose. "I saw his writing. It matches the letters we've been getting to a T."

Elayna's face fell. "Are you sure?"

"Positive. I'd bet my life on it."

Elayna's eyes trailed to the church in the distance. She shivered. "That's creepy. Why, though? What's the motive?"

"I have no idea. Let's get out of here."

The silence hung heavy in the car. Elayna kept her focus out the window and my mind wandered to the letters I had tucked away. *Why.* The question replayed in my head over and over, and I had no answer. We pulled into Elayna's driveway and she made no move to get out of the car.

"Em?"

"Yes?"

"I don't like this. People trust him. It doesn't make sense."

"I don't know what to tell you. I promise you, I will get to the bottom of it."

Elayna unbuckled her belt and turned to face me. Her face grew serious. "Promise me you won't do anything by yourself. I don't feel comfortable with any of this."

I nodded. "I promise."

"I will watch you like a hawk. Promise me, really promise me."

I wrapped my pinky around hers like we did when we were kids. "Pinky swear."

Elayna cracked the hint of a smile. "Okay. I'll call you tomorrow."

"Have a good night."

"You too."

I drove for home as the light faded from the sky. I made a last minute decision to visit the place where Aaron's body went still. I pulled over to the side of the road, zipped my coat up, and stood outside. My eyes lingered to the spot where everything simply came to an end. In the blink of an eye, a life faded from this earth and our lives were changed. We were left forever broken and forced to move on. I shivered from the cold and looked to the sky. How? How does one move on when someone you love ceases to exist? What were we supposed to do? I missed him. I missed him so much. The tears began to blind my vision as I stumbled forward. People told us over and over that time heals all. It does not. The wound is always there, and it always aches. Sure, it's not as paralyzing as it used to be, but it doesn't go away, and it never will. The only difference is we adapt to the emptiness. We learn to cope and march forward without that person beside us. All we have left are the memories.

I stared into the blackness that was now before me. There was nothing left here, nothing but what used to be. Those who passed this stretch of road would never know that my favourite person in the world simply came to a broken end. The world had moved on, nature had healed itself of its blemish. I turned to walk away and fell heavy into the drivers seat. The heat of the car warmed my cool flesh. Aaron's birthday was in three weeks; he would have been thirty-two. The anniversary of his accident would be four days after his birthday. As the day grew closer the urgency to uncover the meaning behind the letters intensified. If I could figure out answers, perhaps I would allow myself to finally feel a sense of closure.

I sighed heavily. I had forgotten something; there were two writers to the letters I'd been receiving. I was sure the one set stemmed from the Reverend;

the other writer I wasn't one hundred percent sure of, but it was laced with a shared sense of sorrow. I had a slight inclination where the other set came from. I just needed to prove it and hope it would lay Aaron's warnings to rest.

CHAPTER TWENTY-NINE

I laid my purchase onto the table. Elayna stared at it and looked back at me. She nodded and smiled. "It could work."

I stared at the get well card and glanced at the letters that were scattered about. I split them into two piles and separated them by the writing. The letters that came from the Reverend were filled with a deep seeded ugliness and anger. They had hidden lessons of revenge and discipline sprinkled within. The other pile, the unknown author at this point, was filled with a sadness and sorrow. I broke my stare and gathered up the papers and the card. It was a simple plan, to get the two I suspected to sign a get well card intended for my mom. I would match the writing and go from there. Other than that, I was playing everything by ear.

"I hope it works." I fiddled with the card and handed it to Elayna. "Can you sign it?"

She did not hesitate. "Absolutely." She handed the card back to me and I scribbled my own message inside. I stuck the card in my purse and stood.

Elayna popped out of the chair. "Where are you going?"

"First things first, I'm going to get the ever caring Reverend to sign."

Elayna grabbed her purse and tossed it over her shoulder. "Not without me you're not." I opened my mouth to protest but Elayna would have none of it. "I'm driving. I'll wait in the car so he doesn't see us together, but Em, I am not letting you go alone."

"Okay, thanks." I breathed a sigh of relief. Truth be told, thoughts of the dim church and being alone with the Reverend left me feeling uneasy.

Moments later Elayna pulled into the parking lot and I marched with steadfast determination to the Reverend's office. I stopped in front of the closed door and rapped my knuckles loudly against the door.

A faint voice called from the other side. "Come in."

I glanced quickly at the get well card for a burst of bravery and entered the office. The Reverend pressed his glasses up the bridge of his nose and looked surprised. "Emmy! What brings you here?"

The cool temperature of the room made me falter. I shuffled from left to right unsurely. The Reverend extended his arm and pointed toward the empty chair closest to me. "Please have a seat."

I moved like a dancer and gracefully settled onto the chilled seat. I crossed a leg over my knee and bounced it impatiently. *Keep calm. You got this.* "As you know, my mom hasn't been well these days." I forced my face to remain soft, and my voice calm. The Reverend nodded for me to continue, I did. "I've made her a personal photo album to keep close to her and its something she can refer to when she's confused."

"That's very thoughtful of you."

I nodded slowly. "Thank you. However, sometimes it can also be comforting to read kind, reassuring words as well. It can act as another reminder of how loved she is. I want her to know that she has a team of supportive people on her side."

"I think that's a fine idea. I'm not sure how I come into this."

"My aunt seems to think my mom finds a level of comfort talking to you when she is shall we say 'gone.'"

He nodded. "She does come to me quite frequently. I'd like to think I help guide her through some of the cobwebs she faces."

I fought to keep my features from twisting. "Right." I lifted the card into view and placed it on his desk. "Would you mind signing this for her? You don't have to write much, I'm just looking for well wishes to keep her going."

The Reverend stared at the card. For a moment, his face went blank. I could read nothing. His left hand gripped hard onto the pen he held; he pressed the end of the clicker on the pen in a repetitive motion. Silence fell heavy in the room. The ticking of the clock and the clicking of the pen became nearly deafening. I uncrossed my leg and leaned back into the chair, folding my arms across my chest as I did so. A surge of victory shuddered in my heart. I knew it was him.

"Are you at a loss for words?" I prodded.

The Reverend's eyes landed on me. His features twisted into something short of a sneer. As he spoke his voice fought to remain collected. "Not at all." His hands pushed the card toward me. "It's a lovely gesture but I think I will pass. I can offer your mother more comfort in person. It's what I do."

I slid the card back to him. "Please, I think it will mean a lot to her."

The Reverend shifted in his chair. "Have your mom stop by and see me. I will keep her in my prayers." He slid the card back and his palm came down on the desk like a gavel.

The calm cover I had tried to keep decayed. I slid the card in my purse and my face hardened. "What's wrong, Reverend? Afraid I'll see something in particular?"

The Reverend's eyebrows drew together and his sneer broke free. "I think we're done here."

"No, we are not." The Reverend stood and I followed suit. We stared at each other from across the desk. A deep rooted darkness broke free from somewhere inside. A strong wave of anger washed over me and the force nearly took my breath away. I smacked my hand on his desk. "Why the hell are you sending me letters? Who do you think you are?"

"I don't know what you're talking about."

"Bullshit you do. Don't hide behind God. Be a man and own up to it. What are you trying to prove?"

"Watch your language, Emmy. I will not have you in here uttering threats my way. Please leave."

"Stay the fuck away from my mom. I don't know what you're putting in her head, but leave her alone. She's been through enough."

"I'm helping your mother find her way. I will not turn her away if she comes to me. You, on the other hand are no longer welcome here."

I curled my fingers into a fist and turned away. Before I was out the door, the Reverend's low voice hit me like a car. "He begged."

I stopped cold in my tracks and turned to him. "Excuse me?"

"A wild, unwillful life can only be lived for so long. There are costs for everything. God knows what is right, and what is wrong."

I stepped closer. "What are you saying?"

The Reverend rolled up his sleeves and smirked. My eyes went wide as I caught a glimpse of color on his forearm. "What is that?" I nearly whispered.

The Reverend studied where my stare was directed and he turned his forearm into view. The snarling bear stared at me with its lifeless eyes. My jaw dropped as my brain forced the pieces together.

"Are you going to leave me?"

I looked up as the Reverend's cool tone filled my ears. He looked smug as he dropped back into his seat. His words echoed in my head, but I heard them as Aaron's. Bile rose in the back of my throat. I forced a swallow and felt it burn down my esophagus. The monster I had locked away broke down the door. Rage came barrelling through my every cell. I picked up a frame from the desk and hurled it with all the power I possessed. The Reverends eyes grew wide as he leapt off the chair just in time. The frame connected with the wall and the glass shattered into tiny fragments. My breathing became laboured and my body shook. The Reverend stared in surprise before I lunged at him. I hit him with the force of a quarterback. His body hit the wall with a dull thud as he tried to fight me off. I pinned back his arms and kept my elbow to his throat.

"What did you do?" I cried.

"Get off of me!"

I shook him like a box of candies. "Why? Tell me why?"

"Jesus Christ!" A voice shot out from the doorway.

I kept my eyes glued to the Reverend. "What the hell did you do?"

Strong arms gathered around my waist. I let out a wild cry and thrashed like a fish on a hook. The Reverend straightened himself out and glared at me as I was carried out. Before he slipped from my view entirely, I caught the distinct look of fear in his eyes.

⌘

I thrashed the entire length of the hallway. I was released once I was outside. I stumbled back from the arms that freed me. Elayna's voice rose the length of the parking lot as I spotted her running toward me. "Oh crap! What happened?"

I glared up as Craig straightened his shirt. "I'm going to kill him!"

"I wouldn't say that so loudly."

Elayna grabbed the front of my shoulders. "Emmy! Talk to me. What happened in there?"

"He wouldn't sign the damn card."

"What else?"

My face grew cold. "He started going off about Aaron and how he basically deserved what was coming to him." My face paled. "He was there, Elayna. I know he was. He said 'Are you going to leave me?' and I knew it was Aaron. I just knew."

Elayna's face paled and she stepped back. "I...I..." she looked from the church to Craig.

I shook my head. "He has a tattoo of a snarling bear."

Craig's voice was low. "For I am the strength you need and don't have. I am what you fear. I am the leader you shall look upon."

Elayna and I shared a glance. "Uh, what?"

Craig gripped his arm where I knew his tattoo lied. "It's what he used to say to me. As I got older, I was the lucky one. I broke free and went my own way. I found my own voice." Craig stared at his arm. "I keep it as a reminder. I am stronger than him. I don't fear him, I hate him."

I gripped onto Craig. "Do you know anything about Aaron? Please, I am begging you."

Craig shook his head and gently pried me off. "I'm sorry, Em. I don't know anything. I only stick around here to make sure Miranda's okay."

I backed away and held my head low. "Elayna, can you take me home?"

"Of course."

We walked in silence and we drove without speaking a word until she pulled into the driveway. "Em?"

"Yeah?"

"What are you going to do?"

"I haven't got a clue." I popped open the car door and slammed it shut. I waved meekly to Elayna as she drove away slowly. I stepped inside the warm house and shut the door quietly. I leaned my weight against the back of the door and stared at the ceiling.

Chase came strolling in and his voice sounded chipper. "I finally have some days off and I was thinking we...Em? What's wrong?"

I met his eyes and broke. Sobs racked my body until I couldn't breathe. Chase wrapped his arms around me and rocked me slowly. I tried to talk but my words came out jumbled. He stroked my hair and pressed his mouth to my ear. "Shh. Shh. Don't talk. Let it pass. It's okay. It's okay."

I held on to him until my hands went numb and my eyes went dry. Chase led me to the couch and I curled up next to him and slowly found the words to tell him. By the end, Chase grew still. "Are you sure?"

"Positive."

"All this time, it's been him?" Chase rose quickly and began to pace. "What are we going to do? He can't get away with this!"

"I have no proof. He's a damn Reverend; half the town practically worships him. I don't even know how much of a part he played in that night. I have nothing."

Chase knelt down in front of me and took my hands in his. "Keep your mom away from him. I don't want you near him until we can figure something out. Promise me."

"I promise."

Chase pushed back a strand of hair. "You look exhausted. How about you head for bed. Do you want me to make you a tea?"

"No, I'm okay. Thanks though." I stood stiffly. "I think a good nights rest is what I need. My head is killing me."

I walked in a zombie like fashion and hit the mattress heavily. It didn't take long for my world to go black.

⌘

"I found him, didn't I?"

"You did. I knew you would. You're almost there."

227

I wiped away the tears that began to fall. I reached out and clasped Aaron's hand in mine. "What did he do to you?"

Aaron gripped my hand back. "Its not so much what he did, as to what he didn't do."

I wrinkled my nose. "What's that supposed to mean?"

Aaron chuckled and ruffled my hair. "You're a smart girl, you'll figure it out."

"I'm tired of puzzles, riddles, and mysteries."

Aaron laughed and stared at the summer sky. The sun was nearly set as the pink and orange began to fade. "Watch out for mom and tell her that I love her."

"You know I will."

"Em?"

"Yes?"

"Never, ever underestimate how far a mother's love will go and what they're willing to do for their kids."

I frowned slightly. "Okay, I'll watch her."

Aaron nodded and wrapped me in a big hug. "You can wake up now. It's almost over."

CHAPTER THIRTY

Not a soul stirred in the quiet of the morning. The barn was still as I turned Ace loose in the sandy arena. He ran out his winter sillies and kicked up his haunches, sending sand flying every which way. It fell quietly like snow. I smiled as he ran with his head low and snaked it back and forth in play. He slowed his body and lowered it into the sand and enjoyed a good, long roll. He rose onto all fours and shook like a big dog. He decided to spook at his own shadow and he sent himself cantering around the arena once again.

"He looks happy." Miranda sat next to me on the empty bench.

I was careful not to look at her. "He is one happy boy."

"I heard what you did."

I flinched, knowing exactly what she was referring too. "I'm not surprised." I straightened my shoulders. "I'm not sorry."

Miranda turned her striking blue eyes on me. I couldn't look away. "You shouldn't be." Miranda's eyes continued to search mine. "You weren't at the funeral." She broke the stare and let her tears fall.

I sat back in surprise, not knowing what to say. Emotion was not something I was used to seeing from her. "No, I couldn't go. I saw enough, I wasn't ready to see the world mourn for him. I wasn't even sure how to mourn for him myself. I was so angry, so lost, so haunted by what I had seen. I didn't want that to be the last memory I had of my brother, but unfortunately that's what I remember the clearest. Even to this day."

Miranda buried her face in her hands and cried. I watched her, stunned. Her small body appeared so frail, so broken. I gingerly placed a hand on her back and rubbed it soothingly. After a few moments, she uncovered her face and wiped the wetness from her now red eyes. "I wish you were there."

"Why?"

"Because then I would have told you everything. But you didn't show up and the moment passed. I've had to carry it with me for so long."

My heart faltered. "Carry what?"

Miranda took a shuddery sigh and reached into her bag. She handed me an envelope and stared ahead, avoiding my gaze. I reached inside and cautiously pulled out a strip of photos taken from a photo booth. My eyes grew wide as I recognized them as the matching set from Aaron's box. In them, Aaron wore his wide, carefree grin. His eyes were glued to Miranda as she laughed and gazed back at him affectionately. I studied her in the photos. I had never seen her look more beautiful. I set the pictures down carefully and unfolded a piece of paper. The neat script unfolded the mystery of the other writer. I read the words eagerly.

You would be thirty-two today. God, how I miss you. My world remains frozen. Not a single day goes by where I don't think of you. My biggest regret was not being able to say good-bye. I'm not sure how to get passed that. How do I move on? Please tell me, how do I let you go? Please. I need to let you go. How in the hell do I let you go?

Miranda watched me quietly. She cleared her throat and spoke so softly. "We were going to tell you all soon. I wasn't sure how you were going to react, but I figured you would get over it. Eventually. Craig knew. He's an ass, but he is very good with secrets. I was scared to tell my dad, I knew he wouldn't approve. He was the only one I was scared to tell. But he found out. Aaron thought I was over reacting but clearly I was not." Miranda stopped to take a breath. "Craig moved out, after my mom died. My dad changed after she passed away. He became obsessed with religion and he took it to an unhealthy level. He was convinced mom died because he was being punished for his past. He tried to get Craig to see "his" ways but Craig refused to get caught up in that world. I, on the other hand felt bad for dad, so I stayed with him. Little did I know that would be the worst mistake of my life, and your family's."

My hands began to tremble as I felt the truth so close it burned. "What happened?"

"Dad seems to think he was chosen to do the Lord's work. He feels strongly that those who do wrong need to be punished. He knew Aaron lived a free spirited life, he felt he had no moral grounds, no roots. He drank, and smoked marijuana. He slept with girls without being in relationships with them. He-"

I held up my hand to stop her. "My brother was a good man. He would have given the shirt off his back to help anyone out. He took care of my mom and I. He was always there. Always."

"You don't have to convince me, Emmy. I know. I saw him. I loved him. He always spoke very highly of you and your mom. His friends meant everything to him. I'm simply trying to get you to see how my dad viewed him."

"Quite frankly, I don't care for your father at all."

"Neither do I. He hides behind his Reverend mask; it has consumed him to the very core. There's nothing left of my father." Miranda reached out and squeezed my hand. Her eyes looked almost wild. "That night was all my fault. I distracted Aaron for one second. One second was all it took. He didn't see the bear until it was to late. He tried to swerve but we hit a patch of ice and he lost control. I mean, can you imagine? A bear crossing the road? What are the chances? I will never in my life forget the sound of metal and glass. I didn't know it could be so deafening. Just before we hit the tree and nearly flipped, Aaron threw out his arm and held me in my seat. He tried to protect me. "Miranda paused for a moment before continuing, deep in thought.

"Parts of that night are still so fuzzy. I remember how Aaron screamed. I remember how I screamed. I couldn't stop. There was so much blood, and it was warm. It was so damn warm against the cold of the night. I tried to take off my seatbelt but my hands were shaking so badly, I couldn't control myself. I wanted to help Aaron. I wanted to make his bleeding stop. He kept muttering for me to get out, he wanted me to get out. I couldn't find my phone, I remember screaming for help.

"Just up ahead a set of headlights came pointed our way. I remember feeling immense relief, knowing that someone was coming to help us. Only I was wrong. It was my dad. He saw us out together that night and he was livid. He opened up my door and he looked at me for only a split second. His eyes studied Aaron like he was a lab rat, and do you know what he did? Do you?"

My eyes had filled with burning hot tears. I could find no words as I shook my head. Miranda gave a bitter laugh. "He laughed at him. Can you believe that? He said 'God works in mysterious ways. You deserve this. This is what you get for trying to corrupt my daughter. You can't live a life without Him and expect Him to save you.'"

Miranda let go of my hand and stared blankly at the floor. "He grabbed me out of the car and I fought him. He tore off my necklace and I screamed for him to call for help. But he didn't. I was so weak and in shock that I let him take me away. I knew that was the last time I would ever see Aaron again, and I did nothing. Absolutely nothing." Miranda stopped and turned to me. "What does that make me?"

CHAPTER THIRTY ONE

The crackling of the fire normally was a comfort to me. Tonight, it was not. The living room was full as Chase, Elayna, Miranda, Craig, aunt Sam and Audrey sat in our living room. I had expected my mother to be absolutely broken after Miranda told her side, but tonight, Aunt Sam won that title. Her faith had been shattered for a man she sought comfort in had ultimately betrayed her. As I studied the look of consternation on my Aunt's face, I hoped her faith would not be broken forever.

Miranda and Audrey had exchanged a knowing glance. Audrey slipped her hand over Miranda's softly. "Miranda kept in touch after we moved away. I knew about her and Aaron. A mother always knows." Audrey turned her eyes to me. "I'm sorry I kept that from you, Em. I made a promise. I didn't know about the accident, only the blooming relationship."

Aunt Sam stared at the fire, lost in thought. "He took away my nephew. That was not his choice to make. He didn't even give him a chance." She turned her teary eyes to me. "You should not have been put through what you did. You should not have ever had to see what you saw. That was not his right. He had no right," she sobbed.

Audrey stood with the strong grace she always possessed. She wrapped her arms around her sister and rocked her gently. "My sweet Sam. You have given up so much of yourself for me; I will not let this rock your faith. It has gotten you through so much. Don't let it breakdown now. He is but one man, one bad, ugly man. He does not represent the things you hold so close to your heart. He is a fraud. Do not let him take this away from you."

My mother's eyes fell to me. "And as for our dear Emmy, no, she should have never had to see what she did. But apart of me is glad. She is a strong young woman, and if anyone could have the strength to get through it, it's her. I'm glad that Aaron was with someone who loved him so much until the very end. He did not go out of this world alone. For that, I am so grateful."

Chase gave me a sidelong glance of pride and spoke softly. "What do we do now?"

Elayna fished through her purse and held out a thin white paper roll. "I say we have a moment to remember Aaron." She pulled a lighter from her pocket and lit the end of the stick. The sweet skunky smell filtered through the room. She took a puff and passed it around. I watched wearily as it reached Aunt Sam. She held it like a foreign object and stared. She lifted it hesitantly to her lips and took a long drag. Her eyes opened wide and she began to cough.

Audrey chuckled and took it from her sister. She patted her back lightly. "Good sport. As for what's next, well, I think it's time we say goodbye to Aaron properly. We need to put all this evil to rest. I'd like to do that while I still can remember who I am. I intend to keep this memory until my dying day."

⌘

Three weeks had passed since we all met in our living room. Aaron's birthday came and went like a passing breeze. Our minds were focused on one task, and one task only. The day Aaron's life was lost. The morning of his anniversary, we all stood outside the church, dressed in our Sunday best. I gripped onto my mom's hand and smiled at her reassuringly. The past week had been rough on all of us as her mind had been vacant. She had been in a state of panic, though she did not know why. She did not accept the comfort of her daughter, for she didn't know who I was. A small, microscopic part of me hoped her mind would forget Aaron all together, and myself. If there was one inkling of kindness this disease could offer her, I hoped it was a fresh slate.

But today, she woke up with a solid grasp on everything. She was once again Audrey, my mother, and she was a protective, grieving mother who was going to demand an apology for a wrong doing that could not be taken back. *Never underestimate the love of a mother and what she will do for her children.* Aaron's voice rang loud in my head as I watched my mom straighten herself out and whisper words of encouragement to aunt Sam. Chase took me by the hand and I reached for Elayna. She linked her elbow in mine and we marched in unity to a building that hosted a liar.

The pews were nearly full as we entered the auditorium. Craig entered behind us and looked apologetic. "Sorry I'm late."

"It's okay. I'm glad you made it."

"Oh, I wouldn't miss this."

As we walked down the aisles, the Reverend's eyes caught mine. He glowered but the anger passed quickly. Unsettlement sparked in his eyes as he took in our group. Miranda sat in the front, next to the stage. She stood and waved us over. "I saved us the best seats in the house."

The Reverend watched us and was visibly shaken. He stepped from the stage and stood next to Miranda. "What's this?"

Miranda didn't falter one bit. "Today marks the anniversary of Aaron's death. Everyone is looking for some extra comfort today."

The Reverend softened his face and placed his hands on Audrey. "Ah, yes. I'm so sorry. I will say a special prayer for you all today."

Audrey slapped his hands off and glared at him with a seething hatred. "Do not touch me. I do not want the hands of death anywhere near me. I am simply here to watch a man fall apart. That man is you."

The Reverend snapped back in shock. His eyes studied each one of us individually. Lastly was Miranda. His face fell and the sting of betrayal took over. "What have you done?"

Miranda glared at her father. "What have *you* done? Do you have any idea how much you have burdened me over the years? Do you have an ounce of compassion in you at all?"

The Reverend raised an eyebrow. "Don't you talk to me like that, child. I have saved you and given you something to live for! The work of God needs many helping hands. I have given you the opportunity of a lifetime; you need to be saved from our past sins. I have given you everything."

Miranda glared and took her seat. "You better get up there. You don't want to keep the people waiting."

The Reverend gave her a studious glare and stepped up behind his podium. He looked at the full house and spoke into the microphone. "Thank you all for being here today." He looked down at his notes and back to the crowd. "I had a set of verses to read, but something has been brought to my attention. Today marks the anniversary of Aaron Jacobs death. His family is here today in the front row. I would like to share a moment of silence and offer a prayer."

Low murmurs filled the room and people lowered their heads in a silent offering of sympathy. Audrey let out a small sob as the reality of the day had begun to hit. Aunt Sam placed her hand in my mothers, and I did the same. I glanced at Miranda and reached out to her as well. We linked as a chain and let the tears slip away. The Reverend began his sermon and his words faded into nothing. As he neared the end, his eyes fell onto us. "I would like to end today with a message for the Jacobs. John 2:15-17 'Do not love the world or anything in the world. If anyone loves the world, love for the Father is not in them. For everything in the world the lust of the flesh, the lust of the eyes, and the pride of life comes not from the Father but from the world. The world and its desires pass away, but whoever does the will of God lives forever.'"

Confusion fell heavy amongst the crowd. People began to whisper to each other as the Reverend left the stage.

"How does that fit in with anything?"

"I'm not sure."

"Perhaps the Reverend is tired. He looked off today, don't you think?"

We ignored the chatter in the room and stood to exit. We followed Miranda as she led us out the back way.

"Where is he?" Aunt Sam huffed.

"Follow me."

Miranda led us into the back lot and the Reverend stood next to his car, gathering up his bag. Audrey stopped and gripped onto my forearm. "I can't. I can't be near him, I don't trust myself. I don't know what I'm capable of."

"Mom, it's okay."

"No, it's not. Please, Emmy. Take me away. I don't like the feeling that's overcoming me right now. Today is not the day for him. It's for Aaron. I'm not ready to face him."

I looked around and succumbed. "Okay. Let's go to the car. We'll meet you guys at the spot, right?"

"We'll be there."

Aunt Sam hesitated. She marched up to the Reverend and glowered. "How dare you! I trusted you; I put my family's trust in you. You will be punished for what you have done."

The Reverend lowered his glasses and scoffed. "Oh, Sam. I will not be punished for a thing. I have done nothing wrong. Don't you see? Your sister is the one who is being punished for raising such a ruthless child. Things are happening as they should. Keep your faith, don't let them take it from you."

Elayna stepped in and whisked Sam away. "He won't get away with it. Come on, today is a day to pay our respects."

Aunt Sam went away without a fight. She let out a heavy sigh. "Are we meeting at Audrey's then?"

"Yes."

"Okay," she said wearily. "I'll see you all there."

I hopped inside Chase's truck and looked around urgently. "I forgot the flowers!"

Elayna scooted in the middle and Chase slid in next to her. "No problem. We can stop on the way to your mom's to get them."

"Okay, thank you."

Elayna patted my knee. "Are you okay?"

"I don't know."

"Me either."

We stopped at the house and I grabbed the bouquet from the kitchen table. The blaring of a horn sounded. I poked my head outside and Chase hollered from the truck. "Em, get in the truck now!"

Fear crawled over me at the sound of his tone. I ran to the truck in lightning speed and launched myself in. "What's wrong?"

"Your mom's gone."

Chase slammed on the gas pedal and the truck launched forward. "What do you mean she's gone?"

"Sam called in a panic. She was preparing food for everyone and she realized your mom wasn't there. She took the car, Em."

My face paled. Aaron's warning rang in my ears. *Never underestimate the love of a mother and what she will do for her children.* "Oh God."

As Chase sped down the back roads, I heard my voice speak in a tinny sound. "Go to where it happened, Chase. Take us to where this all started."

Chase broke his stare from the road to me. His face looked grim as he nodded. "There's the car!" I cried.

Chase pulled over behind my aunt's car. Two women were inside; my mother in the drivers seat and Miranda in the passenger. I hopped out before the truck came to a halt and ran for the driver's door. I hauled it open. "Mom, get out of the car, now!"

Audrey shook from head to toe and was in tears. "Oh, Mom!" I opened the drivers door and helped her out.

I led her to Chase's truck and he hopped out. "Is she okay?"

Audrey turned to glance at the tree and let out a heart wallowing wail. "My baby. It's not fair. Tell me this isn't real. This can't be happening all over again. I don't know how I got here. I just remember feeling this overwhelming urge to be here. I needed to say goodbye."

Chase spoke soothingly. "Just breathe, Audrey. We'll get through this."

The sound of tires crunching tore away our attention. "Son of a bitch. What's he doing here?"

The Reverend stepped outside of his car and his eyes landed on Miranda. He tapped the door and she rolled down the window. Heated words were exchanged, but they were too low to make out. Until Miranda yelled out "Fuck you!"

The Reverend made a disgusted noise and tossed his hands in the air. He slid into the front seat and slammed his door closed. Audrey coiled her hands into fists and let out a ravage yell. She ran toward his car and began pounding on his door. "How could you do this to us? How dare you? Step outside and stop being such a damn coward!"

The Reverend forced his door open and sent Audrey tumbling into the ditch. Chase sprang into action to retrieve her. Miranda stepped outside the passenger door and closed it softly. She sent me a knowing look and I knew what she was about to do.

"Elayna, get in the truck."

Elayna did and I hopped in the drivers seat. I started the truck up and put it in reverse. Elayna watched what was transpiring. "Em, what are you doing?"

"Giving her room." I quieted the engine. Chase held onto Audrey as they scurried out of the ditch. He caught my eye as Miranda started the car. He glanced back at me and I looked away. He scooped my mom up and stepped aside. Elayna and I slid out of the truck together and we all stood side by side to watch.

The Reverend climbed out of his car once more to plead to Miranda. We heard him this time. "Get out of the car now. This is not you. You don't belong with these people. I gave you the opportunity of a lifetime and you're throwing it all away!"

Miranda stepped out of the car and faced her father. "You didn't give me anything! You took my life away. I'm not following you anymore. This ends now."

The Reverend scowled at her. "I should have left you in the car that night." He looked his daughter up and down and shook his head slowly. "It's too late for you. You can't be saved." With that he disappeared into the drivers seat.

Miranda stood frozen for a moment before she stepped back into the car. She closed the door softly. The brake lights went on as she shifted the car into drive. The Reverend was in the midst of turning around when the car Miranda controlled ploughed into driver's side of the Reverend's car. All went still.

Miranda reversed and pulled off to the side of the road. She stepped outside, white-faced. We all stood wordless, watching as the smoke plumed from the hood of the car. I couldn't help but notice the placement of the Reverend's tattered car was strikingly close to where Aaron's had stood. We stared at one another without speaking. We all jumped in unison as the loud honks began from the Reverends car. At first, no one moved but as the honks protested, Chase went first. We followed one by one. The driver's door was bent in to the point there was no way we could pry it open. The window was smashed and the Reverend moaned as blood seeped out his open head wound.

"What are you waiting for? Get me out of here!"

Audrey spoke first. "I remember what you told me, Reverend."

"What do you mean?" he growled.

"Did I ever tell you that I kept a journal?"

"What does that matter?"

"When I don't remember the world around me, I have one consistent habit; and that is I keep a journal. I write about all the things I'll never remember, and I wrote about you and our sessions."

My curiosity spiked. "What? You never told me that."

"I couldn't. You see, the Reverend told me over and over that I was the one who killed Aaron. He told me it was me that caused the accident. He told me that I had killed my own son."

Miranda spoke behind her. "I over heard one of their talks. That's when I started to give your mom private 'bible sessions.' I couldn't bear the thought of the guilt he fed her."

I stared horrified at the man who bled in the car. Flashbacks of Aaron came rushing in and I had to look away. "I don't want to see it again. Please, no more."

Chase stood beside me quickly. "Em, it's not Aaron. Don't go there."

Audrey shuddered. "Nights coming. It's going to be a cold one."

"Somebody do something!" The Reverend screamed.

Audrey leaned close and stared into his eyes. "Is this how my son felt as he asked for your help with his dying breath? And what did you do? You left him to die."

The Reverend closed his mouth and narrowed his eyes. "What are you doing, Audrey?"

"Isn't it ironic how we're all here together in this very spot, on this very day? It's funny how life works out, don't you think?"

"You're walking a thin line, Audrey."

"This is a quiet road. Chances are no one will come by anytime soon."

"You're committing a sin if you leave me here!"

Audrey stood back. "Chances are, I won't remember." With that, she walked away and hopped inside Chase's truck. Elayna was next to follow.

Chase glanced between Miranda and I. "Is this how it goes? Is everyone going to be able to look themselves in the mirror if we do this?"

"For the first time in a long time," Miranda spoke firmly.

I nodded slowly, unable to look away. "A sin for a sin."

Chase ran a hand down his face. "Miranda, you can squeeze in the truck. Emmy, take them all to Sam."

"What about you?"

"I'm going to get rid of the car. I'll call Craig to help, we'll meet up with you at your mom's."

"What about me?" The Reverend hollered. "Are you going to just leave me here?"

Miranda stopped in front of him. "May God be with you." With that, she walked away and hopped in the truck.

Chase and I exchanged a glance. I bit my lip and looked over the Reverend once more. "You don't get to play God. You don't get to decide who lives, or who dies."

My eyes studied the head wound that oozed and swelled. "How many fingers am I holding up?"

The Reverend looked at me with fear in his eyes. "Eight. Are you going to...to...to..." the Reverend began to panic as he tried to use his lips. His eyes darted to his hands and a strange noise escaped his mouth.

"I was holding up two fingers. You hit your head quite hard, and I believe any brain damage you have at this point will most likely be permanent." I leaned close to his face. "You don't get the easy way out; death. I truly hope you will be trapped in this body for a long time, like a prisoner. You will be offered no forgiveness, and not one of us will mourn whatever happens to you. May God be with you, Reverend."

I nodded to Chase as he made the call. He hung up the phone. "We need to get out of here, now."

I stepped toward him, went on my tiptoes and gave him a hard kiss. "See you soon."

"You bet."

We watched Chase drive the broken car away, thankful it still ran. I started the pick up and pulled on to the main road. I let off the gas as we all took one last look at the lone car. Audrey spoke softly. "This never happened, right ladies?"

"Never," we all agreed in chorus.

Audrey nodded. "A day that never happened. A day that I'll never forget."

CHAPTER THIRTY TWO

We never spoke of that day ever again. One week later in the paper, the Reverend's accident was the top story. By the time he arrived at the hospital, his brain had swelled so significantly he had lasting damage. Speech was rather challenging for him, and he would be dealing with a lifetime of memory complications. Much like the same as my mother, however one day, which no one could predict, her mind would entirely be gone.

After the Reverends accident, Miranda left town in the middle of the night. I hadn't heard from her since. Aaron's memorial got put on pause with the hype from the town about the Reverend. It didn't feel like the right time to pay our respects. We decided to keep aunt Sam in the dark about what happened with the Reverend; though her heart was broken by the betrayal of a man of faith, we knew her heart was too pure to keep such a secret. That was a burden we all would take to the grave.

Once the Reverend's news story hit the paper, my mom called. "Emmy?"

"Yes?"

"Did you see it?"

"It's hard to miss."

"Can you take me to him, please? I want to see him."

I knew well enough not to ask any questions. "I'll be there in ten minutes."

True to my word, I pulled up to my mom's and she met me in the car. "Are you ready for this?"

Audrey nodded. "I need to see how he's doing. Just this one time."

"Okay." We pulled up to the hospital and I paid for my parking ticket.

We walked side by side and gave each other reassuring glances. We paused outside his door and counted to three. Audrey shoved me in and she followed closely behind. I glared at her and she swatted me.

The Reverend sat in bed with a bandage wrapped around his head. He stared at his fingers and he appeared to have aged well beyond his years. He looked up as he heard us enter. We both froze as his eyes wrinkled as he stared back at us. Audrey held her head high and stood beside him. "Do you know who we are?"

The Reverend stared and his eyebrows wriggled. Audrey sat on the edge of his bed. "I am a broken woman. My son was taken from me much too soon, and my daughter was there to witness his life drain away. I have racked my brain over and over as to what we did to deserve this horrible act. And I can't think of a single thing. Not one thing. We are good people. The only thing that went wrong was a man who decided he got to play God."

The Reverend stared with his mouth slightly gaped open. He made a noise but no words came out. Audrey tsked. "I'm not sure if you remember who I am, or who my son was. But know this: I will never visit you ever again. I will never forgive you for what you have done. You have taken something so incredibly precious from me, and there is nothing anyone can say or do to bring him back." Audrey took a deep breath. "But I also think you have been punished for what you have done. Your body, like my own, is not our safe place. We are fragile now and at the mercy of it."

Audrey's eyes trailed to me. "Both of your children are alive and well, yet they want nothing to do with you. My daughter is still here with me, and though I may not always be the mother she remembers, or wants, she is still here standing by my side. And I know she always will be."

Audrey stood and looked down at the Reverend. "For that simple gift, I am blessed beyond means. There is something I would like to leave you with however." Audrey pulled a folded piece of paper from her pocket. She cleared her throat and began. "For if we live, we live to the Lord, and if we die, we die to the Lord. So then, whether we live or whether we die, we are the Lord's. Romans 14:8.' I thought it suited you."

Audrey stepped toward me. "Is there anything you'd like to say to him?"

I stared at the tattered man before me. He was now a harmless shell with his lights half burnt out. And still, the monster of wrath and rage that lurked in the shadows of my mind began to take over, for if I closed my eyes, I would forever bear the scar of a life lost, a life I could not save. "There is nothing I have to say to him. Nothing at all."

"Okay, then we're done here. Let's go home."

⌘

The winter snow and icy cold had come to pass. Green shoots of grass had begun to poke through the hard soil, and the sweet smell of life was enough to enlighten the senses as trees began to bud. I shifted in my saddle and the leather creaked from my weight as I ducked under a low lying branch. Ace had pep in his step as the spring air made him giddy. We cut through the trail and opened up into a large meadow. I sat easily in the saddle as Ace broke into a smooth canter. The air still held remnants of winter as a slight chill of wind rustled past, sending the wildflowers dancing. The sun was low in the sky as early evening was near, bringing to life a shade of brilliant orange and pink. I pulled Ace to a stop to admire the view. I gave him his head and let him munch on the young spring grass.

As I leaned over the horn of the saddle, a sense of peace came over me. I studied the landscape and it bore a close resemblance to a past dream about Aaron.

"Does it hurt where you are?" I asked.

"No, nothing hurts anymore."

"That's good. Is it dark?"

Aaron smiled. "No," he said softly. "It's always bright where I am, and I can keep an eye on all of you. I watch out for you guys all the time. I love it when you all laugh."

Tears began to prick my eyes. "I'm glad you're never far away. We miss you so much, all of the time. We don't know how to say good-bye."

Aaron leaned close and draped his arm over my shoulders. "Aw, sis. You don't need to dwell on the goodbye, okay? It will never be goodbye. I'm always here; I will always be a part of you. I do have one request though."

"Shoot."

"Make your life a happy one. Live for me, live for you. Laugh as much as you can, especially with mom. Enjoy her while she's here. Please know, whatever happens, mom will always love you, love us, even when she can't show it. Look after her."

I sighed and leaned my head on Aaron's shoulder. "I promise."

"You're going to be okay, Em." Aaron looked away and pointed in the distance. "Look. He's finally free."

I followed his finger and watched as the black bear stood stalk still in the distance. The wind gently ruffled his gleaming coat. He watched us for a moment and then he turned away. He lowered himself into the grass and began to roll, scratching his back in bliss.

Aaron smiled. "He did good."

I studied the bear. "I don't follow."

Aaron shrugged. "He led you to me. Now you know what happened." He shoved me playfully. "Go on, it's time for you to go. I'll always be here when you need me. I'm happy, Em. I'm at peace. You helped me get there. Now, go."

"Aaron, wait."

"What?"

"We didn't get to say goodbye, not properly. We had it all planned, we had gotten you flowers, and people wrote speeches. We were going to have a proper anniversary for you."

Aaron raised an eyebrow. "Why? Why would you want to remember that day? It was awful. Don't feel so drawn into 'celebrating' that day. I want you to remember the good things about me whenever they cross your mind. Don't save it for a single, crappy day."

Aaron sighed at the face I made. "Em, I'm not there anyways. The stone marks where I lay, but I promise you, that's not the only place you can find me. If you feel the need to visit my stone, by all means, please do. Just know, the ground isn't the only place you'll find me." Aaron grinned. "Besides, you and I both know you would never have attended a memorial service for me. It's not who you are."

I nodded quietly and listened to my steady breath. He was right. I've carried a heavy burden in my heart for so long. I never did find him in the cemetery. I would never go back to that place that holds him in the ground. It is a spot where people go to say goodbye, and I was not ready for that. For you see, Aaron was everywhere. I held him in my heart. He was in the laughter, he was in the fresh powder of snow on the first run of the season; he was everywhere.

I nodded quietly and broke my silence. "Can I read you what I was going to say?"

Aaron grew thoughtful. "Of course."

"I found a poem by Helen Lowrie Marshall. I thought of you." I cleared my throat and continued.

"I'd like the memory of me to be a happy one. I'd like to leave an afterglow of smiles when life is done.
I'd like to leave an echo whispering softly down the ways, of happy times and laughing times and bright and sunny days.
I'd like the tears of those who grieve, to dry before the sun; of happy memories when life is done."

Aaron smiled. "It's perfect." He stepped forward to give Ace a pat. "Now go, Em. Don't take any day for granted, especially with mom. Go, live."

I snapped out of my memory and clucked to Ace. With the sweet scent of spring heavy in my lungs, I pressed my heels into Ace's sides and leaned forward. "Let 'er fly boy." And so, we did.

Life is but a fleeting ride. Embrace the journey; remember the goodbyes. They make the hellos all that more precious.
Katt Rose

Katt Rose

is an aspiring writer who has a love of music, animals, and writing. Katt worked in the health care field but she could not silence the stories inside her head. Once she began to write, she knew there would be no turning back. She was home.